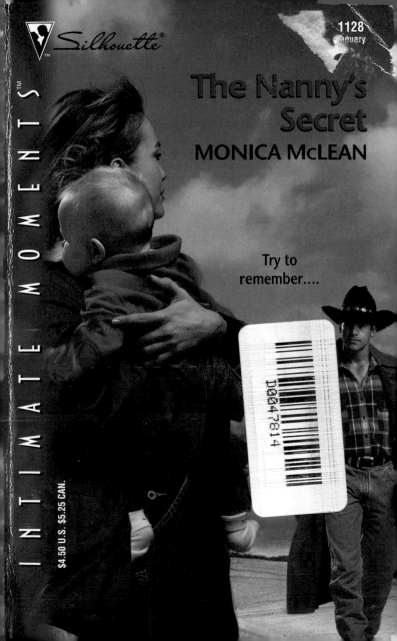

Silhouette®

1128
January

The Nanny's Secret

MONICA McLEAN

Try to
remember....

INTIMATE MOMENTS™

$4.50 U.S. $5.25 CAN.

Silhouette®
Where love comes alive™

ISBN 0-373-27198-0

50450

AVAILABLE THIS MONTH FROM SILHOUETTE INTIMATE MOMENTS®

#1123 RETURN OF THE PRODIGAL SON
Ruth Langan

#1124 THE MAN WHO WOULD BE KING
Linda Turner

#1125 HARD TO TAME
Kylie Brant

#1126 TO WED AND PROTECT
Carla Cassidy

#1127 STILL THE ONE
Debra Cowan

#1128 THE NANNY'S SECRET
Monica MacLean

"I thought you'd changed your mind about staying on as the baby's nanny," Brooks murmured in the darkness.

"I'm not going anywhere," Amelia whispered, looking down into the crib. That much she knew. She was bound to this little boy in a way that defied explanation. He was her anchor in a world turned upside down and inside out. He gave her life purpose, meaning.

"I'm glad," Brooks mumbled, his gaze colliding with hers.

He had the most incredible eyes—deep blue irises fringed with thick black eyelashes. Bold. Hypnotic.

Sexy.

A slow, languorous heat pooled in her stomach. She stepped back, shaking her head. "We should, um, probably get back."

"Yeah. Right." He rubbed the back of his neck. "I don't trust those brothers of mine alone in a kitchen full of pies."

She nodded and led the way, wondering if she could trust herself alone with *him*.

Dear Reader,

Happy New Year! And happy reading, too—starting with the wonderful Ruth Langan and *Return of the Prodigal Son*, the latest in her newest miniseries, THE LASSITER LAW. When this burned-out ex-agent comes home looking for some R and R, what he finds instead is a beautiful widow with irresistible children and a heart ready for love. *His* love.

This is also the month when we set out on a twelve-book adventure called ROMANCING THE CROWN. Linda Turner starts things off with *The Man Who Would Be King*. Return with her to the island kingdom of Montebello, where lives—and hearts—are about to be changed forever.

The rest of the month is terrific, too. Kylie Brant's CHARMED AND DANGEROUS concludes with *Hard To Tame*, Carla Cassidy continues THE DELANEY HEIRS with *To Wed and Protect*, Debra Cowan offers a hero who knows the heroine is *Still the One,* and Monica McLean tells us *The Nanny's Secret*. And, of course, we'll be back next month with six more of the best and most exciting romances around.

Enjoy!

Leslie J. Wainger

Leslie J. Wainger
Executive Senior Editor

Please address questions and book requests to:
Silhouette Reader Service
U.S.: 3010 Walden Ave., P.O. Box 1325, Buffalo, NY 14269
Canadian: P.O. Box 609, Fort Erie, Ont. L2A 5X3

The Nanny's Secret
MONICA McLEAN

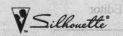

INTIMATE MOMENTS™

Published by Silhouette Books

America's Publisher of Contemporary Romance

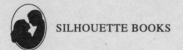 SILHOUETTE BOOKS

ISBN 0-373-27198-0

THE NANNY'S SECRET

Copyright © 2002 by Monica Caltabiano

Books by Monica McLean

Silhouette Intimate Moments

MONICA McLEAN

gave up a jet-set career as a management consultant to pursue her dream of writing romance novels full-time. "What can I say? I'm a sucker for a good love story and a happy ending." A former stockbroker, to boot, she has a B.S. in business law and an M.B.A. in finance. Though she claims McLean, Virginia, as her hometown, she has also lived in New York, Pennsylvania, Maryland, North Carolina, Georgia, Ohio, Michigan, Minnesota...and Texas, if you count living in a hotel (ah, the life of a consultant). She is married—no kids, no pets, no plants—and lists good food, good company and good clothes among life's pleasures.

Prologue

Freezing rain pelted the shattered windshield like a spray of bullets amid the horn's persistent blare. Inside the car, the acrid smell of smoke wafted through the vents.

Gingerly the woman in the driver's seat covered her nose and mouth and lifted her head from the steering wheel.

The baby!

The jagged edge of fear sliced through her foggy brain. She craned her neck and peered into the back seat.

Empty!

No baby. No car seat. Nothing.

Terror gripped her by the throat and rattled her teeth. In a blind panic, she fumbled for the door handle.

Where was the baby? What had happened?

Something crinkled in her hand. Paper. Directions. *Triple H Ranch, Wister, Wyoming.*

The baby! She had to get to him!

She yanked the lever and threw her weight against the door. Gusts of wind roared past like a speeding locomotive.

The handle tore from her grasp. Ice-cold rain spewed inside, stinging her face. She lifted a hand to shield herself and went to climb out. She couldn't. Something held her. Wouldn't let go. She glanced down.

The seat belt.

Clawing past a crumpled map in her lap, she unbuckled herself and wrenched free of the vehicle. She stumbled into the pouring rain and doubled over, gripping her knees as she pulled cold, clean air into her lungs. Shards of ice nailed her from every direction. The deserted four-lane highway, barely visible, glistened like a newly scraped skating rink.

Hunching, she pulled her navy pea coat tighter around her and focused on the ground at her feet. Frozen rain pellets crackled with every step. Twice she nearly lost her balance but managed to keep upright. Rain drenched her hair and seeped through her clothes, but she didn't stop walking.

Around the sharp bend where the car had crashed into the embankment. Down a sloping hill.

She didn't know how far she'd gone when up ahead in the distance, she saw a red neon light.

Teeth chattering, she broke into a dead run.

Chapter 1

The sun had vanished over the Bighorn Mountains when Brooks Hart vaulted up three flagstone steps to his back porch and halted in his tracks. They rarely bothered with locks on the remote ranch, but maybe it was time to start.

The door was open, and he hadn't forgotten to close it all the way. Nor would the others. Not in the middle of a snow storm. And not with their baby nephew crawling around. Which left only one possibility…

More mourners.

With a resigned sigh, Brooks stepped into the mudroom and kicked the door shut. The latch clicked into place, and the wind shrieked like a woman scorned, banging to get back in. Snow had blown inside and scattered across the floor—wet snow, the kind that spelled trouble for calves. It was going to be another long night. With mechanical motions, he hung his coat and Stetson on the deer antlers mounted on the wall, shucked his boots and braced for their latest "guests."

Call him an ingrate, but Brooks wasn't keen on every neighbor within a hundred-mile radius stopping by to pay respects. After two solid weeks, the constant reminders of his loss felt like a steady stream of salt pouring into a wound that would never heal at this rate.

It didn't help to hear gross exaggerations of what a fine young man his older brother had been. Brooks didn't have the patience for small talk, and he damn sure didn't want to discuss his *feelings*.

A Vegas lawman, his prodigal brother had come home for the first time in eighteen years. Then two weeks later, he was dead.

Just how the hell was Brooks *supposed* to feel?

He pushed open the kitchen door and nearly tripped over something in his path. Dumfounded, he stared down at a pair of red, high-heeled shoes. "What the...?" The large country kitchen was empty, but someone "extra" was obviously in the house. He ran down a mental list of women, combed his mind for possible owners and came up empty. Though the calendar said Spring, he didn't know anyone foolish enough to wear high heels in late March in Wister, Wyoming.

Which left the acquaintances of Mitch and Dean.

He rubbed a weary hand over his face. Which little brother and what kind of trouble had he brought home now?

"Hello?" He shoved the shoes aside with the outside of his foot. "Who's here?"

No answer.

He hadn't seen any vehicles out front, didn't hear voices in the house. He stared again at the red, "sleep-with-me" shoes. All right, so he would have used another expression for "sleep-with-me" in the past. All that had changed with his guardianship of their littlest cowboy.

Three men and a baby. A sitcom in the making.

Brooks shook his head and started through the kitchen. He made it as far as the doorway to the great room. Curled up on the couch, was a young brunette, fast asleep.

Jackpot.

Brooks's gaze widened, then narrowed. He frowned as he stepped into the room. He might have found their unexpected visitor, but for the life of him, he had no idea who she was.

Sleeping Beauty wore a knee-length denim dress, black tights and a red-and-black checkered blouse. Did he know her? He couldn't tell with the angle of her head, light brown hair tumbling around her face, small hands folded under her chin.

He cleared his throat. "Ma'am?"

She started in her sleep, mumbling something he couldn't make out. She was a tiny little thing—not short but slight. Needed to put some meat on her bones.

"Hey?" Brooks deliberately spoke louder. "Don't mean to be rude, but, uh, I was just wondering... Who are you?" He waited a full ten seconds then scratched the stubble on his chin.

Something wasn't right.

He leaned down and brushed her hair back from her face. He'd never seen her before, knew for certain if he had, he wouldn't have forgotten. Though her face was streaked with dirt, he could tell underneath, she was pretty as a picture.

She had wide-set eyes with thick, long lashes, a small button nose and perfect, pink lips. She reminded him of a sacked-out kitten. He almost hated to wake her. Almost.

"Ma'am?" He tried again, poking her shoulder. This time, she moaned—the dejected sound of a wounded animal. His senses kicked into high alert. "Uh-oh. What's wrong?" He dropped to his knees beside her, his gaze clinical now, combing over her, taking inventory, searching for answers. "Talk to me, honey."

"Head..." Her voice came thick, raspy. Her fingers shook as she lifted them to her temple. "Hurts..."

A crumpled paper fell from her hand, but Brooks's gaze zeroed in on her forehead and the goose egg he saw there. "Ah, hell." He grimaced, getting up. "Stay put. I'll get ice." On his way to the kitchen, he took the cordless phone from the side table and pressed the button labeled Josephine.

In times like this, it paid to have a doctor in the family. Even though Jo was thirty-one, only two years younger than he was, and despite the fact she had M.D. behind her name, Brooks still thought of her as his *little* sister.

Jo picked up on the forth ring. "Hey, Brooks. Can you hang on a sec? Mandy's in the middle of a diaper change, and— Zach, honey, don't play with the answering machine. You're going to erase the mess..." Deep sigh. "Never mind. I'm sure they'll call back if it's life-or-death. Brooks?"

"Say no more. Do what you gotta do."

"Be right back." The phone clattered to the ground.

Brooks grinned and shook his head, understanding only too well the challenge of performing once-simple tasks with a baby underfoot. And he only had *one* to worry about.

Tucking the phone under his ear, he filled a plastic bag with ice, sealed it and wrapped it in a dishcloth. He returned to the great room as Jo came back on the line.

"Brooks? You still there?"

"Yeah, I'm here." He opened his mouth and searched in vain for words to explain the presence of a mysterious woman passed out on his couch. "I just found her here" might have worked with the stray critters he'd taken in over the years, but in this case, it sounded pretty lame.

Before he could think of anything better, Jo rattled on,

"Great. I'm glad you're home. I was just on my way over with Timmy. Mitch told you I took him for a checkup, right? Anyway, all's well and good news—your new nanny's starting this week. Or so she says. I told her we were desperate, and the sooner the better, but she couldn't nail down a day, so expect her anytime. I gave her directions. Oh, and I told her you'd leave the back door unlocked if you were out. Don't reach for your shotgun if you find a strange woman in the house, okay?"

She laughed.

He didn't.

"The nanny…" Brooks stared down at Mystery Woman. Applying the ice pack to her head, he bent to retrieve the crumpled paper from the floor. *Triple H Ranch.*

Directions from Casper.

At that moment, her eyelids fluttered open, and Brooks found himself staring into bottomless, milk-chocolate eyes with tiny flecks of gold. Sad eyes. Almost…haunted.

He'd barely had the thought when those eyes went wide, like Goldilocks waking up to find the three bears hovering over her.

Suddenly aware of his considerable height, he stepped back, his instincts to protect—even from himself—stirring to life.

"Amelia Rigsby," Jo reminded him. "Best nanny in the agency. And the only one who'd even consider an assignment out here, so you'd better be on your best behavior. My gut tells me it's a borderline call. Won't be surprised if she backs out at the last minute."

"Uh, Jo?" Brooks didn't even try to hide the urgency. "How soon can you get here?"

"Why? What's wrong?"

"It's Amelia. She's here."

"Don't tell me she's changed her mind *already.*"

"I don't know about that, but something's definitely wrong. She must have hit her head. She's conscious but—"

"Oh, geez. Why didn't you tell me? Here I am yammering on. Never mind, I'll be right there."

"Should I be doing anything special? She's lying down, and I've got an ice pack for the swelling—"

"Good. Perfect. Keep her awake until I get there."

"Will do." He hung up and rubbed the back of his neck, shifting under the new nanny's intense, wary stare. "Hey." He inclined his head and took a seat on the coffee table in front of the couch, one hand braced on his knee.

Amelia Rigsby—who would have guessed?

"H-hello." She was sizing him up, probably trying to figure out if she'd made the biggest mistake of her life.

He shifted uneasily, hoping like hell they wouldn't have to wait another month for the next available nanny. "Uh, here." He reached over and took a pillow from the love seat. "Why don't we put this…right…under…"

She tensed like she was holding her breath.

He quickly slid the cushion under her head and scooted back on the coffee table. "Better?"

"Yes. Thanks." She said the words slowly, gauging his reaction, as if he'd asked a loaded question. When he didn't say anything else, she glanced down at her outfit, blinked several times and frowned. The frown deepened as she looked around her, likely wondering what a girl like her was doing in a place like this. But then her gaze returned to him, and he noticed her eyes were bleary, her gaze vacant.

"Where am I?" she asked in a raspy voice.

"The great room." He mustered his most hospitable smile. "You must've crashed in here after knocking your head."

"My head…" She winced. "It *hurts*."

His gut tightened. There were few things he hated more

than watching a person's suffering, to sit by and do nothing. "Don't worry," he said, the only words he could think to say. "Dr. Jo's on the way."

She started to shake her head then winced again.

"Might want to stay still."

"I...don't want...a male doctor." Her voice cracked with strain.

"You're in luck then. Jo's short for Josephine."

Relief flashed in her eyes. Funny, he could have sworn Jo told her she was a doctor in the telephone interview. He eyed the ice pack, wondering if she had a concussion. They'd know soon enough.

"Something to drink?" he offered.

"Yes, please. Cold water?"

"Coming up." He got her a tall glass, but her hands shook when she reached for it, and he didn't think she'd manage without help. "I'll hold it, all right?" At her tentative nod, he sat back down on the coffee table and brought the glass to her lips. "Tell me when."

Instinct had made him ask permission before approaching her again, but she still tensed, and he felt as awkward as he had with Timmy in the beginning, giving him his first bottle.

She took a small sip, followed by another—all the while keeping her gaze on him—until she drained the glass.

"More?"

"No, thanks." She had a faded scar and a tiny bump on the bridge of her nose, barely noticeable unless you were up real close, which he realized he still was and leaned back. As soon as he did, she relaxed somewhat. "Who...are you?"

"Didn't I...?" Well, hell. No wonder she acted like he might be an escaped convict. "Sorry. Brooks Hart." He held out his hand.

She hesitated, then took it, but only for an instant, like

putting her hand in an alligator's mouth just once to prove she could. "Brooks," she said slowly, as if testing the sound of his name on her tongue.

It sounded good to him. A little too good. He shifted and rubbed the back of his neck. "Nice to meet you, *ma'am,*" he said, not only to show respect but to remind himself of their professional, working relationship.

She noticed. "What...do I call you? Mister—?"

"No. No mister. Just Brooks."

"No *ma'am* then. Just..." She stared at him, a crease forming between her brows. "Brooks?" The crease deepened. "Do you know who *I* am?"

He grimaced. "Jo told me. I saw your shoes, but I didn't expect... I had no idea..." He expelled a breath. "Sorry I didn't make the connection right away. You sound different in person." Younger. Sweeter. "'Course, I *was* functioning on an hour's sleep when we spoke. Like I said, calving's our craziest season as it is, so the past month's been...particularly challenging."

"Challenging..."

"Yeah." He combed his fingers through his hair. "The height of calving's over now, so we're anxious to settle into a less frantic routine. Especially with your help."

"I'm...here to *help*..."

"And we're glad to have you. Believe me. Welcome."

She tried to smile. She wanted to say she was glad to be there, except her gaze darted around the room in mounting alarm at the unfamiliarity of everything. She had no idea where she was—and she didn't mean which room.

Brooks Hart hadn't answered her question, as if the answer should have been obvious. Except nothing was obvious.

Not to her.

She swallowed thickly. Calm. She had to remain calm. "I just feel...awful. Like I've been run over by a truck."

He adjusted the ice pack on her forehead, so it wouldn't fall. "You cracked yourself a good one. What happened?"

"I...I'm not quite sure."

"Whatever it was, Jo'll fix you up. She's a fine doctor." He said the words with such conviction, she wondered if the reassurances were more for him than for her.

Something was wrong. Terribly wrong. Far more than physical discomfort. Discord. The world was out of whack, and she was helpless to do anything about righting it.

She stared at the man who seemed her only lifeline, afraid if she took her gaze from him, he might disappear. For the moment, she didn't know which unsettled her worse—his presence or his absence.

He was a very big man—tall and broad. From what she could tell, solid muscle. His size and strength made her uncomfortable despite the fact he'd been nothing but kind.

She couldn't remember her own name, but she remembered a wariness of men in general and large ones in particular. She didn't know where she was, or how she got here, yet she could look into this stranger's rugged, handsome face and know with certainty his eyes were the same deep sapphire as an Alaskan lake, and his hair was as black as midnight without a moon.

How could she know these things and not know something as simple as her own name?

A door slammed, and Brooks rose from the table. "Don't move, Amelia."

Amelia.

The name rang in her ears, like a key on an out-of-tune piano.

"No," she wanted to protest, only she couldn't because she didn't know what else to say. For some odd reason, her brain felt like cotton candy, and her mind was drifting.

When she opened her groggy eyes, she tried to focus on the red-haired woman who introduced herself as Dr. Jo, then flashed a penlight in her eyes.

"Follow my light," she instructed. "Good. So how'd you come across this prize-winning goose egg?"

"I don't remember. It was there when I woke up."

"How many fingers am I holding up?"

"Three."

"Mmm-hmm." The doctor proceeded to check her reflexes. "Can you tell me what day of the week it is?"

She frowned, realizing she had no idea.

"Okay, something easier. How about your full name?"

"Amelia?" She repeated the name she'd heard earlier.

"And your last name?"

She drew a complete blank. She pursed her lips and tried to concentrate but to no avail. Finally she shook her head, feeling the bite of tears behind her eyelids.

Something chased across the doctor's face—something that looked an awful lot like worry—but then, it was gone.

"Hey, that's okay." Dr. Jo squeezed her hand. "Your vitals and responses are great. You have some confusion—retrograde amnesia, I suspect. It's pretty common with head injuries, but there's usually rapid recovery. We'll run you down to the hospital and take some X rays to play it safe."

At the mention of a hospital, a bright, white light flashed in her mind's eye. Bigger and brighter it grew, obscuring blue uniforms…masked faces…sympathetic eyes. The smell of antiseptic filled her nostrils…choking, suffocating, drowning out questions. Endless questions.

"No!" She bolted upright, ignoring the sudden wave of light-headedness. "No hospitals."

"Easy there." Dr. Jo touched a hand to her shoulder. "It won't take very long."

Adamant, she shook her head. "No hospitals. Please."

"Okay, all right." The doctor eased her back onto the

cushions. "It'll probably be moot by morning, but if not… I can't force you, but I *am* known to be highly persuasive— fair warning. Until then, I want you resting comfortably."

She closed her eyes in weary gratitude. "Thank you."

"Brooks, if you wouldn't mind monitoring her condition through the night…"

Across the room, a throat cleared. A deep voice said, "No problem. Just tell me what to do. Mitch and Dean are working night shift, so it's just Timmy and me."

"Oh. On second thought, maybe I ought to keep Timmy."

"Hey. A little faith. I can manage on my own for one night."

She pried open one heavy eyelid, just enough to discern Brooks's tall stature and Dr. Jo's smaller one. The doctor's tone changed when she talked to Brooks. More casual.

"I don't know, Brooks. The three of you weren't doing so hot last I checked. That was, oh, last night."

"Well, you went and changed Timmy's formula without telling us what other changes to expect. We were… overwhelmed."

"So you decided to use a shower hose."

"Worked fine, didn't it?"

"Is my number programmed in the speed dial?"

"Every phone in the house."

"And you promise to call if you need anything?"

"Cross my heart."

"All right then." Dr. Jo reverted to physician mode and rattled off a bunch of instructions. "If there's any change, I want you to call me ASAP."

"Got it," Brooks agreed.

"Amelia, I want complete bed rest from you, okay?"

"Okay." She was too tired to protest, to focus on any of the fuzzy questions running through her brain.

Brooks started a fire in the native rock hearth, and soon

the kindling snapped, crackled and hissed. She took a breath and snuggled against the afghan Dr. Jo draped over her, barely conscious of the hushed whispers moving away....

"She's skittish."

"Hello? She's in a brand-new place, about to start a brand-new job, and she brains herself, knocking out some not-so-trivial facts. You'd be skittish, too, tough guy."

"Maybe. It's just... Never mind. Should I move her into the guest room?"

"In a bit. Let her rest where she is a while...."

Yes, rest. That was what she needed. A nice, long nap. Maybe sleep would clear the cobwebs from her mind. Maybe she was just dreaming anyway. Maybe...

Timmy's nanny cried in her sleep. Half an hour after moving her to the guest room, Brooks watched tears trickle from her closed eyes. She'd curled into a ball, clutching her stomach with both arms. Her brows knitted together.

"Baby," she'd whispered a few times, and he wondered if she meant Timmy, if her subconscious was trying to "work."

"Don't worry," he found himself whispering in return. "The baby's fine." He didn't know if she could hear him.

He thought about waking her, then decided against it. Jo had said she needed to rest between timed rousings, and since she didn't even stir when he'd moved her, he figured she needed it pretty badly. Without a sound, he closed the door behind him. A few steps away, he paused, still amazed at the transformation of the room they now called the nursery.

Toys, books, baby furniture, farm animal wallpaper and border. Still, nothing stamped a brand on the room like the blond-haired, blue-eyed boy who sat in his crib, rubbing his eyes with his tiny fists as he woke up from his nap.

Timmy.

In four short weeks, he'd managed to turn their lives upside-down. Not that he was a burden—he wasn't. He was just a surprise, like an early spring thaw, rendering them excited, though ill prepared.

"Hey, chief. Didn't hear you wake up." Usually he woke up crying, but today, he just sat there looking groggy like he wasn't sure if he was ready to get up yet. "Huh-uh. Can't have you going back to sleep, or we'll be up all night. Look here. What's this?" Brooks took the awaiting bottle from the dresser. "Apple juice. Your favorite. Mmm-umm."

As Timmy reached for the bottle, Brooks scooped him up and changed his diaper, careful to put it on the right way—diapers were trickier than they looked. He put Timmy down on the carpet and went to wash up in the bathroom. As he dried his hands, a thump came from the guest room. Reeling around, he retraced his steps to find Amelia sprawled on the floor.

She looked up when he entered, that same Goldilocks-startled expression on her face, only she didn't make him feel like one of the Three Bears, but the Big Bad Wolf.

As he stepped forward, she scrambled back, coming up against the bed. He was trying not to take it personally, told himself she was still out-of-it. But he didn't like it. Not one bit. Something about her expression reminded him of the way his mother had looked at his father, the way Brooks had sworn no woman or child would ever look at him.

With fear.

It made him want to compensate, earn her trust. Prove he was different. He scooted back, wanting to give her as much room as she needed. "You okay?" He crooked his head. "I heard you fall."

She glanced down, as if to make sure for herself, then

up at him, as if she didn't trust him enough to take her eye off him for more than a second. "Where am I?"

"The guest room."

"Whose?"

He thought it obvious but answered anyway. "Mine."

Her gaze swept around the only room in the house with a feminine touch. Curtains, bedding and rugs in pastel colors. Dry flowers in vases. *"Yours?"*

"Well, formerly Jo's," he explained. "She kinda went overboard with frou-frous, being the only girl in the family. We thought you'd be more comfortable—"

"And these...?" She smoothed a hand over her new bedclothes. A pair of sweatpants Jo had left over here and a thermal shirt Brooks had accidentally shrunk. Jo, rooting through his drawers, had pulled it out and guessed it would fit Amelia. She was right. It did. And the sight brought an unexpected tightness to his throat.

Jo had said she looked underweight—not eating disorder range, but enough she'd suspected recent stress or illness and recommended extra helpings of Clara's home-cooking. At once, Brooks understood what his sister had meant.

The soft, stretchy weave hugged two arms he could have circled with a thumb and forefinger, a waist he could tuck between his hands, breasts that would barely fill his palms.

If she'd been a stray, he would have taken her home in an instant, hand-fed her until she fattened up and kept her for his own. But women weren't like critters, and he never entertained the thought of keeping one.

He couldn't afford to, given his family history.

"The shirt's mine," he answered, wondering if he didn't sound like a three-year-old.

Mine, mine, mine.

Only the woman herself was not his, nor would she ever be. She was here for a job, hired because he had no choice. For Timmy's sake, he hoped she'd stick it out a few years.

"That is, it *was*," he amended on the shirt, "before I shrunk it. The sweatpants are Jo's. She changed you," he clarified. "Thought you'd be warmer. Couldn't find your luggage anywhere. Just some wet clothes in a garbage bag."

Amelia pursed her lips as if trying to remember, then shook her head.

"Here, why don't you let me help you back into bed."

"*No*. Thank you." She held up a hand. "I can manage." She grasped the edge of the bed and rose on shaky legs, her gaze shifting between him and the task at hand.

He picked the edge of the down comforter off the floor, keeping his distance as she eased under the covers. The last thing he needed was for this woman to think he was putting the moves on her. Living out in the back of beyond, they had enough trouble appealing to city folk, never mind single women willing to care for another's child. He wasn't going to screw this up for Timmy.

"We figured you took a bus from the airport and caught a ride from town." He adjusted the bedding. "I would have picked you up if I'd known you were coming. Were your bags delayed?"

She stared at him, her expression blank.

"Never mind. I'll run down to Casper when they show—"

"Casper?"

"Yeah, Sheridan's closer, but if you don't like puddle-jumpers, you're better off flying into Billings or—"

"Casper." She threw off the covers and started to get up. "I have to go. I have to find…"

"What? Your bags? I'm sure the airlines—"

"No, not what. *Whom*. I have to find…" She frowned and rubbed her temple. "I'm not sure."

"Tell you what." Brooks placed a restraining hand on her shoulder. When she jerked back against the pillows, he stuck the guilty hand behind his back, feeling like a leper. "When you can get out of bed without falling, you can go wherever you like. Until then, I gotta answer to Dr. Jo, and frankly, I don't relish the thought of my head on a platter."

At a high-pitched squeal of delight, Brooks turned to see Timmy set his diapered butt down in the entryway. He clapped his hands and gave them both a gummy grin, proudly displaying his two new bottom teeth.

"Yep. This is why we don't leave the safety gate open." Brooks chuckled and shook his head. Once king of his palace, he'd abdicated the throne to an infant. Then his gaze went to Amelia, and the smile slid from his face.

She'd gone stark white, gripping the sheets up to her neck with two knuckle-drawn fists. Her gaze darted between Timmy and him.

"Amelia? What's wrong?"

She shook her head. "I—I don't know. Seeing…your baby gave me a jolt. I can't explain it."

"It's okay," he said, though he suspected it was more than a jolt. In her interview, Amelia had told them she couldn't have children—the reason she'd first decided to become a nanny. "Jo said you might be a little confused." But it wasn't just confusion, and he knew it.

He'd recognized the unmasked yearning in her eyes when she looked at Timmy. Brooks had been there himself, around his friends' wives and kids. Wanting something and seeing it, knowing all the while, it could never be yours.

But where he'd worked long and hard to stomp out his needs, Amelia flung herself smack dab in temptation's path.

In a way, he admired her, but he also questioned how safe it was, emotionally, for her to become involved with other people's kids. But then, the nanny agency had sent glowing letters of recommendation. Brooks had phoned each family personally. No one had any reservations whatsoever.

"Well, we better leave you to rest." He scooped his nephew into his arms. "Timmy needs his nanny back on her feet as soon as possible, don't you, little guy?"

"Nanny?"

Timmy craned his head around as if trying to locate who had spoken. Seeing Amelia, he beamed and extended his arms.

"Whoa. Where do you think you're going?"

In response, Timmy lunged. Brooks latched onto him, preventing a nosedive onto the bed.

Amelia smiled. "He's a beautiful baby."

"A beautiful baby who appears to prefer women."

"How old is he?"

"Nine months." Hard to believe they'd had him a month. Sometimes, it seemed like yesterday. More often, like he'd been there all along. "Obviously getting an early start on skirt-chasing. Timmy, come on." He jostled the now-fussing baby. "Stop flirting. Amelia's not feeling well. We need to get you out of here, so she can rest. Say bye-bye."

"Bye-bye." Amelia waved.

Timmy started whimpering. As soon as the door closed behind them, he let loose a full-fledged wail, turning back with one arm outstretched.

"There, there, chief." Instinctively Brooks rubbed Timmy's back. "Amelia's going to play with you later on. She needs to get some shut-eye first, okay?"

But it took more than a few minutes to soothe Timmy. His plaintive sobs reminded Brooks of calves bawling for their mothers during fall weaning. Poor little buckaroo.

There was nothing Brooks wouldn't do to make things right for him.

She couldn't lie still. There was a strange, buzzing anxiety inside her. A void she needed desperately to fill. What was it?

She tossed and turned in her bed, first hot, then cold. She

threw the covers off, then pulled them back. Was it the wind that moaned, or was it her? Through the fog of bizarre dreams, Brooks Hart's deep, steady voice lured her out of the darkness, coaxing her to respond at scheduled intervals.

Brooks Hart.

She didn't know him. His name meant nothing. Neither did hers. Surely it would come back to her in the morning. She wouldn't panic until then. She wouldn't panic…

She awakened to the sound of a baby's cries. Her eyes flew open, and she stumbled to her feet. "Coming!"

"Amelia?"

"I'm coming!" She tried to run for the door, but her body and her mind couldn't connect. Limbs tangled, and she collapsed in a heap on the floor.

A small lamp clicked on, blinding her with its sudden brightness. She blinked as two strong hands pulled her up. And then she was back in the bed, Brooks tugging the sheet to cover her.

"No, don't." She flailed her arms, gesturing toward the door. "I have to go. The baby."

"Shh, it's all right." His now-familiar voice came low and comforting, but she wasn't the one who needed the comfort. Didn't he understand?

"Please." Her voice cracked. "I have to go to him."

"I'll go. You stay."

"But…but he needs me."

"I'll go. You stay," he repeated in a tone that left no room for argument. He took her shoulders and nudged her back against the pillows. "I'll take care of him. Don't worry. Get your rest. You'll need it while he's teething."

"He…he's teething?"

"That's why he's crying. He needs a nightly fix of numbing gel for his gums."

She bit her lip and watched him leave. Outside, the wind roared, rattling the windowpanes. She shivered and rubbed her arms, racking her brain for something, anything that would fit together her fragmented thoughts and right her world again. But there was nothing. Nothing except these powerful feelings with no memories on which to hang.

She wanted to see the baby, *needed* to see him with her own eyes. Determined, she got to her feet, steadied herself and headed for the door. This time her arms and legs obeyed her brain's commands, and she made it without mishap.

As she turned the knob, she braced for opposition, but no one was there. Relieved, she slipped out undetected.

A faint patch of light spilled into the hallway from an open door. There were four doors in total—including her bedroom and a bathroom—off this first floor hallway. She took a cautious step, followed by another, until she could peek inside.

It was a nursery. A Cat In the Hat night-light cast a warm, cozy glow over the room, illuminating the form of a large man in a comparatively small rocking chair. With his foot, he pushed the rocker back and forth, and in his arms, he cradled a little bundle as if it were his most precious possession.

At his obvious devotion, a tightly wound coil loosened inside her, releasing an unbearable pressure. Every muscle in her body eased, and she nearly sagged against the door.

Brooks's lips were moving, and she wanted to tell him not to talk when the baby woke up in the middle of the night, that he wouldn't fall back asleep. Instead she held her tongue and strained to distinguish the quietly spoken words.

"Uncle Dean asked about the meaning of life today. Can you believe that? Seems like just yesterday he was asking me to tie his shoes. Now he's talking about the meaning of life.'' He shook his head. ''I didn't know what to say. When a man sees life and death every season, you'd think he'd have an answer. Truth is, I haven't given it much thought. Why *are* we here, each of us?'' He frowned. ''Heck if I know.''

Timmy gurgled and reached for Brooks's face, clapping his tiny hands on his uncle's cheeks. Brooks chuckled, a rich sound that wrapped around her heart. ''All right, we're way too awake, chief, but I can fix that.'' He reached for the bookshelf beside them and took a magazine from the stack. *Farmer's Almanac.* He gentled his voice and started to read.

Watching them, calmness settled over her.

It was all right. Everything would be all right now.

Silently she crept back to the guest room and crawled into bed, too tired to even pull up the covers. Every bone in her body ached, not just her head.

Sometime later, when she started to drift off, she felt the soft covers being drawn over her legs, tucked around her. She waited a minute, then opened her eyes to see Brooks by the window, holding the curtain aside so he could look out.

Lamplight filtered through the glass pane, exposing his unguarded expression, one of pain and worry.

She knew that look. She'd seen it countless times. Her own face in the mirror.

''They say you can't run forever, but they're wrong, aren't they?'' she whispered.

He turned to her. Their gazes met and held like two laser beams. But sleep beckoned, and she could fight it no longer. So she closed her eyes and let the darkness carry her to a place where pain and worry weren't her constant companions, driving her to keep running time and again.

Chapter 2

The woman in the mirror looked no more familiar to her the next day. But when Dr. Jo again pressed for X rays, she begged her to hold off a little longer. For the life of her, she couldn't shake a deep-seated fear of having to go to the hospital. She didn't want to go; moreover, she felt stupid.

Certainly no one gave her any reason to feel this way. In fact, everyone had gone overboard to see to her comfort. Brooks had sacrificed his own sleep to keep a night-long vigil over her, then topped it off by bringing her breakfast in bed. Dr. Jo not only made house calls but lent her clothes.

Such kindness for a stranger was hard to believe. She felt as though the checkout clerk at the grocery store had accidentally forgotten to charge her for something, only she didn't know *what,* so she couldn't attempt to fix the mistake.

Carefully she touched the bump on her head. It was still

tender, but the swelling had gone down, and she wasn't nearly as woozy after dozing on and off all morning and into the afternoon. That was something. She tried to keep faith the rest would soon follow. In the meantime, she did have a job to do....

It had surprised her at first to learn she was a nanny, but then, she couldn't deny her instant connection with her ward. It felt right that she was here to care for him. She certainly had a nanny's radar, judging from last night.

With firm resolve, she put a lid on her worries, tossed aside her towel along with her paranoia and changed into her new clothes and new attitude.

Drawing back the curtains, she feasted her sight on a panoramic view of vast, open land. Ahead and to her left, rolling hills appeared to stretch all the way to the sky. Cows speckled the snow-covered landscape like dark polka dots. To her right, steep foothills gave rise to majestic mountains, behind which the sun poised to sink. Its fiery glow painted the high wisps of clouds in brilliant pinks and outlined the profile of a man riding horseback, checking the cows in a nearby corral.

She recognized Brooks from his broad shoulders and tall, commanding presence. The blanket of freshly fallen snow contrasted with his golden, sun-bronzed face. Chaps covered long, jean-clad legs, and a black Stetson tipped low over his forehead. He rode the powerful animal with the easy assurance of a man thoroughly accustomed to it, and when he turned and headed toward a big, red barn, her breathing grew shallow at the mesmerizing silhouette—a man and his horse riding into the sunset.

In that moment, she understood the appeal of the mythical cowboy.

Flushed, she unlatched the window and cracked it open for some fresh air. A nippy breeze blew in, carrying the smell of winter wrestling its way to spring. She inhaled, filling her lungs with crisp air, when the tinkle of wind chimes mingled with a baby's cry.

Her diaphragm froze. Alarm jolted every vertebra in her spine. She whirled for the door, her instinct to go after the baby stronger than ever. But the instant she turned the knob, the cries stopped.

What happened?

She raced back to the window, straining to hear past the pounding in her ears. Something, anything…? Nothing. And then…yes…a high-pitched squeal. A happy sound.

An elderly woman came into view. In her arms, she held Timmy, playing peekaboo with his bright red hood. Hearty giggles punctuated his delight.

Oh, thank God. She covered her thudding heart and sank boneless onto the edge of the bed. Boy, she obviously took her job seriously, if her still-shaking limbs were any sign.

"Okay. Breathe," she coached herself. "In. Out. In. Out. You can do this." She'd done this breathing exercise before; there was familiarity in the routine.

Once she'd regulated her breathing, she forced herself to finish getting ready, drying her hair and brushing it out with slow, easy motions. Again, she grounded herself in tasks that seemed second-nature. By the time a rap sounded at the door, she felt much better. "Come in," she called.

The door swung open, and Brooks's tall frame filled the entrance. Slightly bow-legged, he wore his faded Wranglers longish, the denim stacked from his knees down, frayed cuffs dragging at his heels. His silver belt buckle was D-shaped, like a sideways horseshoe, a horizontal bar hinged to the vertical bar of the D. His Western-style shirt accentuated his broad, muscled shoulders, a flat belly and a trim waist. He'd left two pearl snaps undone, and a white T-shirt peeked from below the hollow of his throat. There were splotches of orange paint on his jeans. His short, dark hair was matted with sweat, and he carried the scent of the earth and freshly fallen snow, of leather and horses and an honest day's work.

Oh, yes. She understood the appeal very well now....

"You're up." He smiled. "And dressed."

She wore a pair of his sister's denim overalls and a cream-colored, ribbed turtleneck. "Clean, too."

"One up on me." His smile widened, and he hitched a thumb over his shoulder. "I was about to hit the shower. Thought I'd check on you first. Clothes fit okay?"

A smile tugged up the corners of her own lips as she recalled the tinge of color in his cheeks that morning when he'd set the package of new cotton underwear alongside the stack of clothing Jo had dropped off.

"Yes, thank you," she said. The secondhand garments were baggy but comfortable, and she wasn't going to complain.

He tipped his head. "Feel up to joining us for supper? It's your call. I'll fix you another tray if you'd rather—"

"No, no. I've had enough room service. I'd like get out, see the baby."

Brooks turned his gaze to the window. Had she not been deliberating the hue of his eyes again, she might have missed the way they softened. Her gaze followed his to the backyard where two men stood. One of them held Timmy.

She straightened. Where had the elderly woman gone?

A buzzing uneasiness mounted inside her, fueled by an inexplicable protectiveness that made her shudder from the sheer force of it.

"You're cold," Brooks said, as if drawn by the abrupt movement. "I'll close the window."

"No," she answered a bit too sharply. "Th-thank you."

"Sure?" At her jerky nod, he said, "Weather's crazy in March. Rain, shine, sleet, snow. Runs the gamut."

Vaguely she registered the snowflakes that started to fall,

but she was more concerned with the men with the baby. "Who are they?"

"That's Mitch with the chief."

"Chief?"

"Er, Timmy. They're talking to a neighbor who helped out during the height of calving. It's the best and worst time. Hours are long, and sleep's short. But it's the start of a new cycle, so it's exciting despite the hassles." His deep, husky voice was a salve on her frazzled nerves.

She was starting to get used to him. Maybe even like him a little. He did have kind eyes and a nice voice. But like a stray sniffing a stranger's hand before approaching, she couldn't explain her wariness, only knew she wasn't ready to trust anyone too much. "Mitch...? Next in line after Jo?"

Brooks nodded. He'd told her the "pecking order" of Hart siblings. His two brothers Mitch and Dean brought up the rear at twenty-seven and twenty-five.

"How is he with Timmy?" She tried to sound casual.

As if sensing her concern, Brooks reassured, "Real good. Always had a gift with horses—tames even the wildest beasts. No real wonder he's a natural with babies, too."

Was that a pang of envy beneath his obvious admiration?

"My expertise is limited to ranching," he said in answer to her unasked question. "I'm kinda counting on you to...help me figure out this baby stuff." Shifting, he dropped his gaze momentarily, and she was struck by the flash of vulnerability in this towering hulk of a man who for all appearances wasn't intimidated by anyone or anything.

"I'll do everything I can," she said, hoping she'd have something of value to offer him, after all he'd done for her.

"I appreciate it. So, you hungry?" He rubbed his hands together and grinned, revealing the long slash of a dimple in his left cheek.

A shiver of awareness that had nothing to do with food danced up her spine. She swallowed. "I—I think my appetite might be coming back."

"Good, because Clara's the best cook in the county."

"Is that who was out there earlier with Timmy?"

"Yep, and let me tell you, that woman bakes a mean apple pie. She's got three in the oven as we speak."

"Three? Wow. We'll be eating pie all week."

Brooks laughed, a hearty, rumbling sound. "Don't bet on it. Three's nothing around here. They'll be gone inside thirty seconds, so if you want a piece, you'd best be at the table by the time they cool." He eyed the clock on the bedside table. "I'd say another fifteen minutes, tops."

"I'll be there."

"Timmy will be glad to see you. He's had his ups and downs, but meeting you was a definite up."

She raised an eyebrow. "He told you this, I suppose."

Brooks grinned. "Not in so many words, but trust me, you made a great first impression. I thought he'd camp outside your door the way he fussed. He's had a rough start," he said by way of explanation. "Luke—his daddy, our oldest brother—just died. His mother bailed on them a few months before that, so the kid's pretty much an orphan."

"How awful. The poor baby. Thank goodness he has you." Before she knew it, her eyes teared up. "Oh. Oh, my." She blinked rapidly, startled by her emotions. "I didn't expect this." Embarrassed, she dabbed the corners of her eyes, but Brooks just smiled.

"Got a soft spot for babies, don't you?"

"I must." She gave a nervous smile. "Sorry—"

"Don't apologize. That's why we hired you." His gaze held hers a long moment, and she wondered what he saw when he looked at her, if he could make any more sense of the stranger who looked back at her in the mirror.

He shifted then, lifting one large hand to his shoulder as if to work out a knot. "I've got calls in to the airlines about your luggage. Can't imagine what happened to your purse or handbag or whatever women always have with them."

"Maybe I left it somewhere?"

"If it's with your ride, they'll figure it out soon enough. Might want to check with the bus company, too."

"I'll do that," she said. "If you could point me in the direction of the phone book later...?"

He nodded. "By the way, we call the noon meal 'dinner' around here, the evening 'supper.' Didn't know if you knew."

"No, I...I didn't."

He face slipped into a frown then as if something just occurred to him. "I hope this wasn't some kind of foul play, clobbering you on the head and taking off with your money."

Her eyes widened. She'd never considered that. "You think...?"

"Nah." He shook his head. "Now that I think about it, what are the chances of someone whacking you on the forehead?"

"I...I don't know."

"Slim to none. Usually you get clubbed on the side or the top or even the back. Front? That's likely accidental."

She narrowed her gaze, studying him. For a nonmedical type, he sure knew a lot about head injuries. "Maybe the bus driver—or my ride—slammed on the brakes. I banged my head, and in my daze, I forgot my purse."

"Now *that* is a highly probable scenario. We've got a constant problem with hitting deer out here." He rocked back on his heels, visibly impressed. "You're good with puzzles."

"So are you. From what you know about head injuries, you could have been a doctor yourself. Or a cop maybe."

At the offhand remark, a shadow chased over his face like a storm cloud drifting overhead. A muscle in his jaw pulsed, then relaxed.

Had she said something wrong or was it her imagination?

"I'm going to take that shower now." He inclined his head toward the door. "Unless you need anything here?"

"I'm fine. Thanks." She rubbed her temple and watched his retreat. Not a bad retreat, she mused, surprising herself. It wasn't until the door started to close that she thought of something. "Wait. Sorry. There *is* one thing I meant to ask before. Do you, by chance, have my résumé?"

He drew his brows together. "Of course."

"I mean, handy. I…I'm curious about myself." She shrugged, hoping he wouldn't find her request too strange.

"Oh, right." He snapped his fingers as if he should have thought of it. "Hang on." He strode from the room, then returned carrying a manila folder. "Here's everything I've got. You're welcome to look through it." He extended his hand, ropes of muscle like whipcords in his arms.

"Thanks." Gingerly she forced herself to reach out and take the offering, to hold steady and not shrink back. "I— I appreciate it."

"No problem." If he'd noticed her resistance, he didn't show it. "See you in a bit."

"See you." She forced a smile. The second the door closed, she emptied the contents of the folder onto the bed, fanning the papers so she could scan them in one sweeping glance.

Résumé, letters of recommendation, an application for employment through the Triple H Cattle Company. She read every word—twice. Every last shred of evidence indicated she was absolutely incredible at what she did—even if she couldn't remember any of it.

She replaced the papers in the folder and sighed in frustration. She hated living in a vacuum, hated all these questions with answers just out of her reach. Her thoughts turned to the hospital, and she worried her lip.

Dr. Jo had assured her the tests would be strictly outpatient, that she'd likely be in and out in a few hours, but Amelia's chest still tightened painfully at the thought.

When the urge to hyperventilate struck, she closed her eyes and forced several deep, calming breaths. Above all, she could *not* risk letting her new employer think she was a nutcase while she awaited the return of her elusive memory.

What if he sent her packing? Where would she go? She obviously didn't have a home of her own. She hadn't listed any relatives on her application, giving the main number at the agency as her emergency contact. No family to speak of. And no money, as far as she knew.

She hated to admit she needed to go to the hospital, needed to get those X rays. *Why*, she wondered, did the idea of something that could possibly help her scare her to death?

"Death by apple pie." Brooks closed his eyes and inhaled the mouthwatering aroma. "Clara, if you weren't already married..."

"Get outta here." The sixty-five-year-old wife of their longtime foreman swatted his hand with a twisted towel. Her short, white curls always had a windblown look, and her face had softened more from the great outdoors than age. "Brooks Hart, there ain't a woman in three counties wouldn't take you up on an offer of marriage."

"But none that can bake an apple pie as fine as yours."

"I'll make you a deal. You find yourself a filly, and I'll give her my secret recipe."

"How about you give it to me?"

"No deal."

"Come on, Clara. It's not fair to keep holding out on me like this. You know I'm a confirmed bachelor."

"And it's a sorry state, I tell you. A man can't go through life alone. Ask Pete. He tried and see what he was missing out on?" She indicated with a flourish of her hand.

"No argument here." Brooks grinned and pecked Clara on the cheek. "But you're already taken, darlin'."

Clara made a noise that told him he wasn't fooling her, but she beamed all the same at the endearment.

One fine morning when Brooks was fourteen, a year after his mother took off for parts unknown, the old man finally went and drowned himself in his bottle. Luke was oldest at seventeen, not old enough to serve as legal guardian, so Pete and Clara stepped in to keep five kids from being split into foster homes. Best thing that ever happened to them.

"It's breaking Pete's heart to miss calving this year," Clara said. "I tell him a man's gotta retire sometime, but if he hadn't broke his leg, I know he'd be out there 'round the clock. Don't nobody call him an old stove-up cowboy."

"Hmm. Now who does that sound like? Let me think." He rubbed his chin thoughtfully.

"All right, smarty-pants." Clara put a hand on her hip. "You made your point." Though she was past due for her own retirement, she claimed cooking as a hobby, "not work," and took exception to every cook he tried to hire, finding some perceived fault that made them unacceptable.

But he'd drawn the line when she offered to watch Timmy full-time. With no children of her own, she didn't have any more experience with babies than he did. And though he could use a hand every now and then, he didn't want Clara spending her golden years changing diapers, if he had any say in it.

Truthfully he could tell she'd been relieved when Jo recommended—and he'd concurred—they should hire a nanny.

Brooks pulled out a chair from the long oak table and straddled it backward, watching Timmy in his walker. "Easy on the bouncing, chief." He reached out a hand. "All that action after a feeding makes me nervous. Call me skeptical, but I know your tummy."

Timmy gave an enthusiastic squeal and maneuvered away, heading for the doorway. Brooks glanced up to see Amelia standing there. Arms folded, she had a crease between her eyebrows as if unsure she'd made it to the right place.

Timmy, on the other hand, had no such reservations. Half bouncing, half dragging, he steered a path to his new best friend, arms outstretched.

"What are you, the Pied Piper?" Brooks asked in wonder.

Clara stood at the stove, clucking at Timmy's response.

Amelia shook her head as if she, too, couldn't believe such a warm reception. But in mere seconds, her expression shifted from wary curiosity to pure delight. A broad grin broke across her face as she squatted, extending her hands toward Timmy.

Brooks stopped breathing. He'd thought she was pretty before, but her smile lit up her entire face, erasing worry lines and bringing a glow to her cheeks. She was more than pretty when she wore that smile. She was an angel.

"Is it okay?" She glanced up at him, the look in her eyes—open, honest and pure—unlike any he'd seen.

His tongue stuck to the roof of his mouth, and it took him a second to realize she was asking permission to hold Timmy. "Please." At this point, Brooks was afraid of what would happen if she didn't. Timmy had some powerful pipes, as she was going to find out if she *didn't* pick him up soon.

Thankfully she did. "Hi, sweetie." She lifted him into her arms, crooning in a voice filled with magic and life.

"How are you? Are you being a good boy for Uncle Brooks? Yeah?"

Like an orphaned calf grafting on a surrogate mother, Timmy dropped his head on Amelia's shoulder and stuck his thumb in his mouth.

"Aw…" Her arms curved around him, one hand rubbing the back of his blue corduroy overalls as she rocked from side to side. "What flavor is that thumb? Strawberry? Or maybe chocolate?" She brushed her cheek against the thatch of hair at the crown of his head. "I'll bet it's yummy."

If not for Jo, Brooks wouldn't have known jack squat about the way it was supposed to be between women and their babies, and though this woman wasn't a mother herself, every instinct he possessed told him she had what it took.

For a heart-stopping moment, he damn near asked her to marry him right there on the spot. And from the look Clara shot him, she had half a mind to ask on his behalf.

Belatedly he remembered himself and his manners and rubbed a hand over his face to break the spell. "Amelia, this is Clara. Clara, this is Amelia."

"Hi." Amelia smiled and extended her free hand.

Clara smiled back and took her hand, nodding at Timmy. "That's some sampling of your services. I can see why the nanny agency says you're the best. Gonna have to keep you around long as we can. Right, Brooks?"

"Yes, ma'am."

At the buzz of the timer, Clara turned to the stove. "You know how to bake apple pie, Amelia?"

Amelia pursed her lips and appeared to search her memory banks. Finally she frowned. "I don't think so."

"Not to worry, dear." Clara patted her arm. "I got this great recipe. Been passed down through generations. Might even be inclined to share it one day." She gazed pointedly at Brooks. "Under the right circumstances."

"You play dirty, Clara."

"Yep, and don't believe anyone who tells you otherwise." She winked at Amelia. "You like ribs?"

Amelia gave a helpless shrug. "I'm sorry, I don't remember."

"Well, you'll like these ribs. Cured and smoked. Meat falls right off the bone and melts in your mouth."

Amelia moistened her lips. "My stomach's growling, if that's any indication."

Clara gestured toward the table. "Sit. Make yourself at home. No formalities here. Brooks—"

"I'll check." He was already in motion. "Here, you want to try giving him the rest of this?" He held out the bottle of formula.

"Sure." When their fingers brushed, her gaze cut to his. But instead of the full dose of caution he had come to expect, there was something new in the mix. Something good.

She was warming to him.

Good. He smiled and stepped back, not wanting to push his luck. "Be right back."

"Where...where are you going?"

"Just around the corner." He inclined his head toward the window. "Mitch and Dean are smoking the ribs out back. I'll get a status report."

"Oh. Okay." She nodded and gave a shy smile.

Progress indeed.

Brooks grabbed his coat from the hook on his way out. On the porch, he zipped up and glanced back at the window.

She'd taken his usual place at the table, one knee bent, so Timmy could lie across her lap. When her lips moved, the soft lilt of her voice replayed in his head. She chose that moment to look up. Spotting him, she smiled and waved.

His stomach hitched in a knot.

She looked good, sitting there with his baby nephew. She looked *damned good,* as if she belonged. For one crazy instant, he imagined the possibility of having more than a working relationship with her. Then he remembered all the reasons he couldn't, and reality crashed down.

Ah, hell. He shook his head in disgust, gave a halfhearted wave and jammed his hands into his pockets. Stepping from the porch, he cursed himself for even thinking about it.

Timmy's nanny was hardly material for a discreet, no-strings affair, and despite what he'd said to Clara, there was no way he'd ever risk anything but.

Amelia might have been the perfect match for Timmy, but Brooks could never be the perfect match for anyone.

Amelia grazed Timmy's rosy cheek with the back of her index finger. The corner of his mouth lifted as he dozed, and a sense of rightness settled around her for the first time since she awoke in this strange, unfamiliar world.

She draped a cloth over her shoulder and gently lifted him. The motion brought him out of his light catnap, but he seemed content to hang out in her arms. Mewing and kneading her overalls like a kitten, his sweet, baby scent and sounds filled the empty spaces in her heart if not her mind.

Just then, the door opened, and three tall, dark-haired men entered the kitchen one after another, the tantalizing aroma of barbecue wafting from the covered pans they placed on the counter. They stood side by side in line for the sink, their broad shoulders forming a formidable wall of muscle and sinew. Where before she'd found the large, country kitchen airy and spacious, it now seemed crowded.

Instinctively she held the baby a little closer.

"Guys, this is Amelia." Brooks reached for a towel to dry his hands. "Amelia, meet Mitch and Dean." He nodded at each brother respectively before throwing the towel to Dean, who caught it midair.

"Hey." Dean wiped quickly, slung the towel over Mitch's shoulder and stuck out his hand. He had boyish good looks and a bashful grin that belied the devilish sparkle in his eyes. "Nice to meet you."

"You, too." She took his hand. "You're the one who gives riding lessons at a neighboring ranch?"

"That's right." Dean tugged on Timmy's foot and was rewarded with a smile. "Gets me outta summer chores." He winked at Brooks who shook his head but grinned back.

"Not entirely, cowpoke." Brooks carried a pan to the table and uncovered the smoked ribs. "But I suppose anyone who willingly bonds with greenhorns deserves a few perks."

Mitch chuckled and thumped his younger brother on the back. "'Course it's not just any greenhorn who's got our Dean going back there every year." He extended his hand to Amelia. "Welcome. You'll get to meet Dean's girlfriend in a few months when her family comes out for their annual dude ranch adventure."

"She's not my girlfriend."

"Yeah, right." Mitch's playful grin revealed the long slash of a dimple identical to his older brother's. "That's how come you're blushing ten shades of red, right?"

Dean ducked his head.

Amelia smiled, relaxing a little at their good-natured ribbing. "Any chance of a nanny discount on riding lessons, Dean? I'm pretty sure I qualify as a greenhorn, too."

"Yep. For you, one hundred percent."

"Oh, I don't want to take advantage—"

"Standard nanny contract. Check your paperwork. And she's not my girlfriend," he insisted, setting silverware at everyone's place. Head bent in task, he watched Brooks from the corner of his eye.

"Need a shovel there, Dean?" Mitch chuckled.

Amid the jesting, Brooks raised an eyebrow and shot a measured glance at his youngest brother. Though his smile was good-natured, his voice carried a serious undercurrent. "Next time I read Timmy the story of *Country Mouse and City Mouse,* you might want to sit in for a refresher."

"All right, boys." Clara whipped off her apron and wiped her hands. "Let's table this subject. Amelia doesn't need to hear jaded cowboy philosophies over supper. Not to mention if the two of you had anything vaguely resembling love lives, you wouldn't feel the need to meddle in Dean's."

Three mouths dropped open, then snapped shut.

"I know, Dean." Amelia patted his hand, surprised by her heightened comfort level. "She's not your girlfriend."

"Thank you."

"Don't mention it." She scooted her chair back and stifled the urge to laugh. She was still an outsider and didn't want to overstep her bounds on their inside jokes. "The little one needs to freshen up."

"Uh-oh." Brooks eyed his nephew with apprehension.

"Rock, paper, scissors?" Mitch suggested.

"I, um, I'll help Clara fix up plates to take Pete." Dean tugged nervously at his collar. "Better pack extra, Clara. Pete's gotta be hungry as a bear, laid up in his cast. Here, let me get that for you."

With a resigned sigh, Brooks grimaced and held out his arms. "I'll take him."

"That's okay," Amelia reassured. "It's my job."

"Jo just changed his formula," he explained. "It might be a bigger job than usual."

"I'm sure I've seen worse."

"Maybe in a toxic waste dump." Mitch chuckled.

Clara whacked his elbow. "Mitchell Hart."

"Ma'am." He bowed his head, though one corner of his mouth curved.

"Please, go ahead and start." Amelia rose to her feet. "We'll catch up."

"I'll show you where everything is." Brooks gestured for Amelia to follow him. At the door, he paused. "Don't say we didn't warn you."

"Lead on. We're right behind you." Halfway down the hallway, she took one of Timmy's chubby hands and kissed his knuckles. "Look at that, sweetie. You've got a big, strong cowboy shaking in his boots."

The back of Brooks's neck turned red. He glanced over his shoulder, and for the briefest of seconds, she held her breath, regretting the impulsive quip. But he wore a humble grin, and to her surprise, something unmistakable flickered in those sapphire eyes—a glimmer of physical awareness.

Without conscious thought, an answering warmth spiraled through her. But just as swiftly, an alarm went off in the hidden corridors of her mind, as if someone had tripped the motion detector of a security system. Her muscles tensed.

Timmy started to squirm. She realized she was holding him too closely. Easing up, she gave herself a mental shake.

Snap out of it already.

"Here you go." Brooks stepped into the nursery, took a diaper from the changing station and popped the lid on a box of wipes. "All yours."

"Thanks." She whipped through the changing like a pro. Giving him a look that said no-big-deal, she sashayed past Brooks and into the hallway. In the adjacent bathroom, she turned on the faucet, washed both hers and Timmy's hands and splashed water on their faces.

Timmy stuck his tongue out to catch the water, then

lunged for the faucet. Amelia lowered him to sink level, so he could hold his hand under the stream for a few seconds.

"Okay, that's it." She turned off the water and dabbed a towel on Timmy's button nose. He cooed and reached for the soft cloth. She laughed and did it again, then glanced up to see Brooks lounged in the open doorway.

One ankle hooked over the other, he watched their exchange with curiosity. He had a lazy sensuality about him, a look that said "step into my parlor," instead of "ready or not, here I come," which did nothing to lessen her awareness of him but did make her feel more in control.

"Taking notes?" She folded the towel and hung it back on the rack.

"Sorry," he said but made no move to leave. "I don't mean to stare, but you have this way with him I can't help noticing. Like Mitch with horses. You seem to speak the same language."

"Ah, yes." She smiled mysteriously, as a wise woman who knew the secrets of the universe. "That would be the highly acclaimed language of baby talk. All nannies are proficient, I'm sure, but the skill isn't limited to the professionals. I have every confidence you, too, will learn in time." She sounded like an infomercial.

For once, Brooks didn't return her smile. He averted his gaze, his voice skeptical. "What if I'm illiterate in baby talk?"

"You're not."

"You don't know that."

"I do." When he frowned, clearly not convinced, she shifted Timmy to her hip and said, "I saw you last night."

That brought his head up, one brow raised in question.

She nodded. "I watched you rock him, even after he'd fallen back asleep. I don't know if it's a soft spot for children in general or this one in particular, but it's there, and I saw it. You'll make a good father, Brooks."

At her words, an unfathomable emotion darkened his eyes. He looked at Timmy for a long moment, as if he wanted to say more, then braced his hands on either side of the door frame.

The gesture suddenly made Amelia aware of the confining space in the bathroom...and the fact Brooks blocked the only exit.

Like the Coyote in the Road Runner cartoons, she didn't start to fall until she realized there was no ground beneath her feet.

All at once, the bathroom walls seemed to contract with Brooks's presence. Her vision tunneled. Her throat closed. Panic clawed its way to the surface. Air. She needed air.

"Please," she choked out, holding Timmy a little closer. "I—I'd like to leave." Her voice rang hollow in her ears, as if she were underwater.

Brooks straightened, looming even larger at his full height, confusion etched on his face. "Something I said?"

"No, no." She swallowed, fighting the urge to shrink back, to retreat into herself. *Use your words. Stay calm. Stand up for yourself.* "Please, can you let us out of the bathroom?"

"Oh. Right. Sorry." With a sheepish expression, he backed into the hallway, giving her a wide berth. "Didn't mean to hold you prisoner like that."

In the open space, a rush of cool air funneled around her. Her head cleared, and she regained her equilibrium.

"It's okay." She pulled in another deep, cleansing breath and summoned a smile. "I'm fine now." Which didn't change the fact she hadn't been fine a second ago. *Prisoner.* That summed up how she'd felt. Like a captive with no clear escape route. "I...I might have a touch of claustrophobia." Again, she felt embarrassed, but Brooks took it in stride.

"I'm the same in the city," he said. "All those people

everywhere, sticking to you like burs. Spend enough time in wide, open spaces, you get used to your own personal supply of air."

"I never thought of it like that."

"I'm glad it was only claustrophobia. You had me going for a second there. I thought you'd changed your mind about staying on as Timmy's nanny."

"No," she whispered, though she did wonder if it was *only* claustrophobia. "I'm not going anywhere." That much she knew. She was bound to this baby in a way that defied explanation. He was her anchor in a world that had turned upside-down and inside-out. He gave her purpose. He gave her life meaning. He gave her a great, big smile, and her insides turned to tapioca. "Aw." She kissed his forehead. "If you aren't just *the* cutest baby..."

"He likes you," Brooks said.

"I like him, too." She stroked his hair. "I can see the strong family resemblance. He's a minireplica of his uncles. Your square jaw, Mitch's lopsided smile, Dean's twinkling eyes. Except for this blond hair..."

"A trick of Mother Nature. All five of us started off as towheads, then Jo turned red, the rest of us dark brown. Everyone but Luke. He was the only one who stayed blond."

"Hmm. I wonder what'll happen to Timmy."

"No telling. Just have to stick around and find out."

"I'd like that," she said softly.

"Me, too," he mumbled.

Her gaze collided with his, and she found herself reluctant to look away, even when she knew she should.

He had the most incredible eyes—deep blue irises fringed with thick, black eyelashes. Bold. Hypnotic.

Sexy.

A slow, languorous heat pooled in her stomach. She

stepped back automatically, shaking her head to clear it. "We should, um, probably get back."

"Yeah. Right." He rubbed the back of his neck. "I don't trust those two alone with Clara's pies."

She nodded and led the way back to the kitchen, wondering if she could trust herself alone with *him*.

"Thanks." Amelia passed the mashed potatoes across the table to Brooks, took the tongs from him and put a half-rack of ribs on her plate. Timmy sat between them, his high chair at the head of the table. He'd already eaten, but the challenge of chasing and catching Cheerios kept him busy.

Looking around, Amelia noticed Brooks and his brothers had tucked their napkins into the necks of their shirts and were using their fingers.

When in Rome...

She folded down her turtleneck, tucked in a napkin and rolled up her sleeves. After cutting off a section, she put down her knife and picked up the rib. Thick, warm sauce oozed over her fingertips. Delicately she leaned forward and bit into the meat.

A burst of flavor exploded in her mouth, awakening her taste buds, and a tiny sigh escaped her lips.

"Good?" Clara asked.

"Great," she said. "Everything you promised and more."

At the moans of agreement from around the table, Clara smiled in satisfaction.

The smoked, tangy flavor of barbecue was addictive, and they sported evidence of their testimonials on their hands, faces and wadded up napkins. The more Amelia ate, the more she wanted to keep eating.

Clara waited until they made a dent in the main course, then brought out the pies. No sooner did they hit the table than they disappeared, as Brooks had predicted. Saving room for dessert obviously didn't pose a problem if you treated it as a side dish.

Amelia took her first bite and thought she'd died and gone to heaven. Though she couldn't be certain, she didn't think she'd experienced earthy indulgence like this before. She surreptitiously licked her fingers, then glanced up to see Brooks grin and lick a dab of sauce from the corner of his lip as he joked with his brothers.

What kind of hedonistic fantasy was this? Indulging in the world's best ribs and apple pie while drooling over a handsome cowboy and playing earth mother to his baby nephew?

Part of her wanted to laugh, while another feared once she started, she'd soon find herself crying. It felt so normal here, close-knit, like families were supposed to be. She didn't know why she would expect anything else....

She spooned a bite of pie filling to Timmy, to which he grunted his satisfaction, drumming his hands on his plastic highchair tray and kicking up a storm. Happy feet.

"All right, boys—and Amelia," Clara said. "I'm taking off. You stay out of trouble."

"We'll try." Brooks raised his napkin to his mouth and pushed back his chair, but before he could get up, she put a hand on his shoulder.

"Sit and finish your supper."

"But—"

"Sit and finish your supper." Her obvious affection shone through her firm insistence.

"Ma'am." He grinned and pulled his chair forward again. "Tell Pete we'll swing by at the usual time tomorrow."

"He's got you all hooked on that game show, don't he?"

Dean coughed into his napkin. "No comment."

Clara gave a hearty laugh. "That's okay. I've got him watching my soap now. Says he can stop anytime. We'll see about that…'' Her laughter turned into a playfully devious cackle that left them all chuckling in her wake.

"Do they live nearby?'' Amelia asked Brooks.

"Just down one of the ranch's roads, not quite within spitting distance. Mike Morgan's old place.'' He told her the Triple H ran a thousand head of cattle and was among the last family-owned ranches of its size in Wister County, one of the richest agricultural regions in the state. Their outfit included several empty houses in various stages of neglect—the homesteads of smaller ranches their ancestors had annexed in the days before wealthy individuals and corporations started buying up land and driving up prices, making expansion impossible. To this day, they referred to these houses by the names of their original owners. "We renovated one of them for Pete and Clara two years ago.''

"Back when we had money,'' Dean said under his breath. When Amelia glanced up in question, he told her, "We got a loan to help pay off the Blond Widow's debts.''

"The Blond Widow?''

"Timmy's mom. Laura hung Luke out to dry before she headed for the hills, and *we* ended up footing the bills.''

Brooks gave his brother a pointed look. "And we'd do it again in a heartbeat.''

"Right.'' He scoffed. "Like the interest alone ain't killing us.''

"Man.'' Mitch shook his head. "If she ever shows her face around here…'' Tough words, but the slight waver in his voice betrayed him.

Dean, too, cast an anxious glance at Brooks.

This was their worst fear—that Timmy's mother would show up and want him back. "Nah,'' Brooks said with more confidence than he felt. He didn't want his brothers to worry. He was worried enough for all of them. "Chances are, she's probably moved on to her next victim.''

"Yeah.'' Mitch hopped onto the bandwagon. "It's her

nature. Like a black widow spider's. Eat your mate and move on to the next sucker.''

"Good riddance to bad rubbish," Dean chimed in.

All of a sudden, Timmy's face scrunched up and turned beet-red, but before he could let his wail rip free, Amelia hoisted him out of the high chair and onto her lap. Rubbing his back, she crooned softly to him until he settled down.

"Better?" she whispered, stroking his hair. And then she turned her gaze to them. "He picks up on your tension," she said, her own voice unsteady, as if the baby wasn't the only one. "I don't think you should talk about…the Blond Widow—" she dropped her voice to a whisper "—around him."

At her quiet voice of reason, Brooks felt two inches tall. He could still remember the icy dread in the pit of his stomach, sleepless nights he'd spent as a boy, lying in bed, overhearing his father's angry voice. Sometimes loud, sometimes not, it never mattered if he could hear the words. The tone had spoken volumes. And made Brooks's skin crawl.

"Sorry," he said. "It won't happen again." He looked to Mitch and Dean for agreement and saw a reflection of his own shame on his brothers' faces. They'd been too young to share his memories, his nightmares, but each would have gone to hell and back for Timmy, and they were trying, as Brooks was, to raise their nephew to the best of their abilities.

"It's okay," she said. "We…all stumble sometimes."

He doubted it. Not her. She didn't seem the stumbling type when it came to babies. Memory or not, she was blessed with a built-in instruction manual.

He only hoped he could learn from her.

Chapter 3

"Doing okay?" Brooks asked as he moved Timmy's high chair aside to pull his playpen to the head of the table.

They'd finished eating a while ago, but no one was in any rush to get up and go just yet.

Amelia handed Timmy a ball. "Doing fine." She smiled a little too quickly and a little too brightly. When Brooks narrowed his gaze, she glanced around, searching for an accomplice to help her change the subject, but Mitch and Dean were discussing weather as a genuine topic of interest rather than filler, absorbed in conversation.

"You're not a very good liar," he said, and she could tell he was genuinely concerned.

She bit her lip. "I'm scared about this memory loss."

"I'd be surprised if you weren't. Me, I'd be climbing the walls, but you're cool as a cucumber. On the outside," he noted. "Gotta wonder what's going on inside."

Inside, her brain felt like scrambled eggs. But she wasn't going to tell him that. "I feel *things,*" she said. "But I have no explanations for what I feel."

"Hmm. Nothing's rattling around?"

"Oh, there's lots of rattling, but nothing giving way." She saw dried pie on Timmy's face and reached for a napkin, dipped the edge in her water glass and wiped his mouth. Her gaze lingered, her heart warming as he happily clapped two plastic cups together, his brow furrowed in concentration.

It was odd, but she drew strength from him. She was motivated to get well not only for herself but for him, so she could provide him with the best possible care. She *did* take this job personally. That realization helped her work up the nerve to acknowledge the inevitable.

"I should get those tests tomorrow," she said, hiding her shaking hands in her lap. It didn't matter if she was scared. This was the right thing to do, and she wanted—needed—to do the right thing.

"I'll go with you."

She glanced up. "You would?"

"If you want."

Of course, as her employer, he was concerned for her health. And as a woman with no memory of her past, she couldn't risk jeopardizing her present much longer—she *had* to get better. "I...I'd like that. If you could spare the time..."

"Hey, guys?" He caught his brothers' attention. "You mind handling the maternity ward on your own tomorrow, so I can run Amelia into town?"

Mitch leaned back and patted his stomach. "No problem. We got it covered."

"Great." Brooks turned to her. "Looks like a date."

A date. Why did the word on his lips make her mouth go dry? She swallowed and shifted in her seat. "I, um, really appreciate everything you've done. You hardly know me—"

He held up a hand. "We know what we need to know."

He tipped his head toward his nephew. "The chief here's a real good judge of character, and he's given you the thumbs-up."

Timmy piped up with an encouraging string of babble, tossed his cups and started banging on his play piano.

"See?" Brooks smiled. "He's never been this happy for this long. It's like he can tell—the long, hard winter's over, and spring is in the air. Isn't that right, chief?" He reached over the edge of the playpen and picked up a beanbag turtle. "Who's this? Is it Myrtle the Turtle?"

Amelia smiled. There was something endearing—and attractive—about a big, strong man gentling his voice to talk to a baby. She didn't know why, but she wanted to thank him for it. Instead she issued a blanket thanks, for everything. "I mean it. I don't know how to repay you—"

"Look, we all pitch in around here. You take care of our little buckaroo, and we'll call it even. Deal?"

"Deal."

They played with Timmy a while before Amelia broached the subject Brooks suspected had been on her mind.

"So, how bad are the finances?" she asked on a note of caution, as if stepping in known land-mine-ridden territory. "I-if it's none of my business—"

"Your paycheck's your business. But don't worry, we can afford to pay you. It *is* tight," he said, "but we'll figure something out. We went through this when our old man kicked the bucket. Estate taxes nearly crippled us—we're still paying off those loans. But we weathered the worst of that. We'll weather this, too."

What he didn't say, but what he and his brothers knew was with each generation, ranches changed ownership. Some sold out willingly; most had no choice, their outfits gone belly-up.

In the back of his mind, Brooks always wondered if and

when their house would be added to the collection of vacant homesteads of former ranch families.

The old Hart place...

"We could run a feedlot for extra income," Mitch said, stretching back in his chair. "Ranchers who want to plump their calves a bit before shipping can send them here. Or, we could diversify into sheep..."

Dean coughed. "Dude ranch."

"Then again," Mitch said, wiggling his eyebrows. "We could sell out for tourism, seeing how certain city slickers have a thing for cowboys, don't they, Dean?"

"Wouldn't know, hoss." Dean's foot found its way to his brother's chair and gave it a shove.

Mitch's arm shot out to grab the table's edge before he toppled backward. Grinning, he lowered the legs of his chair to the floor with a resounding thud. "What you say, Brooks?"

Brooks shrugged and rubbed his face. They'd had this conversation more than once. Though various possibilities intrigued him, the prospect of throwing good money after bad scared him worse. While he liked the idea of dude ranching, he didn't know the first thing about hospitality. He was a cattleman, not an innkeeper. Nature, not choice. He wasn't like Jo, whose book smarts opened a world of possibilities, enabling her to live on the land, not off of it. Nor was he like Luke, who'd traded life in the saddle for the big city and a badge. Brooks couldn't see *changing* his calling to stay on the ranch any more than he could envision leaving.

He was born a cowboy, and he'd die the same way.

"Whatever we do, we need to look before we leap, so we don't wind up in a bigger pile of..." He glanced at Amelia. "I don't want to make any hasty decisions we'll live to regret." Leaning over the playpen, he lifted Timmy into his arms and stood up, cutting short the discussion. "If you'll handle cleanup, I'll go run the chief's bath and put him down.''

Mitch and Dean nodded, and Amelia got to her feet, too. ''Why don't you let me do that?'' She held out her hands. Timmy took one look at the offering and swiveled toward her, making his preference of caregivers known.

''Easy, chief.'' Though regret poked Brooks's ribs as he lowered Timmy into Amelia's waiting arms, he told himself it *was* her job. He should be happy she was so good at it. He *was* happy. It just unnerved him to have Timmy choose her over him so soon, like he could tell, even at nine months, Brooks didn't have a clue, and Amelia was the real deal.

''Hey, sweetie,'' she said, an undercurrent of excitement in her voice. ''Guess what? It's bath time. That's right— your favorite.''

Brooks frowned. ''How'd you know that?''

At his question, she frowned, too. ''I don't know. I guess I just noticed he liked playing in the water earlier.''

''He does.'' Brooks nodded. ''If it were up to him, he'd stay in the tub until he shriveled up like a prune.''

''Well, we're not going to let that happen. Are we, little one?'' She caught one of Timmy's hands and planted a noisy kiss on his knuckles. Timmy laughed and tried to stick his hand in her mouth. She tipped back her head and escaped, her own laughter spilling from her throat.

At the sound, a faint ripple skimmed through Brooks's gut, like a stone tossed along the surface of a lake. Her laughter was like music. It made him want to pull her close, to dance with this woman who had brought sunshine and smiles into his nephew's life in the span of a few hours. It made him want to frame her face between his hands and thank her. It made him want her in a way that had nothing to do with gratitude and even less with good sense.

Mitch and Dean looked on curiously.

Brooks's instincts to protect kicked up, stomping out any desires he had to possess. Suddenly he wanted Amelia *out* of the kitchen, away from his brothers. Away from *him*. He coughed and cleared his throat. "Let us know if you need anything." His voice was rougher than intended, dismissive.

She took the hint. "Good night, everyone."

"'Night," they said in unison.

After cleaning up, Brooks and his brothers went out and checked the drop. Typically they fed pregnant cows more in the evening to encourage day calving. It might have been an old rancher's tale, but it seemed to work. The cows ate and went to sleep.

They had seventy-two cows left to calve, and with the weather cold and damp again and the corrals sloppy, they were back to checking on them every few hours. Newborn calves lost body heat quickly. Add to that coming into the world wet and slimy, and they could turn into Popsicles and freeze to death if they didn't get warm and dry fast enough.

When at last Brooks poked his head into the nursery late that night, he found Timmy sprawled in his crib, tiny fists by his ears. He laid a hand on his tummy, taking comfort in his deep, even breathing, in the steady rise and fall of his small body. Amelia had left a note on the counter saying he'd gone out like a light after his bath, and she'd taken his baby monitor with her to bed.

Relieved on all counts, Brooks smoothed Timmy's hair from his face, then ducked out and headed for the great room. He fired up the computer and caught up inputting calving data, then turned to other neglected paperwork.

He tried in vain to work at the desk, but despite the years, he still couldn't concentrate anyplace but the kitchen table, where they'd learned to gather every night after supper, doing homework under Clara's supervision.

Finally he gave up. He printed what he needed, shut down the computer and gathered his things to take into the kitchen. He didn't know how much time had passed when he blindly reached for his mug and took a large gulp of stone-cold coffee. With a colorful oath, he grimaced and glanced up, then did a double-take.

Amelia stood in the entrance, wearing a blue-and-green plaid flannel nightgown that had belonged to Jo. Gone was the light he'd seen in her eyes as she played with his baby nephew. Gone was the healthy glow of filling her belly with Clara's home-cooking. Face pale, dark smudges beneath her eyes and worry lines around her mouth, she looked like hell.

Brooks set down his mug, the remaining coffee sloshing around the bottom, and got to his feet. "Can't sleep?"

She shook her head, the straight ends of her graham-cracker-colored hair brushing her shoulders. One small hand gripped the door frame, her knuckles white. "I didn't realize you were working. I saw the light, and… Sorry, I didn't mean to interrupt." She ducked her head and turned to leave.

"Wait." He couldn't very well tell her how strange it felt to have a woman barefoot in his kitchen. A woman who might have worn his sister's nightgown and slept in his sister's bedroom but very definitely *wasn't* his sister.

With a nod, he gestured to the chair across the table.

She hovered at the door. "I—I don't want to intrude."

"You're not." He stacked the clippings and brochures strewn across the table. "I'm not getting anywhere anyway. Want some coffee? It's unleaded. Jo made us quit drinking caffeine after six. Caught on we'd turned into junkies."

"No, thanks." She glided across the hardwood floor, slid onto the chair and drew up her legs, making a tent of the nightgown. Eyeing the spread on the table, she asked, "Dude ranches?"

"Yeah. I'm studying the market."

"May I?"

"Help yourself. They're all working cattle ranches. About the size of ours. Different parts of the country."

"Does this mean you're considering…?"

"I don't know." Brooks rubbed a hand over his face.

"But you're open to the possibility."

"Desperation makes a man open to anything, I suppose."

She put down the brochure and opened her mouth to say something, then appeared to reconsider.

"Go ahead."

"I want to help. Any way I can."

"You are."

"I mean, in *addition* to Timmy. If there's anything I can do, to help with the ranch's finances…"

He studied her a full minute. "Thanks, I'll keep that in mind." His response was obviously important to her. He angled his head, again taking in her obvious fatigue. He considered his next question carefully, decided *what the hell, he was up anyway.* "You, ah, want to talk about it?"

"What?"

"Whatever's keeping you up when you look like you're ready to drop. Is it the hospital?"

She hugged her legs and rested her cheek on her knees. "Actually, I've been thinking about my job. Timmy's grown on me, and I was just wondering…" She looked at the brochure. "I was wondering about his parents."

Brooks steeled himself, realizing he'd gone and stepped in it knee-deep. He didn't want to talk about Luke. Not to Amelia. Not to anyone.

"I'm curious about his mother in particular."

"His mother?" Brooks frowned. "Why?"

"Job security."

"Your job's secure."

She nodded and worried her lip. "I guess I'm trying to understand what brought me here. Also, what circumstances might...change things for me. The big picture so to speak."

Brooks couldn't begrudge her need to know. As Timmy's nanny, she had every right. But truth to tell, he was still struggling himself to wrap his brain around the past month's bizarre chain of events.

"If you'd rather not—"

"No, it's okay." He drew a breath and exhaled sharply. "It's okay," he repeated, knowing sooner or later, he'd have to cough up the answers. "We...didn't even know Luke had married until he showed up on the doorstep a month ago. He left home at eighteen. We knew he would, just a question of time. He was a hell-raiser, always getting in trouble. After the old man died and Pete and Clara stepped in as guardians, I guess he figured there was no real reason to stick around any longer. He was finally free to go. He surprised us all, ending up on the right side of the law."

"You missed him," she said.

Brooks shrugged. "In the beginning. He'd send cards and letters—birthdays, holidays. I don't remember when they stopped. Out of sight, out of mind, you know. He moved on, built his own life, didn't have time for visits. And after a while..." He swallowed and rubbed his neck, the pain of the past still alive inside him. As boys, he and Luke had been inseparable, like two pups in a basket. But as they grew up, they grew apart. And now, his death had sealed the distance between them forever. "We were all so wrapped up in our own lives. *I* was so wrapped up..."

"Brooks, I'm sorry. I didn't mean to—"

He shook his head. Saying the words aloud took away

some of their power, like clipping off the sharp edges, so the pain dulled to an ache.

He stared out the window into the darkness. "We didn't see him for eighteen years. Then one day, there he was—on the back porch with Timmy. Said he fell hard and fast for a cocktail waitress at a casino—Barbie-doll blonde, he called her, though I could tell that was the pain talking." He always could read his brother's eyes—not even eighteen years' separation had changed that. "They weren't married long before things went sour. The pregnancy was unexpected." He remembered the flash of anger in Luke's eyes before he'd turned away. "I don't think she wanted the baby."

"He said that?"

"Not in so many words. Not like he had to. She went out one day and never came back. Turned out she'd emptied their bank accounts and skipped town. He asked us to keep Timmy for a while, so he could try to piece his life back together. She'd left him in ruins." Brooks's throat felt raw, and it hurt to swallow, but he did it anyway, knowing the worst pain lay ahead. There was more to the story, but he wasn't ready to say it, didn't know if he ever would be.

She drew her lower lip between her teeth. "Any note?"

Anguish stabbed at him. He closed his eyes. "No. No note."

"And Timmy?"

"We don't know the specifics, just that she left him at day care." He scowled, remembering the way Luke had clammed up, clearly not wanting to get into details, as if they were too painful to repeat.

She just up and left, like Mom, okay? Luke must have known that was all they needed to hear. Based on that alone, they would keep Timmy for as long as he needed, no questions asked.

"How sad." Amelia lowered her lashes. "I have this

image of an innocent little baby crawling from room to room, crying out for his mother, not knowing where she is…not knowing where *he* is.'' Two tears leaked from her eyes, spilling down her cheeks. She sniffled and dabbed the corners of her eyes. ''Sorry. That just really got me. Makes me want to go hug the kid for the next twenty years.''

Brooks's chest tightened. He didn't know what to do with his own emotions, let alone someone else's, but seeing her tears made his arms ache to hold her, to ease her pain as she'd eased his, getting him to talk when he usually didn't and shedding tears he'd long forgotten how to shed himself.

''Sorry,'' she whispered again.

''It's okay. You don't have to apologize for…having feelings.'' Man, it felt weird to even say it. He glanced out the window waiting for a bolt of lightning to strike him dead for being a hypocrite, then plucked the tissue box off the counter and set it down in front of her.

''Thanks.'' She took one. ''I…actually think I might have had a baby once.''

What? Brooks opened his mouth, but no words came out. She could've knocked him over with a flick of the tissue in her hand. When she told them she couldn't have children, he had assumed that meant *past,* present and future. But this… This made him wonder if there was a significant man in her life—a man whose significance extended to her present and future as well as her past.

The idea didn't sit well. He couldn't pretend it did. He closed his mouth and swallowed, waiting for her to go on.

''I'm not sure,'' she said. ''I've been having this dream. It might be just that…a dream.''

''Or it might be a memory.''

''It does *feel* real.''

''Tell me about it.''

She hesitated. ''There isn't much. I come to in the seconds after a car accident. I'm in the driver's seat. I turn around, expecting to see a baby in a car seat. Only there's nothing there. I…hear a baby crying in my sleep.''

''Is that what happened last night?''

''I think so.'' She nodded. ''I felt an emptiness inside me when I first came here, when I first woke up. I thought it was the memory loss. There's that, too. But that's more *confusion*. This was something else… It hurt, in a bone-deep way. But then I held Timmy, and it went away. That's why I don't understand what would possess a woman to leave her own child, especially one as young as Timmy.''

''You and me both. I don't know how *any* parent can up and check out.'' He shook his head. ''Seems I've thought about it all my life, and all I can figure is it's some genetic defect in nature. You see it in cows, too. Some just aren't suited for motherhood. They drop their calves in snowbanks and wander off. That's what our mother did. Left five kids to fend for themselves. Of course she left to get away from the old man, but she never came back, and the bastard's long dead.''

''Oh, Brooks. I didn't know—''

''I was older than Timmy. Old enough to remember.''

''I'm so sorry.''

''Me, too.'' He stared at the table. He hadn't talked about this in… Hell, he'd never talked about this. Why *was* he dredging it up now anyway? ''I guess I'm just glad Timmy's young enough. He won't remember the leaving part.''

She bit her lip. ''What if his mother wants him back?''

Blood rushed in his ears and pounded through his veins. Red-hot fury spiked with ice-cold fear. ''Over my dead body,'' he said between clenched teeth, shoving from the table with enough force to send his chair crashing into the wall.

Amelia flinched. Her hands flew up to shield her face, her entire body leaning to the side.

The unexpected reaction stole the breath from Brooks's lungs swifter than a gelding's kick to the gut. "Amelia. God, I'm sorry. I didn't mean—"

"No. No, of course not." She lowered her hands and grimaced in embarrassment. "I don't know what came over me."

"Nerves?"

"Nerves." She nodded, but her smile didn't reach her eyes.

Regret over his lost temper cut him far deeper than she knew. To say his father wasn't a role model was putting it mildly. In routinely beating the hell out of their mother, he'd taught his children a thing or two about the darker side of mankind. Enough to make them fear emulating it in their lifetime.

With two exceptions, Brooks had never struck another person in anger, and never anyone smaller or weaker. Once, he cold-cocked a guy for forcing himself on Jo. The other, he twisted a cowhand's arm to make him apologize for a lewd remark to Clara. Both fractures were accidental, but they taught Brooks to be careful of his strength—and his temper.

Trying to put the memories out of his mind, he dumped his mug of cold coffee and poured some hot, repeating his offer to Amelia, who again shook her head. "Not a coffee drinker, huh? How about those flavored ones?"

"I don't think so."

"Jo's crazy for flavors. You never get plain coffee at her place. Vanilla, hazelnut, cinnamon." He made a face. "Might as well stick a colored straw and a little umbrella in there." He took in her rigid posture, crossed the kitchen and opened a cabinet. "How about hot chocolate?" When she raised her head and appeared to reconsider, he added, "We've got fresh whipped cream."

"That does sound good."

"I'll take that as a yes." At her nod, he fixed her a mug and placed it in front of her with a spoon. "I'd offer to spike it with a shot of whiskey, but—"

"No, thanks."

"The house is dry," he said. "The old man was a drunk. A mean drunk."

Understanding flickered in her brown eyes, and he felt an odd connection with her, even before she spoke. "Alcohol can bring out the worst in people sometimes."

"Yeah." He sat back down, studying her, wondering what it was about her. He was suddenly very aware of her as a woman. A very attractive woman. Barefoot in his kitchen. "The, uh, warm milk ought to do the trick and knock you out."

"Don't hold your breath." She gave a rueful smile.

"If you get desperate, I'll read the *Farmer's Almanac*. Works like a charm for Timmy."

"I heard. Last night," she reminded him. "He doesn't care what you read. It's the sound of your voice."

The sound of *her* voice made something shift in his gut. He frowned. "Just how long were you there?"

"Long enough." She ate the whipped cream first, then took a tentative sip, closed her eyes and drained the mug. "Thanks. I needed that." She used a napkin to wipe her mouth.

Nice mouth, he thought before he could stop himself. Full lower lip. Perfect for—

"I'm sorry if I brought up a sore subject," she said. "I'm just a little apprehensive. It's hard to believe... Timmy is such a joy. Why any woman wouldn't fall in love with him on sight... Well, it's beyond me."

"Maybe that's because you're different." He raised his gaze from her mouth to her eyes.

Nice eyes. Was it the color? No, something else. The shape maybe?

"You don't strike me as the kind of woman who'd go on a shopping spree and overspend every last one of your credit cards, or skip mortgage payments to put a down payment on a fancy new car, or leave your husband so far in the hole he wouldn't see the light of day for the next decade."

"No. I'd never do any of those things." Her eyes clouded. "Brooks? What *will* you do if she comes back?"

He hiked his shoulder in a careless shrug, aimed at disguising his worst fear. "Pistols at dawn?"

"How chivalrous." She stared into her empty mug.

He could have let it go then; she would have let him drop the subject. "She has no reason to return. She's free and clear of all responsibility. Financial and otherwise."

"Maybe," she said, her hands wrapping around the mug. "But speaking only for myself here... I think the pain of loss is something that lingers. Your body remembers even when your mind shuts down. I know you don't want to think about her changing her mind..."

"Are you kidding?" He gave a short, humorless laugh. "I can't think of anything else. I've seen a lawyer, and he's prepared to petition the courts to have her declared unfit, if it comes down to it. But like he told me, courts favor the parent." It broke his heart to admit, "I'd move heaven and earth to keep that kid, but it could get ugly. There's only one thing we can do at this point, and that's pray. Pray the Blond Widow never darkens our doorstep."

Amelia swallowed. "You have my prayers."

"Thank you." He resisted the impulse to reach over the table and touch her face, to see if she was really there, or just a figment of his sleep-deprived imagination.

At the sound of muffled sobs from the baby monitor, he got to his feet. So did she. Across the table, their eyes met and held.

"I'll go. You stay," she said with a shy smile. "It's my job, and I've taken up enough of your time." She made it sound like he'd made some huge sacrifice, and he turned his gaze to the clock, surprised to see how much time had passed.

It had felt strange opening up like that, talking about his problems, let alone to a stranger who listened as if she cared. Of course, now that she was employed here, she had a vested interest. With a nod, he forced himself to sit down.

But as he watched her leave, her bare feet soundless on the hardwood floor, folds of shapeless flannel billowing behind her, a prickle of awareness shimmied up his leg.

He straightened abruptly and stomped his foot a few times, the same way he did when his leg fell asleep and needed circulation, but it didn't help. The prickling continued, turning from a tingle to an insistent, slow-burning heat.

Ah, hell. Brooks groaned and rubbed a hand over his late-night stubble. He should have been relieved six weeks' sleep deprivation hadn't permanently killed his sex drive after all. Instead the resurgence felt more like a nuisance.

How long had it been? Three months? Four? It wasn't like he kept track. Whenever he got the itch, he scratched it. It had always been as simple and uncomplicated as that.

Staring at Amelia's vacated space, he wondered if Clara was right about his love life. Not in the way she meant, of course, but in the fact he'd gone too long without a woman.

That alone explained his unwanted pull toward Amelia. It wasn't *her,* he reasoned. Any attractive woman in close proximity would have triggered the same primitive response. The sooner he took care of the itch, the sooner it would stop.

* * *

By eight the next morning, Brooks had lined up a date for Friday night. Two more days and he'd be renewing his acquaintance with Rachel Tanner, former classmate and on-again, off-again flame.

Like Jo, she'd gone to school in Colorado, then returned to Wyoming. An environmental lawyer, she was married to her career and had no desire to compromise her first love. For Brooks, she was as safe as safe could get.

One night with her, and he could stop seeing Amelia's heart-shaped face in his dreams, stop imagining the feel of small, delicate breasts in his hands, the taste of his name on her lips, the scent of her skin—

"Brooks," Amelia called. "I'm ready whenever you are."

He gritted his teeth. Thanks to the late-night adult movie that had played in his head as he slept, he was ready all right. Ready for Rachel to put him out of his misery.

"Be right there." He grabbed his coat and hat.

Two and a half more days, he reminded himself. Surely he could make it through the next sixty hours....

He had some concerns about staying out late before all their calves were on the ground. Though there wasn't much Mitch and Dean couldn't handle, you never knew about these things—it was better to be prepared.

Rachel had offered to swing by the Triple H, but he'd nixed that idea right fast.

There were two things Brooks Hart never kept in the house: his booze and his women. Add to that he and Rachel had two standing rules: they always met on neutral ground, and they never spent the entire night together.

His ranch was *out*.

Brooks put on his Stetson and pulled the brim low, then gathered a few more of Timmy's toys to take over to Pete and Clara's, where they had arranged to drop him on their way to the hospital.

Amelia had fed and changed Timmy, while Brooks packed his diaper bag. He'd thought he was getting pretty good in the coordination department, but Amelia had raised the bar. It was as if the woman had eight arms the way she whisked through chores and kept Timmy entertained.

She made his breakfast disappear in record time, like a magician waving her wand. She let Brooks in on her secret: as long as she put something sweet on the front of the spoon, Timmy would eat almost anything, including the squash they hadn't been able to get down him yet. Then, there was the frozen waffle trick for teething pain—she broke off a piece for him to nibble. But perhaps most impressive was the fact she didn't bat an eye changing messy diapers that, thanks to Timmy's new formula, smelled ripe enough to flatten a bull.

"You sure do remember how to take care of a baby," he commented when they were in the truck, watching her buckle the chief into his car seat and check to make sure he was secure before fastening her own belt.

"Thanks." Pride softened her eyes. "I have to admit the little guy's been second-nature to me. He's terrific."

So are you.

Brooks tried to ignore the way his chest tightened at the thought. He'd watched Jo with her babies, seen his friends' wives with theirs. He was immune to it by now.

Or so he told himself.

He didn't want to admit there was something about *this* woman interacting with *his* nephew that was messing with his mind, making him think of the wife and children he'd always sworn he would never have.

He'd buried those desires like hazardous material in a place deep inside him, where they couldn't hurt anyone—not himself and not the people around him.

Just because Timmy had fallen into his lap didn't mean Brooks could throw a lifetime of caution to the wind.

Setting his jaw, he started the truck, forcing his mind to clear and his gaze to stay on the road where it belonged, instead of mooning over things that would never be his.

Within minutes, they were at Pete and Clara's log home. Amelia came inside and met Pete, who looked comfortable as could be leaning back in his recliner, the latest issue of *Western Horseman* resting on his potbelly. He had wise gray eyes, neat silver hair, and a quick, easy smile to match his soft-spoken charm. Though he grumbled plenty about his lack of mobility, it was clear to everyone he didn't so much mind all the extra attention.

"You take Amelia around the range?" Pete asked him.

"Not yet," he said, crouching down to help get Timmy settled. "We're saving the tour for later in the week."

"All right, well be sure and take her out to the west pasture. Best sunset you ever did see. Ain't that right, Clara?"

"Always been my favorite." She squeezed his shoulder, and he patted her hand.

"Rode out there the evenin' I asked my girl to marry me," he said to Amelia with a wink.

Uh-oh. Brooks caught the twinkle in Pete's eye, knew right away Clara had supplied him with an earful of crazy, romantic notions about marrying him off. He'd tried humor; he'd tried honest logic. It didn't matter how many ways he told Clara she was wasting her matchmaking efforts on him, the woman never gave up. "On that note..." He straightened and hitched his chin toward the door.

Amelia took his cue. "Nice meeting you," she said, but as she stood to leave, her gaze lingered on Timmy. Sensing their departure, he tossed aside his board book and started whimpering. "You sure it's okay...?"

But Clara just squatted and picked him up, planting him on her hip as she shooed them to the door. "Don't you worry none. He'll be just fine in a minute."

"Thanks again for taking him." Brooks kissed her cheek, then Timmy's forehead.

"No thanks needed, and I meant what I said. Don't you worry about a thing. Either of you," Clara included Amelia in her reassurance, as if she, too, had noticed the way the nanny hovered over her new ward. Even when talking to one of them or in the middle of doing something, Amelia still kept an eye trained on Timmy. "These old bones are still good for short bursts. Like helping out with baby-sitting in a pinch. You take care and tell Jo not to work too hard."

"Will do," Brooks said. "But I doubt she'll listen."

"Ain't it the truth." Clara laughed and wished them well again.

Amelia waved and headed with him to the truck. From her quick steps, he could tell she was trying to make it without looking back. Brooks opened her door first. She hopped in, closed her eyes and expelled a heavy sigh of relief.

"Safe." He grinned and closed the door, then rounded to the driver's side.

As he climbed behind the wheel, she crossed her arms and arched a brow. "Are you making fun of me, Brooks Hart?"

"No, ma'am." He turned the key in the ignition. "I'm remembering a time not too long ago when that was me holding my breath as I hightailed it back to the truck. I couldn't stand to have Timmy out of my sight for a minute. I'd watch him when he slept to make sure he was still breathing."

Her lips curved then, the sweetness of that slight smile making his mouth go dry. "Doesn't take long before they wrap themselves around your little finger, does it?"

"No," he said and dragged his gaze away. "Not long at all." Soon, they were cruising down a windy, two-lane road, passing cottonwoods with fat buds ready to burst, heading toward the highway that would take them to Sheridan.

"I like them," Amelia said, almost as an afterthought.

"Babies? So I noticed." He raised a finger from the steering wheel to wave at the driver of an oncoming pickup.

"No, not— I mean, yes, them too. But I was talking about Pete and Clara. I like those two."

"They're the best," Brooks said simply.

"They're the parents of your heart, aren't they?"

He slanted a glance at her. "Never thought of it like that, but yeah, I reckon you're right."

She nodded, her expression wistful before she turned toward the window.

He wondered then about her family, what had become of them. He obviously couldn't ask her, but he *was* finding himself more and more curious about her. He could only imagine the questions that must have been eating at *her*.

Hopefully she'd get her answers soon.

They rode all the way to the highway in companionable silence before Amelia shifted and cleared her throat. "So, um, who takes care of Jo's kids?"

"Her mother-in-law. She moved in about two years ago, after the twins were born."

"And Jo's husband?" She fidgeted some more, clasping and unclasping her hands. "What does he do?"

Besides any genuine interest she might have had, he could tell she was nervous and needed to talk to keep her mind off the hospital. He wasn't used to idle chitchat, but he tried to oblige as best as he could. "He was a rancher."

"Was?"

"Kev died a little over a year ago."

Amelia swiveled in her seat, clearly caught off guard.

"Inoperable brain tumor," he said. "Went in his sleep one night."

She sucked in a breath, covering her mouth with her hand. "Oh, how tragic. Jo must have been devastated."

"She was. She'd been prepared for years, but there's no real preparation for losing someone you love."

"She *knew* he was dying?"

"Yeah. Married him right after the diagnosis. Same night in fact. Said to hell with the engagement. She didn't know how much time they had left, but she wasn't wasting another second of it. The doctors gave Kev anywhere from a week to six months, but it turned out to be two years. He saw the birth of his children, watched them take their first steps."

Amelia's eyelashes fluttered, as if trying to keep her tears at bay. "That's incredible. I can't even imagine..." Her voice dropped to a hoarse whisper. "Loving someone that much... Being that brave... Knowing you have to let go."

Brooks's throat worked, and he flexed his hand on the steering wheel. "Me, either."

They made it to the hospital in record time. In the parking lot, he cut the engine, opened his door and hopped down. But in the time he'd rounded to the passenger side, Amelia had yet to unbuckle her seat belt.

Without a word, he opened her door and offered his hand, but she continued to stare straight ahead, oblivious to him. They stayed like that a full minute before she closed her eyes briefly, then turned to him. When she opened her mouth, he fully expected her to balk.

"I can do it myself," she said instead, reaching for the seat belt.

"All right." He stepped back.

She shook her head. "I mean inside."

"Oh." His hands shot to her waist, helping her down, then jammed into his pockets the second she planted both feet on the ground. "You sure?"

She nodded. "I'm sure."

"Okay." Brooks pointed them toward the hospital, one hand starting for the small of her back before he caught himself. "I'll just sit in the waiting room until you're—"

"No." She stopped, lifted her chin and turned to him. "I'll call you when I'm done."

He wasn't going to win this one. "All right. Hang on a sec." He jogged back to the pickup, rooted around in the glove compartment and unearthed a gum wrapper and a chewed pen. It would do. "Beep me when you're done."

"Beep you?"

He felt her gaze on him as he scribbled two numbers and showed her the pager clipped to his belt after he finished. "I got it for Timmy. You know, in case of emergencies. I'm giving you the cell number, too. But sometimes the battery runs low, or I'm out of range. The pager's best."

She smiled and took the wrapper, tucking it into her back pocket. There was a look in her eyes that unsettled him, a look he wasn't used to seeing.

"What?" he asked. "You're looking at me funny."

"Sorry. It's just… I feel…" She gave a nervous laugh and lifted a shoulder. "Proud?"

"Well, sure. That's understandable—"

"Of you."

His head jerked back. "Of *me?*"

Her smile widened, and she nodded. "You might have started from ground zero with this baby stuff, but you've come a long way in a short time. Not everyone could have done it. I'm proud of you."

"Thanks." The single word stuck to the roof of his mouth like peanut butter. "That, ah, means a lot coming from you, this being your field of expertise and all." He stuck his hands into his pockets and squinted at the hospital doors. "I'm…proud of you, too. I know this wasn't easy for you, coming here." Nor was it easy for him to be having this conversation. He shifted uneasily.

"Thanks. I'd better go now, before I change my mind."

He heard the catch in her voice, noticed her smile slipped a notch. He straightened to his full height. "I don't mind waiting, you know."

"I know." She glanced down at her hands, now clasped together, one on top of the other. "But I need to do this myself." Squaring her shoulders, she met his eyes directly. "Please don't be angry with me."

"Angry? Why would I be angry?"

"Because I had you clear your schedule, and—"

He waved her away. "Never mind that." He rubbed the back of his neck, thinking of a way he could pass the time, kill two birds with one stone. "Tell you what. I'm going to stick around town a while longer, so don't hesitate to call. I was planning to hook up with an old friend Friday night, but there may be a chance of getting together sooner rather than later."

Amelia smiled. "I hope it works out."

"Yeah. For you, too." He forced himself to turn, not to watch her leave. He wasn't going to let himself fall for this woman, *couldn't* let himself think of her in any way but as Timmy's nanny.

Amelia Rigsby wasn't the kind of woman a man took to bed and forgot shortly afterward, the kind who could walk out the door one day and hardly be missed.

No, she was the kind of woman a man envisioned as the mother of his children. The kind he'd want to make love to not once, but every night, for the rest of his life. The kind he'd move heaven and earth just to keep by his side.

That was the reason he steered clear of her kind. His exact same fear with hard liquor. Losing control. He didn't know if monsters were made or born, only that his father had been one, unable to control his dark side. No way could Brooks see himself following in the bastard's footsteps, but some risks plain weren't worth the gamble.

* * *

Amelia didn't know why the idea of Brooks accompanying her into the hospital had suddenly made her nervous. She'd been fine with it—even reassured by it—before they pulled into the parking lot. But once she'd seen the building, all she could think was she didn't want anyone speaking for her, or listening to what she said. She needed *privacy.*

Luckily Brooks hadn't needed explanations.

She waited until the blue Ford pickup pulled out of sight before she headed for the entrance, trying to ignore the odd, prickling sensation creeping up and down her spine.

An unaccountable urge compelled her to tug up her collar, tuck her chin and glance over her shoulder a few times. Jittery hands tapped her pockets in search of sunglasses to shield her eyes, but there were none.

As she slipped inside the automatic doors, a whiff of antiseptic odor made the breath catch in her throat. She'd smelled it before. She knew for certain. But where? When? Why?

Adrenaline pumped fast and furious through her veins, roaring in her ears. With small steps, she forced herself toward the water fountain to take a sip. Then she eyed the long corridor and started toward the information desk.

With each step, her jaw clenched tighter, every nerve in her body throbbing with a dull ache. From the corner of her eye, she saw something blue and stopped in her tracks. A uniformed police officer breezed past her. She went numb.

He approached the information desk, standing with his legs braced apart, gun holster and billy club on his belt. As he talked to the person behind the counter, perspiration beaded on her lip. She started shaking.

Run! Before he sees you!

Her gaze darted around, searching for an escape, but he turned before she could move.

Their eyes met, paralyzing her with indecision. At his slight frown, the hands of panic wrapped around her throat, squeezing until she couldn't breath. Spots danced before her eyes. Her head swam. Her vision tunneled. A low, dejected whimper slipped free.

The policeman's frown deepened. He shifted, the silver of his badge glinting under overhead florescent bulbs.

As a vampire blinded by sunlight, Amelia recoiled and spun away. Back, toward the sliding doors. Shoes clicked the tile. Faster and faster. She broke into a dead run.

A blur of brown emerged from the doors, catching her up short. She raised her hands to shield her face but couldn't stop her body from colliding into the rock-solid barrier.

In the next second, she heard someone saying "Amelia," felt strong hands grip her arms, pinning her, dragging her out of the way, away from the doors.

"No…please." She struggled, a sickening sensation churning her stomach. "Have…to…go." Muted words assailed her. Indistinguishable. Like a tape played at half speed. "Please," she begged. "Don't hurt me."

Chapter 4

Brooks swore under his breath. "I'm not going to hurt you. I would never…" She wasn't listening. She pounded on his chest with her balled fists. "Amelia, it's Brooks." Her arms flailed, striking his shoulders and arms. A panic attack. He should have known, should have seen it coming.

He'd been there himself once.

"Look at me, honey. *Look*," he said, catching her chin, but she refused to meet his eyes.

She kicked his shin instead.

"Ow." Damn, she was going to hurt herself if he let go. He tightened his grasp, avoided what blows he could, and took the rest. She was stronger than she looked, but one slip of a woman was hardly equipped to kick the stuffing out of him. Sooner or later, she'd wear herself out. Just like Timmy.

Brooks had gotten the baby past his hysteria at being handled by strangers; he'd get Amelia past this.

He tapped his wellspring of patience and softened his

voice as much as he could. "It's okay," he murmured, over and over. "You're all right. No one's going to hurt you."

Though he'd pulled her out of the way of the entrance, the few passersby craned their necks to get a better look. He ignored them and concentrated on Amelia, repeating his reassurances. "You're safe, honey. Everything's okay."

Bit by bit, the fight siphoned out of her. Each time, he loosened his hold, until finally, he wasn't restraining her at all, but stroking his hands up and down her back.

"Brooks?" she whispered, her voice so reedy he almost didn't hear her.

"Yeah."

"Oh, God." She squeezed her eyes shut and burrowed deeper into his open coat, her face pressed to his chest, her trembling fingers bunching the material of his shirt. "What…what just happened to me?"

"Shh, it's okay." He raised his hand to the back of her head, smoothing the silken strands of her hair. "Just rest for a minute. Lean against me and catch your breath."

She drew a shuddery breath, and he felt tiny ripples racking her body like hiccups, dampness against his skin where her tears had soaked through his shirt. Fishing into his pocket, he pulled out his handkerchief. With a muffled thanks, she accepted the offering and blew her nose.

Just then, a police officer came up to them. "You folks need any help?" His gaze alternated between them.

Amelia took an almost-imperceptible step closer to Brooks, her fingers tightening on the wads of his shirt.

Instinctively he dropped a hand to the small of her back and turned his body to shield her. "Yeah, actually. My sister's a doctor on staff here. Josephine Hart."

"Sure, I know Dr. Jo." He smiled.

Brooks didn't know what to make of his smile, but now wasn't the time to think about it. "If you could tell her

Amelia Rigsby's here, we'd appreciate it. She's expecting us.''

''Will do.'' The man nodded and retraced his steps.

Brooks turned his gaze to the woman nestled against him. One of his hands was still in her hair, the other at the base of her spine. Her cheek rested on his chest, her knuckles pressing against his stomach. She'd relaxed when the cop left, but she didn't move away, and neither did he.

Every so often, she sniffled, and he held his breath. Damn, but she felt good—not just her body, but her trust. Brooks knew he didn't deserve either, knew this was a one-time, limited offer, so he wasn't in any hurry to let go.

''You came back,'' she whispered after a time.

''I was going to sneak into the waiting room.''

''Why?''

''Didn't want to get my head bit off. You were pretty insistent—''

''No, why did you come back?''

He'd asked himself the same question as he'd turned the pickup around not even halfway down the road. ''Would you believe me if I said I wanted to give blood?''

She shrugged and glanced up. ''Do you?''

''I'm a card-carrying Red Cross donor. I usually give every month.'' He was avoiding the real answer. He sighed. ''I thought you might need me.''

Her lower lip trembled. ''I'm sorry.''

''Don't be.''

''But I *am*. I can't believe I flipped out—''

''Stop right there.'' He brushed her hair back from her face. ''We knew you were afraid of hospitals. I was stupid to leave in the first place.'' *I was too busy hoping to get laid.* ''I'm the one who should apologize.''

She gave a humorless laugh. ''How can you people be so incredibly kind to me?''

''You're Timmy's nanny,'' he said, knowing even as the

pat answer rolled off his tongue, it didn't tell the whole story.

She pressed her face to his chest and inhaled deeply. "Did I...did I hurt you?"

His chin came up. "In your dreams, woman."

"Good, I couldn't bear it if I..." She pulled back and winced.

"Hey, now." With the curve of his finger, he raised her head. "You've gotta buck up, buckaroo. You passed the first hurdle. That's cause for celebration, not a long face."

"Right." She stirred up a wobbly, halfhearted smile. "As if my employer doesn't already think his new nanny's a nutball."

"I don't. I think you had a panic attack. But we'll let the good doctor decide."

Brown eyes searched his, wide and uncertain.

He dropped his hand to his side. He hated the thought of turning back when they'd come so far. "There was this time when I was fifteen," he said. "I was riding fence in the north pasture when my horse got spooked by a rattler and threw me, but good. Now I'd been thrown plenty, but this time, I got wrapped in the coils of my rope."

Amelia drew in a sharp breath. "Were you hurt badly?"

"Depends on your definition of bad. The gelding stomped on me, kicked me in the head a few times, cracked four of my ribs and dragged me half-unconscious until the leather holding the rope to my saddle horn broke."

"Oh, no..."

Brooks shrugged. "Took me four months before I'd get back on a horse again. And the only reason I *stayed* on was because Pete and Luke nearly hog-tied me in the saddle."

"Did you...did you fight like I...?"

"Hell, yeah. Not to mention I'm bigger and tougher than you. Luke decked me, so I wouldn't spook the poor horse."

She shivered. "I'm glad you didn't…"

"Slug you?" He shook his head. "Not an option."

Relief flashed in her eyes before she closed them. "I am so embarrassed—"

"Hush." He laid a finger over her mouth, then yanked it back just as fast, not wanting to wait until he was burned before deciding not to play with fire. "You think that's a tale any cowboy worth his spurs goes around bragging about? I've never told anyone besides you. Only people who know were there." He drew a breath, still unable to believe he *had* confided in her. "You're not the only one who's been spooked. Not to mention, every one of us has lived through our share of embarrassing moments."

Her lips curved a little then. "And if a big, strong cowboy can pick himself up and dust himself off…"

Something about the way she said that big and strong stuff made the back of Brooks's neck grow warm every time. He straightened his arms and put her away from him. They were through the crisis. He needed some distance and fast.

"I can wait in the truck."

She turned her gaze to the windows. "Looks like snow."

"Rain," Brooks said and hiked his shoulder. "Doesn't bother me. Your call."

"Maybe…maybe you could go give blood, then sit in the waiting room?"

He smiled. "I could do that."

"Brooks?"

"Yeah?"

She returned his smile with a shy one of her own. "I'm glad you came back."

Her quiet words cinched the knot of longing around his belly and pulled the slack. He shoved his hands into his pockets. "Don't mention it," he said, fighting to look like a man who didn't give a damn one way or another what she thought of him. And trying like hell to deny he had a thing for his baby nephew's nanny.

"It's the strangest thing." Amelia drew a shaky breath and hoisted herself onto the examining table. "I don't know why it keeps happening."

Dr. Jo flicked on her penlight. "It happened before?"

"In the bathroom at the ranch." Her eyes followed the penlight as instructed. "The small space...overwhelmed me. But this was worse. A lot worse."

Dr. Jo checked her vitals and reflexes, removed her stethoscope and confirmed, "You had a panic attack." Her voice was calm and matter-of-fact, yet still compassionate. "It's not uncommon."

"But what *causes* panic attacks?"

"Any number of things—stress, anxiety, an unpleasant experience, an innate phobia. We'll probe the source as we investigate your memory loss. I do want to run some tests, if you're still willing."

"I am." Amelia nodded. "I want to be normal again."

"Atta girl." Dr. Jo smiled, then lowered her voice to a conspiratorial whisper, "You realize normal's a relative term."

Amelia glanced over her shoulder to catch the doctor's wink.

She spent the day going through a battery of tests and numerous consultations with specialists, after which Dr. Jo delivered good news and bad news.

On the upside, she was healthy as a horse, with no evidence of brain damage whatsoever. On the downside, the doctors could find no conclusive explanation for her memory loss and offered no sure-fire prognosis for recovery.

While the latter both frustrated and alarmed her, for a while there, she'd feared irreparable, physical damage. Dr. Jo had gone strangely quiet upon examining several X rays of her head, after which she'd ordered a bone survey, which she explained was a scan of her entire body. But in the end, she'd delivered her final verdict as a clean bill of health.

"So where do I go from here?" Amelia worried her lip.

"Casper. I'd like you to see a colleague of mine. A specialist." She handed over a card. Emma Andersson, M.D. Psychiatrist.

Her head snapped up. "You think I need counseling?"

"I think we could *all* benefit from counseling." Dr. Jo smiled. "In your case, I just want to cover all the bases. The goose egg sent me in one direction, and I don't want to overlook the other."

"Meaning I might have mental problems?" She swallowed.

"Meaning we have nothing to lose by seeking another professional opinion. Psychological trauma has been known to cause a certain type of amnesia we call psychogenic."

Images from her dream flashed in her mind.

Could it have been a memory after all?

"Dr. Jo?" She drew a breath. "There's something I've been wanting to ask you. Is there any way doctors can tell if a woman's given birth before? I mean, from her body…?"

"It's possible. Why?"

She told her about the dream. "Did you see anything today that might indicate…?"

"There's nothing obvious, like stretch marks. But I wasn't looking for the nonobvious. If you want me to—"

"Not today." Amelia shook her head. "I think I've reached my limit."

"Let me tell you something," Dr. Jo said, taking a seat. "Now Dr. Andersson's the authority here, but I suspect she'll back me up on this. If we *are* dealing with psychogenic amnesia, you don't want to play detective to unearth your answers. They'll surface when your mind's good and ready.''

''So if it's true, if I really did...lose a baby, it's better if I remember on my own than if you tell me?''

''Exactly.'' Dr. Jo indicated the card in her hand. ''I took the liberty of having you scheduled.'' On the back, she had written Friday—1:00 p.m. The day after tomorrow. ''Are you all right with this?''

Amelia forced a smile. ''Do I have a choice?''

''Yes, you do.'' Dr. Jo's gaze held steady, her green eyes solemn. ''It's your decision, Amelia. Give the office at least twenty-four hours' notice if you want to cancel.''

She stared at the card. Jo was right—she didn't have anything to lose. And she did so want to be well again. She remembered what Brooks had told her on the way over about Jo and her late husband and marveled again at the depth of Jo's compassion and courage. How did a woman become so strong?

Amelia didn't know, but she wanted to be like that, wanted to confront her fears head-on, instead of running, being a victim, feeling captive.

''I'll go,'' she said, tucking the card into her pocket. When she looked up, she noticed the doctor's eyes had taken on a faraway quality. But before she could blink, Dr. Jo smoothed a hand over her hair and snapped her attention back to her patient.

''Atta girl,'' she whispered, patting Amelia's hand.

At the first opportunity, Brooks pulled Jo aside and grilled her. They were in the hallway outside her office. ''Well? What do you think?''

She narrowed her gaze and tucked Amelia's file under her arm. ''*I think* you should tend your cattle and let me tend my patients.'' She poked his stomach to prod him out of her way. Though she neither confirmed nor denied anything, one look at her, and Brooks knew she'd found something.

Amelia's tests had taken longer than expected, and he'd spent the afternoon pacing the waiting room. Uneasily he glanced toward the room, where she was now waiting for him.

"What is it, Jo? You know something. Come on." He bent his knees, so they were eye-level. "She doesn't have any family."

"I know." Jo frowned, her fingers kneading the tendons on the side of her neck, clearly grappling whether or not to confide in him.

"We're it." Brooks reached out a hand to work out her kink. "If it would help her…"

"It would." She angled her neck. "I know it would. It's just so tricky with her amnesia. She's the patient, but if she had family, they're the ones I'd be counseling right now."

He didn't say anything more, let her reach her own conclusion.

"Wait here. I'll see if she'll sign a release." She disappeared around the corner, then returned a few minutes later. With a brisk nod, she looked him square in the eye. "This stays between you and me. No one else. Understood?"

"Got it."

"Not even Amelia."

He frowned. "But—"

"No buts, Brooks. I'm the doctor here. You need to trust me."

"I do. I just don't get why—"

"You will." She drew a breath and tugged him into an empty examining room. Only after closing door did she let him see the depth of her concern. "Amelia's been hurt."

Panic reared up and kicked him in the chest. "Bad?"

"Yes. But it's not recent."

"What do you mean not recent?" He searched her eyes. "She just cracked her head the other day."

"The X rays show more... Older injuries. There's a clear pattern."

Pattern?

"No..." Brooks shook his head, but that age-old, icy dread was roiling in his gut.

"You'd know it as well as I would."

"No." He gritted his teeth and braced one hand on the wall, the other covering his eyes.

"It's not accidental."

He swore viciously. Cold fury oozed into his pores until it filled every inch of his body with rage, until he shook with the effort of holding himself back from putting his fist through the wall.

"She has numerous fractures," Jo said. "Some weren't set and didn't heal properly, like her nose—you can see a bump there, on the bridge. The others aren't as obvious."

"God Almighty." He rubbed his face.

"I don't think her injuries were sustained over a long period of time, but it looks like more than one incident. I think she spent a good amount of time in hospitals, probably with her abuser sitting right by her side, supplying doctors with phony stories to cover his ass."

"I want to find him." Brooks clamped down on his jaw. "I want to hunt him down and show him exactly how it feels, that son of a—"

"I know," Jo whispered. "I do, too. Every time I see a woman, a child... Don't think for a second I don't feel the same way. Everything we do is shaped by our past. I can't get away from it any more than you can." She reached out then and took his balled fists in her hands, looking up into his eyes. "That's why it's so important to channel our experiences into something productive. We can help Amelia,

perhaps better than those who didn't have a front-row seat
to what she's been through."

His eyes stung, and his voice came hoarse. "What can
we do?"

"I don't know for sure what's caused her memory loss.
I've recommended a psychiatrist. My guess is her mind's
shut down in order to process something difficult. Maybe
it was triggered by the bump on the head. I don't know.
But she's shut out the good as well as the bad. If I'm right,
if she is suffering from psychological trauma, we have to
be careful not to plant suggestions or press her to remember. The mind shuts down as a natural defense. She'll remember in her own time, when she feels safe."

"What…can I do?" He was afraid of the answer.

Jo's gaze never wavered. "You know the profile of a
battered woman. You know what she needs. Give it to
her," she said as if it was the most natural thing in the
world.

Brooks yanked his hands from hers as if scorched. He
backed up, smacking the examining table, its sterile paper
rustling. "You don't know what you're asking."

"For you to be her friend, not just her employer."

"No." He shook his head. "Not me. Mitch or Dean."
They'd keep it platonic. *He* would make *sure* they kept it
platonic. "Let me talk to them tonight."

"*No*. Between the two of them, one's likely to blow it,
and I'd put money on Dean. Bless his heart, he's too much
of a straight-shooter to pay mind to discretion. Or tact. And
Mitch isn't that far behind. They're too young. They don't
know things like we do. They didn't see what we saw."

"Isn't that better?" He was grasping. He knew he was.
He groaned. "I can't. Not her. *Especially* not her. No," he
said again. "No way."

Jo didn't reply for a long moment, simply stared at him.
A long, measuring stare. Arms crossed. Jaw set. He could

see the wheels turning in her mind as she prepared to pull out the big guns. "Brooks Hart," she said quietly. "I have never asked you for anything in my entire adult life."

"Not this, Jo. Please. Not this." *I don't know if I can be just her friend.*

She saw his plea and upped the ante, "You can help her. I know you can. Please, do it for me. Do it for Mom..."

Bull's-eye. Like an arrow straight through his heart, she got him where he lived. As children, they hadn't been able to help their mother. As an adult, Brooks had to stop himself whenever he wandered into the endless wasteland of would have, could have, should haves. "It won't bring her back," he said. "Nothing can bring her back."

"You're right," she said. "But there's catharsis in helping others, others like her. I've seen it, done it."

"God, you make it sound so easy." He paced the small room like a penned bull.

"It's not *that* difficult. All you have to do is let her lead. Just follow wherever she goes. Give her the chance to regain her self-confidence...her faith in men."

He closed his eyes, pinching the bridge of his nose. What if their *friendship* turned into something more? A small voice told him in the best of scenarios Timmy could have a real mother, but he couldn't let himself go there.

He'd resigned himself long ago to the fact he would never be a husband or a father. Timmy's arrival made him break one of his rules, but he wasn't budging on the other.

Amelia might have known nothing about her past, but he knew far too much about his.

It was the *worst*-case scenario he feared. With reason. He'd never been tested, didn't know what would happen if he was. Would he turn into Amelia's worst nightmare, into *his* worst nightmare—a man who would sooner sell his soul than live without the woman he loved?

* * *

Lightning flickered like a faulty flashlight in a gray, overcast sky, the rumble of thunder vibrating the ground.

Brooks halted under the covered entrance as the storm broke and splattered fat raindrops on the blacktop. "Well, that's different," he commented, then explained to Amelia. "This is more like a summer storm. Spring's usually misty with sleet."

"I like it." She inhaled deeply, and he did the same. "Nice to breathe fresh air again, isn't it?"

"Definitely," he said. "You, uh, want to wait a bit? Rinse out our lungs?"

A slight smile curved her lips. "That'd be great."

They watched the rainfall, trading sweet, damp air for the hospital's antiseptic smell.

"So," she said after a time. "Jo told you everything."

"Yeah."

"Including her recommendation of another opinion."

He nodded. "You'll like Dr. Andersson."

"You know her?"

He stuck his hands into his pockets. "I went to see her after Luke died. Jo did, too."

"Did it help?"

"I didn't think so at the time. I wasn't ready. Last night with you, that's the first I've talked about it. But the things Dr. Andersson said... She was right, looking back."

"Thanks for telling me." She didn't say anything else but stole furtive glances at him through the corner of her eye, as if trying to figure out what he *wasn't* telling her.

Brooks kept his expression carefully neutral, not wanting her to read anything on his face or glimpse the true depth of his feelings. Damn it, he didn't want to have *feelings*, not for any woman and especially not this one.

She bit her lip. "Have you called the nanny agency?"

"No, why?"

She lifted one shoulder in a delicate shrug. "I didn't know if you were planning to…request someone else."

"Another nanny?" he asked, incredulous.

She nodded and stared down at her feet.

"Well now." He tipped back his Stetson, wiped his brow and pulled the brim down again. "After a comment like that, I can see why they'd want to check your head some more."

She glanced up, unsmiling. "I may have issues—"

"Hell, we've all got issues."

"Brooks, I'm trying to think of what's best for Timmy. God knows, I want that to be *me*. But if that's selfish—"

"Selfish?" He sucked a breath between his teeth and blew it out in a hiss. "Damn, woman. You're the best thing that's happened to my kid since I got him. You think we haven't *tried* to accomplish the things you have? You've got something special—he responds to you. So no, I don't think it's selfish. And I don't want another nanny. I want *you*."

Her gaze shot to his, brown eyes wide with wonder.

He scowled at his word choice, the double meaning far closer to the truth than he cared to admit. "Look, Jo would never put Timmy at risk. If she had reason to question your abilities, she'd say so. Now did she even imply…?"

"No." She bit her lip.

He rocked back on his heels. "So unless I'm mistaken, the only one here with doubts is you, so let me ask you this straight out. Do *you* think you're a threat to Timmy?"

No sooner had he spoken the words than her expression turned fierce, like a mama bear protecting her cub. "I would *never* let anything happen to that little boy." Her intensity appeared to startle her, but it didn't faze Brooks in the least. She'd put to words what he'd seen with his own eyes.

"Great, then that's all we have to say on this matter."
He peered at the sky. "Doesn't look like it's letting up."

Amelia blinked at the change in subject, then followed
his gaze, pulled up her collar and shook her head.

"Stay here. I'll get the truck." Without waiting for her
response, he took off across the parking lot. His long strides
shortened the distance in no time. He fired up the engine,
let it idle a minute, then turned on the headlights and windshield wipers and pulled to the curb.

The canopy was several feet back, so he took out his
slicker and held it over her head, so she wouldn't get
soaked. "Watch your step." He took her elbow and made
sure she didn't slip climbing into the cab.

"Thanks." She turned in the passenger seat, shook her
head at him and smiled—the first real smile he'd seen from
her since the episode in the hospital.

"What?" He leaned down to see her better.

She reached out a hand, and for an instant, he thought
she meant to touch his face, but she held her fingers under
a stream of water that poured off his hat.

"You have the world's best manners," she said.

He squinted. "I do?"

"Yes, you do." At his sour expression, she gave a small
laugh. "That was a compliment." She flicked her fingers
and splashed a few raindrops at him. One caught him in
the eye, and he reflexively blinked and pulled back. She
paled. "Oh. S-sorry. I didn't mean to…"

His heart tightened painfully. What kind of bastard took
offense at something as innocent as that? God, how he
wanted to pummel the damn jerk into the ground. But as
his temper spiked, he thought of what Jo had said and tried
like hell to let it go, to channel it into something productive.

"Some compliment." He flashed an easy grin and
flicked her back. "Ranks up there with telling a guy he's
nice."

Just like that, her smile came back, loosening something in his chest. "I, um, hate to break this to you, but you are very—"

"Whoa." Brooks grimaced and held up a hand in protest. "You don't want to go there." He stepped back and gestured for her to tuck all her body parts inside before he closed the door and rounded to his side.

He wasn't about to admit helping her in and out of the pickup afforded him a spectacular view of her butt, a fact he was fairly certain landed him on Santa's naughty—not nice—list. So he climbed beside her and tried to think nice thoughts, none of which included how intimate the cab felt after nightfall…especially in a storm.

He checked the digital clock on the dash. Forty-eight more hours until his date. Could time crawl any slower? The day felt like a week, during which he hadn't eaten a bite. He was well beyond famished, in dire need of fortification before he keeled on the spot. He didn't know if a man had ever died of sperm retention, but he didn't want to find out.

"Brooks?" The soft lilt of Amelia's voice threatened to drop-kick him over the edge. "Is there anything I can do for you?"

His fingers tightened around the steering wheel, and he struggled to come up with a suitable response.

"I just thought since you spent all that time at the hospital with me…"

Not his idea of quality time. No, the kind of time he wanted to spend with Amelia—

Gave him half a mind to pull over, jump out and send her on without him. A fifty-mile hike through frigid rain would do him a world of good right about now.

"There must be something…" she whispered.

"There's something," the words came out from between

clenched teeth, the muscles in his jaw tight with the effort of his restraint. "You can take care of Timmy."

"Besides—"

"No," he said with more force than intended, then added hastily, "thank you."

But at his clipped tone, Amelia bit her lip and stared out the window, making him feel like an even bigger jackass.

Damn, he wanted to wrap his arm around her waist and haul her across the cab, settle her next to him and shelter her from the world. But he also wanted to lift her face to his, nibble on that ever-tempting lower lip and satisfy his curiosity about its softness.

How the hell was he supposed to protect her from *him?*

All right, damage control time. He had to lighten the mood, let her unwind after the ordeal she'd suffered today, get his own mind back on track before he blew it big time.

He relaxed his death-grip on the steering wheel, reached over and handed her a mini Mylar balloon taped to a stick. "From the hospital's gift shop. Not a lot of selection."

"For Timmy?" she asked, taking the balloon from him.

"Congrats? I don't think so." He pulled onto the long ribbon of highway that would take them back to Wister. "It's for you."

"For me?" Disbelief tinged her voice.

"Sure. I didn't want to show up empty-handed after your big day. I figured you were too old for lollipops."

She gave a small chuckle—a soft, sultry sound that washed over him like warm, apple brandy in the winter and gave him the same rush. "You're kidding, right?" She stuck a hand into her coat pocket and pulled out a sucker. *"Ta-da."*

"All right, nix that." Brooks rubbed a hand over his face. *"I'm* too old for lollipops."

"No way. I got one for you, too."

"For me?" It was his turn to sound surprised.

She nodded and pulled a second sucker from her pocket. "Cherry or grape?" She held one in each hand, offering him first choice.

Brooks gave her a sidelong stare.

"What? Why are you looking at me like that?"

"I haven't had a lollipop since I was a kid."

"That long, huh? Did they even make them back then?"

"Hey! It wasn't *that* long ago."

"Uh-huh." She peeled off one of the wrappers. "You probably don't even remember what you're missing, right?"

He cast her a suspicious glance. "What flavor's that?"

"Cherry. My favorite."

"In that case, I'll take grape."

She smiled and unwrapped the second one for him.

"Thanks."

"Thank *you* for my balloon." She popped her sucker into the side of her mouth, waited until he'd done the same, then smiled in satisfaction.

Brooks shook his head. She was quite a sight when she eased up even the least little bit, and damn if she didn't have the finest smile. A smile like hers could brighten up the gloomiest of days.

"Don't tell me. I know." Amelia pulled up her legs and leaned sideways on the seat. "I'm easily amused."

"Hardly. This is a rare treat."

"It is good, isn't it?" She'd misunderstood, but he let it go.

"Yeah, it's good." He grinned. "Real good." When her smile widened, a gut-deep hunger roared inside him. He scowled and rubbed his thigh, as if he could work out his desire like a sore muscle at the end of a hard day.

Amelia wrapped her arms around her legs and dropped her head back against the rest, fatigue evident in the telltale way her eyelids drooped, reminding him of Timmy.

"Why don't you take a nap? Mitch already picked up the chief, so we're headed straight home. I'll wake you up when we get there."

"No, thanks. I don't want to choke on my lollipop."

"You just want to make sure I stay on the road."

"The thought occurred to me."

"I've driven in a lot worse than this." He told her about the time Dean broke his leg—major plaster—and the drought that had given way to a flood with the first real downpour in over a year. "Roads were washed out. You couldn't see two feet in front of you."

"Don't leave me hanging. Finish the story. There's a happy ending, right?"

"You didn't notice his wooden leg?"

She opened her mouth to reveal a bright, red tongue.

"Kidding."

"Not funny." She snapped her mouth shut.

"Sorry." He cleared his throat. "Sugar makes me punchy. By the way, your tongue's red."

"Is it? Yours is purple."

He frowned and stuck out his tongue in the rearview mirror. "Purple." He nodded. "And I have you to thank."

"You're welcome. Eyes on the road. Finish the story." No sooner had the words left her mouth than she grimaced. "Sorry. That sounded really pushy. I didn't mean to—"

"Yeah, you're real bossy, lollipop. Gotta work on that." He brandished his sucker. "Can't have you fitting in with the other two tyrant females running our household. A real tragedy that would be, answering to three of you."

She looked pensive at first, like she didn't know what to make of him, then a tentative smile played on her lips. "You *were* making fun of me that time."

"Maybe." He stuck the lollipop back into the side of his mouth. "So you want to hear a happy ending or chew me out? Because if it's all the same to you, I'll pass on—"

"Finish, smarty-pants."

"Yep. Gonna fit right in." Brooks grinned and shook his head, then finished narrating the trials and tribulations of getting Dean situated. "Jo set his leg, and he had a full recovery. Aside from occasional aches and pains, he's good as new. You'll see come summer. He hasn't slowed down on riding lessons one bit." He scowled, thinking of the city girl to whom Dean had taken more than a passing fancy. The first few summers hadn't concerned him much, but this was the third, and she was graduating from college next year. They weren't kids anymore.

"So you saved the day."

"What?" He pulled his thoughts back.

"Dean. The accident. You trudged through a torrential downpour and saved the day."

"Right." He tipped back his head. "Forty days and forty nights. Did I mention that part?"

She chuckled. "All right, Noah. I trust you to get me home in one piece." She leaned her head against the window and closed her eyes. "I do love the sound of rain."

And *he* loved the sound of her calling his ranch "home." More than he should. He clamped down on his jaw. "Rain'll be snow by the time we hit the gate. Weather's fickle as a woman in these parts."

"As a man, you mean. *Men* are the fickle ones."

"Yeah, that's what I meant." He grinned and slanted her a dubious look.

Her eyelids fluttered. "I thought so." She yawned. "Maybe I'll just rest my eyes a bit…"

"You do that."

"Brooks?"

"Hmm?"

"What you did for me today… I won't forget it."

He wished *he* could, wished he never knew how her

body felt against his, the softness of her hair, or the beat of her heart.

"Rest your eyes, lollipop."

Outside, the wind howled, slapping against the truck. Rain softened to mist, then sleet. The rhythmic back-and-forth swish of the wiper blades mingled with the heater's whir. Amelia conked out within minutes.

Brooks reached over and took the lollipop stick from her mouth, his gaze lingering on the slight curve of her lips. She was soft and sweet, and she deserved to find peace. And in that instant, he knew he would help her.

He would be Amelia Rigsby's friend.

Chapter 5

As Brooks expected, sleet turned to snow before they reached the Triple H: another nuisance storm that dumped a couple inches. Cows in the pastures would find sage and bushes to bed down their calves. He would go out after supper and spread more straw in the corrals, so the stock forced in wet, sloppy areas had a dry place to lie down.

He eased up the rutted driveway to the house, checking his herd and inspecting fence lines. Built on a hillside, the big, bungalow-style ranch house was made of cut sandstone with cobblestone pillars on front and back porches. From habit, Brooks started to pull up to the back porch, then turned around so Amelia's door opened to the steps.

He cut the engine, but she didn't stir. "We're here."

He got out and went around to her side. He tapped the window with his key. Nothing. He unlocked her door and carefully opened it. Her head slumped against his chest. Thick, clean hair spilled across his arm like spun silk.

A ripple of heat curled in his gut. He drew a breath and braced himself, leaned over and unbuckled her seat belt.

He ignored the soft whisper of her breath on his cheek and the sweet scent of cherry. He told himself to wake her, to let her walk into the house on her own two feet. His mind rattled off a dozen reasons why he couldn't let himself touch this woman, under any circumstances. And still, he found himself slipping one arm around her waist, the other under her knees.

He lifted her easily into his arms and kicked the door shut with his boot. Her body was soft and pliant against his, and the heat that had started in his gut slowly spread outward. He gritted his teeth and carried her up the steps to the porch, trying not to jostle her too much.

At the door, he reached for the knob and came within inches of flattening his nose when he found it locked.

Oh, sure. *Now* they decide to lock the door. He shook his head, reflecting on the day he'd come home to find the red shoes and his mystery woman asleep on the couch.

His mystery woman.

Brooks swallowed and stared down at her. She wasn't his. Not by a long shot. But she *was* a mystery, one that intrigued him more each day.

He couldn't deny the fact he liked her. More than he should have. More than he wanted. He liked the way she smiled, the way she walked, the way she talked, the way she didn't…the sound of her laughter, deep in her throat.

In the golden light of the lamp post, he studied her face, relaxed in sleep. The tension around her mouth and eyes had eased. The shadow of her eyelashes fell against her cheekbone. Even closed, something about her eyes drew him.…

Was it the perfect symmetry in the way the arch of her eyebrows framed her eyes?

For the briefest of seconds, he found himself imagining she was his woman, envisioned laying her down on his bed and pictured her hair fanned across his pillow. As the unbidden image burned in his mind, his gaze fixed on her lower lip.

Then her eyelids fluttered, and he jerked back with a silent oath. "Are we home?" Soft, brown eyes gazed up at him through lowered lashes, and damn if his insides didn't turn to mush.

"Yeah." He swallowed. It wasn't like he was going to *do* anything. But he'd thought about it. Oh, man, had he thought about it. And if she kept looking at him the way she was, he was going to keep right on thinking.

Put her down. Open the door. Go take a cold shower.

"Brooks?"

"Hmm?" he grunted.

Her eyes were searching his, as if looking for answers. He wanted to tell her not to look too close, that she wasn't going to like what she saw. But then, her gaze lowered to his mouth. And lingered. Slowly her fingers wound into the hair at his nape, and she lifted her head to brush her lips against his. The contact was brief, fleeting, over before it even fully registered she had kissed him.

She had kissed him.

Brooks held his breath for the span of three heartbeats. Three loud, unsteady heartbeats.

Around them, snowflakes flurried, and the wind blew. But in the shelter of the covered porch, time stood still.

"Thank you," she whispered. "For everything."

With a curt nod, he closed his eyes and swore softly.

"I—I'm sorry. I didn't mean to—"

Neither did he. As if his will belonged to someone else, he bent and swept his lips across hers. Just once. One more innocent taste was all he intended, all he needed to dispel the god-awful, gnawing curiosity. This time he paid attention. This time he made note of everything—the satin smoothness of her lips, the sweet, fragrant smell of her skin, the warm tickle of her breath against his face. He etched every detail into his mind to remember later.

"You're welcome," he said, lifting his mouth, forcing himself to end the kiss. But when he did, a muffled whimper followed in his wake. To his surprise, it came from her—not him—and her head trailed after his in protest.

Protest, as in she *wanted* him to kiss her.

"Damn, woman." His voice vibrated with desire. He wasn't strong enough for both of them. He licked his lips and tasted her. "Cherry." He groaned. "My favorite, too."

"More?" Whether it was a plea or an offer, the single word wasn't more than a cracked whisper.

Brooks didn't know who moved first, only that their seeking lips found their way together again, joining and molding, neither brief nor casual this time, but long and purposeful.

She tasted like heaven, like balmy summer nights and carefree laughter and a million stars twinkling above. She was everything and nothing he'd imagined, and the thought of anyone hurting her turned the fire in his loins to a searing ache in his heart.

Tenderly he kissed her chin, her cheekbone, her eyelid, the bridge of her nose. "Ah, Amelia." He sighed, wanting more than anything to lay her down someplace soft and take his time touching her as she'd never been touched before, to show her there was good in this world, and she deserved it.

But it was her lead; his job was to follow.

And he would, wherever she wanted to go.

"What do you want, honey? Tell me, and it's yours."

With astonishment, he felt her cup the side of his face and lifted his head to gaze into heavy-lidded eyes that held equal measures of desire and uncertainty. When she touched his lips with her fingers, he shuddered and closed his eyes. "Grape's good, too," she whispered, and it took every ounce of his control to keep from crushing her mouth with his.

Instead he caught her index finger between his teeth, nibbling as he flicked his tongue against the sensitive pad.

Her eyes widened, and her lips parted. ''Oh.''

Brooks smiled in satisfaction. Dipping his head, he caught her lower lip and sucked gently, forcing himself to savor her slowly—ever so slowly—like the last piece of holiday candy, knowing when it was gone...

The cold air swirling around his head told him to stop, warned this was going nowhere, that they were only complicating an already-complicated situation. But futures didn't concern him with the warmth of her body so close, so he turned a deaf ear to logic and held her even closer. He would give her whatever she wanted, touch her as long as she let him, and deal with the consequences later. Much later.

His tongue traced over the seam of her lips, and when they fell open, he gave a strangled groan and accepted her silent invitation. She kissed him with tender hesitation, growing increasingly bold, gripping his collar.

He eased her legs down, sucking in a sharp breath when her thigh brushed against him. But when he expected her to draw back, she moved even closer, her hands splaying across his shoulders, fitting herself to him. He bit back a groan.

''You feel...so good,'' she said between breaths, as if voicing a deep, dark confession.

He gripped her hips and swallowed hard. ''So do you.''

When she whispered his name, he thought for sure he was a goner. No way was he going to live to see Friday. Every cell in his body was crying out for completion, screaming that he needed to be inside this woman, to make slow, sweet love to her and show her in the most primal way how it was supposed to be between a man and a woman.

When she stretched up and lifted her face, he complied and kissed her thoroughly. "Brooks…?" She gasped, hands clutching his shoulders, hips moving restlessly against him. Driving him out of his ever-loving mind.

He swore softly and pulled her more fully against him. When she moaned, his control snapped. He caught her arms and pressed her against the door, kissing her long and deep.

But something had changed, almost right away, intruding on his passioned haze. Her body had gone rigid as a board—the only one getting anything out of the moment was him.

Brooks jumped back as if she'd branded his chest with a red-hot iron—D for dumbass.

His breathing shallow and choppy, he stared at her in dazed confusion. Eyes shut, face contorted, head tilted away, she looked as though he'd made her trek through cow dung in those blasted high heels.

"Amelia, I'm sorry, I… Ah, hell." He rubbed a hand over his face. What could he tell her?

That he'd been thinking about her in ways he shouldn't have? That when he held her in his arms, all sense of logic stampeded from his brain? That she was a boy's fondest wish and a man's carnal desire?

Big, brown eyes flickered open then, guarded and wary as a spooked colt's. One strong gust of wind, and she'd likely bolt for the barn.

One step forward, five steps back.

Damn it all to hell. Brooks cursed his own stupidity. He rode into dangerous territory the instant he'd put her down. He *knew* he wasn't like her, content to sample what she couldn't have. He had to curb his impulses, stamp out his needs before they took over. Before it was too late.

Before he *couldn't* be just her friend.

"I'm sorry," he said again, lifting his hands in appeal. "I was out of line. Way out of line. It won't happen again. I swear."

She frowned and drew her coat closer around her.

Something in her eyes disturbed a remote, shadowy place inside him. The image of his father's hand flashed in his mind. Angry welts. Empty apologies. His mother's tears.

Brooks knew of men whose apologies rang hollow, and he couldn't blame Amelia for doubting him.

He lowered his own hands, vowing from that moment on, he would show Amelia with his actions—not just his words—that aside from this slip, he was a man of honor and integrity.

He fished in his pocket for the keys, unlocked the door and held it open for her.

"Thanks," she whispered and stepped inside. "Brooks?"

"Yeah?" He closed the door behind him.

"I didn't plan that. I…I don't want you to think I intended to lead you on and then—"

"Stop." He clenched his jaw, barely resisting the urge to bash his head against the wall. "Gotta stop apologizing for things that aren't your fault, honey. I'm a grown man. I'm responsible for my own—"

"I kissed you. I told you what I wanted. I…asked for it." She looked down, fidgeting with her coat zipper.

Brooks frowned and took off his Stetson, combing his fingers through his hair. "You didn't ask for it, Amelia. Believe me, I know asking." He knew begging, too. "And that ain't it. You had a rough day. You needed a little comforting. You didn't need to be pawed." *He* was the one who needed that.

"But I started it.…"

"And I should have ended it. Better. I won't put you in that position again." His voice was gruff, his jaw set in determination. "You don't know me well enough to trust my word, but it's good. You'll see."

"It's not you, Brooks." She wrung her hands together, the self-recrimination in her eyes making his heart heavy. "It's me. I don't know if I trust *myself* right now...."

A muscle ticked in his jaw. He told himself he didn't want or need this woman's trust, but the demons of the past wouldn't let him off that easily.

He needed to prove himself if only to keep them at bay. He wasn't like the bastard who hurt her, and he wasn't like his old man.

He could control himself.

Clearly she was insane. Certifiable. Wacko.

Any minute now, Brooks would rethink his position on keeping her on as Timmy's nanny. She knew this. She was dreading this. And what does she do? She goes and kisses him. Not once. Not even twice. But again and again—and *again,* for pity's sake!

And now, having splashed cold water on her face for five minutes straight, she'd think her head would have cleared.

But no. She still felt dizzy, light-headed, all these muscles she didn't realize she had still pulsing, throbbing, *clamoring* for attention. Her body didn't seem to notice or care she wasn't playing with a full deck.

Her body had a mind of its own.

And it wanted Brooks Hart.

Aargh. She cupped her hands and kept dousing her face. Sooner or later, it had to pass. Didn't it?

Okay, so he made her heart beat faster, sent shivers of awareness dancing along her nerve endings. He was extremely virile, in a rough-hewn sort of way, like a tamed beast, a fierce mountain lion who had been domesticated.

From the moment he'd held her at the hospital, his gentleness had moved her in a way she just couldn't get over.

Of course she was attracted to him. What woman in her right—or altered, for that matter—mind wouldn't be? All it took was a pulse, and she obviously had a strong one.

She turned off the faucet and stood with water dripping down her face, staring at her reflection in the mirror. The woman who looked back wasn't that bad-looking, nor was she particularly eye-catching. She had the kind of face people might find pretty if they liked her, bland if they didn't.

She knew this because it was her own experience.

But Brooks… A man like him would have his pick of women, and she'd never have expected him to be attracted to *her*. She pictured him with a wild, adventurous woman, an equally rough-and-tough, outdoorsy type who rode bareback with him through a torrential downpour, fearlessly lifting her face to the heavens, both of them giddy with laughter.

A gutsy lion tamer, not a mousy nanny.

Oh, but for those few minutes…

For those few minutes, it hadn't mattered. Because she had been pretty. Not just to him, but to herself. She had been the kind of woman who deserved a little happiness, a little pleasure, to be held so exquisitely and kissed by a man like Brooks—a good man, a kind man, an unbelievably sexy man who looked at her with a combination of desire and reverence she would have sworn she'd never seen before.

A woman couldn't forget such a feeling, could she?

Like a flower turning toward the sun, she'd craved his touch, needed to feel his lips on hers, with an instinct as natural as breathing. She had wanted him enough to ignore reason, to block out the niggling fear, even to fight her mounting anxiety. Until the insidious claustrophobia washed over her full force, and she'd been powerless to shake it.

It had happened when he trapped her arms, sandwiching her between the solid barriers of his hard body and the door. Though rational thought told her this man would never hurt her, in that moment, she'd felt only the instinctive panic of a wild animal snared in a hunter's net.

If he hadn't backed off when he had, she would have struck out. She was sure of it. Hysteria had bubbled in her. One more second and...

She gripped the towel in her hands, eyeing the woman in the mirror with increased suspicion.

"Who are you?" she asked. "What are you running from?"

Supper was awkward. Amelia fed Timmy first, then tried to turn him loose in his playpen, but he was too love-starved with them gone all day and wanted to be where the action was. Even the high chair failed, so she and Brooks took turns with him in their laps, keeping their plates well out of reach of little fingers that were into everything.

Clara stayed long enough to get everyone settled, then begged off on joining them so she could get back to Pete. "Dampness," she said. "Gets into broken bones something fierce with old age."

"I've been a little rickety myself the past few days," Amelia said. She glimpsed a flicker of emotion in Brooks's eyes before he turned away, as if he couldn't bear to look at her any longer than absolutely necessary.

Only he did keep looking. He stole glances in her direction when he thought she wasn't looking, and she did the same thing with him. But whenever their gazes collided, they skittered away just as quickly. Silent messages crackled in the air: Whoops. Excuse me. Pardon me.

But even as the apologies whispered through her mind, an entirely different chorus played in the background.

What you did to me before…? It was incredible. You were incredible. Please, can we try it again? I don't know what happened to me there at the end. Don't give up on me.

"Amelia?" Mitch asked.

"Hmm? Sorry, did you say something?"

"Could you pass the fruit bowl?"

"Oh, right." She passed the bowl down the table. "So, how's *your* leg, Dean?" she asked a while later. Each of the brothers had polished off second helpings of Clara's hearty beef stew before she even put a dent in her first.

Timmy had settled down a bit, so she tried the high chair again, this time with success, the peas she'd put on his tray helping keep him entertained.

Dean shrugged. "Can't complain."

"There's a first." Mitch grinned and rubbed a shiny, red apple on his sleeve.

Dean shouldered him. "Oops. Don't drop your apple there, Mitch," he said, deliberately reaching across him for the fruit bowl.

Mitch stuck out his elbow, blocking his brother, then tossed him a banana from the bowl, which Dean caught with the smooth reflexes and good nature of a boy raised in a family of older brothers and horseplay.

A perfect environment for Timmy.

"So, everything go okay today?" Dean asked, eyeing Amelia and Brooks. At the ensuing silence, he turned his gaze to the banana in his hand, focusing intently on the task of peeling it. "Mind my own business. Got it."

"Thank you," Brooks said with a tight smile.

"No, that's okay," Amelia said at the same time, then shifted uneasily at their contradiction. "I…it went fine today," she felt compelled to answer. "Thanks for asking."

How would she explain her latest panic attack to Jo? *"So I was kissing your brother…"*

Dean nodded but said no more on the subject.

They weren't big talkers, the Hart men. Sure, they conversed amicably enough at the dinner table—they certainly never missed an opportunity to tease each other. But there seemed to be an invisible line no one dared cross, as if they could be footloose and fancy-free splashing around in the shallow end of the pool but judiciously avoided the deep end.

"Got a bunch of those brochures you ordered on dude ranches," Mitch said to Brooks. "Stuck them in the desk drawer with the others."

Before Brooks could respond, Dean raised an eyebrow. "I thought you said 'no way, no how' to putting up dudes."

"I said *likely* no way, no how." Brooks spooned a few more peas onto Timmy's high chair tray. They all rolled in different directions, and Timmy grinned, going after one. "Can't hurt to look into it."

"Yeah, good idea, Brooks. Wish I'd thought of it."

"Hey, I almost forgot." Mitch crunched into his apple and slurped the juice. "Rachel called to confirm. She's still on for Friday night."

"Thanks." Brooks tipped his head and took a bunch of grapes from the fruit bowl. He glanced at Amelia for the briefest of seconds before popping one into his mouth.

That lone second was enough. Pinpricks of apprehension stuck at her. Brooks had neglected to mention his plans were with a woman. Was it an insignificant detail?

"So, when are you going to make an honest woman of her anyway?" Dean asked casually, tossing his banana peel onto his empty plate. At Brooks's mutinous glare, he coughed and muttered under his breath, "Never mind."

Not so insignificant after all.

Humiliation stung Amelia's cheeks, shame fast on its

heels. Who was she kidding? Of course there was someone else. Men like Brooks could easily keep a stash of ready and willing *someone elses* on hand.

What do you want, honey? Tell me, and it's yours....

God, had it been pity that motivated him to say that? The reason he kissed her? Correction: let her kiss him?

She bit her lip, trying to ignore the petty jealousy she had no right to feel. Underneath the table, her hand clamped around her napkin, wadding it into a ball.

Damn it. She'd been feeling particularly brave after today's events. Brave enough to ignore the Don't Feed The Animals sign, so she could pet the nice lion's mane.

Brave? Ha.

Try: deranged.

"It's time you and I had a talk, partner." Brooks clapped a hand on Dean's back. "Especially with summer around the corner. We need to revisit a couple things."

"Lucky me. Can't wait. Want to join us, Mitch? Need to brush up on the birds and the bees?"

"Nah, I'm pretty well squared, thanks." He tossed the apple core onto his plate and laced his fingers behind his head. "The thought of my brother talking dirty doesn't do a thing for me. Sorry."

Amelia pushed back from the table. "Excuse me." She carried her plate to the sink and turned on a blast of cold water. Sticking her hands underneath the spray, she willed herself to come to grips.

It had been a tumultuous day. Her emotions were on overload. She needed to go to bed early. She needed to forget the way Brooks had held her when she'd fallen apart, the security of his arms and the comfort of his banter.

She *definitely* needed to forget the way he'd kissed her. Holy smokes, did the man ever know how to kiss....

But kissing him had been a mistake. One she wouldn't repeat. It was one thing to lose her memory, another to toss aside common sense. She had control over the latter. She needed to exercise it.

Thankfully she and Brooks had already apologized and agreed to put the incident behind them. Now *she* needed to fulfill her end of the bargain.

Brooks had a life before she ever got there. For that matter, so did she. Even if she couldn't remember it. Maybe she had a beau somewhere. Maybe someone was waiting for her to check-in. Maybe someone actually cared for her.

With an empty, hollow feeling, she realized none of the scenarios rang true. She felt her rootlessness in her bones.

But when she would have slinked off to a corner to lick her wounds, she thought again of Jo agreeing to marry a man she knew would soon die. Women like Jo didn't sit around feeling sorry for themselves. They didn't question their worthiness, or obsess about their limitations. They took charge of their lives and their happiness.

Amelia turned off the water and lifted her chin. She could wallow in her shortcomings, or she could be grateful for what she had—good people around her, a good job and a little ward whose baby blues melted her heart. As for her employer, he was just that—an employer. So far, he seemed pleased with her job performance. And so was she.

"What do you say, chief?" Brooks tugged Timmy's foot. "Can you stay awake long enough for a bath? You definitely need one since you're wearing half your supper. Is that…? Yeah, that's smushed peas in your hair. Yum."

In response, Timmy made a tired *mmm* sound and rubbed his tiny fists over his eyes, smearing a glob of peas on his eyelashes. Stunned, he blinked in rapid succession, a bewildered wail already forming.

"Hang on." Amelia wet a clean dishcloth at the sink and crossed to Timmy's high chair. "Look here, sweetie." She mopped his face. "Yes, you do need a bath, I'm afraid. I know you're wiped out. But you'll feel so good after a bath.'' She brushed his cheek with the back of her finger. ''You'll be all clean in your jammies. Won't that be nice?''

Timmy smiled and stuck up his arms. ''Mamamama.''

Everyone went still. Three sets of eyes shifted between her and the baby. Amelia tried to swallow around the knot of emotion in her throat.

''Did he just say…?'' Mitch cocked his head.

''I think he did,'' Dean said in wonder.

Brooks nodded in agreement. ''He did.''

''Mmm!'' Timmy gave a tired groan, wiggled and kicked in his high chair, demanding to be picked up at once. ''Ahhh!''

Amelia forced a smile, while inside her heartstrings pulled so tightly she thought for sure they'd snap. ''You're just making noises, aren't you, sweetie?'' Once in her arms, he dropped his head on her shoulder, and stuck his thumb in his mouth. She closed her eyes and rubbed his back. ''Yeah, you like to talk with the grown-ups. Nine months old, you'll be a big boy soon with lots of words to impress everyone.''

None of which would include Mama. Poor kid.

She kissed his forehead, smelling that wonderful baby scent, and swore as long as she was around, she would care for him as her own. ''I'll go run his bath.''

Brooks stood. ''Need help?''

''No, thanks. I've got it covered.''

He nodded and sat back down.

Half an hour later, she'd bathed Timmy, read him a story and put him down for the night. She stood by his crib for long moments, mesmerized by his peaceful innocence and struck by a desire to keep him that way. Bone-weary, she returned to her room, crawled into bed and burrowed beneath the covers.

Tomorrow was a new day, and she was determined to be a new woman. At least until she located the old one.

* * *

"Hi, my name's Amelia Rigsby, and I was wondering if you had any record of a fare to Wister in the past week?" She gave the Triple H's address and sat with her pencil poised at the kitchen table, using Timmy's naptime to go down the short list of cab companies listed in the phone book. "I think I might have left something in the cab." *Like my memory.* "But I'm not sure which company I used."

"Wasn't us," said the man on the other end—the same response she got each time. "We don't run out that far."

"Would you mind double-checking for me?" She wanted to cover all her bases since nothing had turned up yet with the airlines or the bus company, nor had any "ride" had called. "Maybe someone made an exception?"

"I doubt—"

"Please, it's very important. I'll leave my number if you could ask around."

"Well, do you remember what the driver looked like?"

"No, I…I wasn't paying attention. Here, if you could just take my number. I'd really appreciate it." She talked him into it, then hung up, fighting her discouragement.

At a rap at the mudroom door, she glanced up to see Brooks peering through the glass. Her spirits lifted, and she smiled and waved, ignoring the flutter in her stomach.

Not a big deal. Not a big deal. *Not* a big deal.

He turned the knob and stuck his head inside. "No luck, huh?"

"It's *not* a big deal!" She slammed the phone book closed.

"Geez. Sorry I asked."

"No, no. I'm sorry." She blew out a breath and tucked her hair behind her ears. "I'm a little tense today. Don't worry, I've been fine with Timmy—"

"I'm not worried." He shucked his boots and kicked

them to the side. "If you want, I'll put a call into the sheriff after dinner. He's an old friend of mine, and—"

"No." She shot up from the table. "I mean, no thank you. I don't think that's necessary. It's only been a few days." Although missing luggage usually turned up within twenty-four hours. "I'm sure someone will get back to me soon," she said brightly, rounding the island in the center of the kitchen where she'd laid out the dinner fixings.

Brooks closed the mudroom door and strode into the kitchen in his stocking feet.

Her gaze swept over broad shoulders that tapered to a narrow waist and denim-clad legs that went on forever. Every inch of his considerable height radiated masculine strength like heat. His large hands had the power to snap her like a twig, yet she couldn't forget how he'd cradled Timmy as he rocked him to sleep. Or how he had held *her*.

There was such gentleness in his touch. So much more than she would have guessed.

"I'm sure you're right," he said. "Still, it wouldn't hurt to put in a call."

She blinked and swallowed. She'd lost the thread of conversation. "Call…?"

"To the sheriff. About your missing luggage."

"No," she said again, following her instincts. No police of any kind, not even friends of the family. Not until she knew why… "I do appreciate the offer, Brooks, but you've pulled enough strings for me. Thanks anyway."

"All right, but if you change your mind…"

She nodded. "You'll be the first one I run to."

At the bold declaration, the sapphire of his irises darkened a few shades to a deeper, richer jewel tone, and her mouth went dry on the spot. She recognized the almost-imperceptible spark of desire in his eyes because she had seen it last night, in the instant after she kissed him.

She hadn't imagined it. At the memory, her insides quivered, and she raised a hand to her mouth.

When Brooks's gaze followed the absent gesture, she dropped her hand to her side. Still, he didn't look away. Swallowing hard, she gripped the counter with both hands, trying to combat the dizzying warmth veering its way through her senses—the same yearning she'd felt last night, when she'd touched her lips to his, and she'd forgotten herself.

She wanted to forget again.

No, she didn't.

God, what was happening to her?

She didn't *want* to feel this way about her employer—about any man—but she did anyway. When he'd held her, something inside her had awakened, and squashing it down required ever-increasing amounts of willpower.

This time, however, Brooks compensated for her lack. Clearing his throat, he turned away. "Where's Clara?" he asked, taking a gallon of milk from the refrigerator.

She smoothed a hand over her hair and clothing, as if straightening herself after a real—not imagined—encounter. "Um, Jo called and said she found an earlier opening for Pete to get his cast off, so Clara ran him into town."

"Great. I'll swing by later and see how he's doing."

She nodded. "I fixed sandwiches."

"You did?" He gave her a lazy grin of appreciation.

She crossed her arms and forced a light, breezy tone that belied the butterflies in her stomach, "Don't worry, it's kind of hard to mess up PB and J."

"Peanut butter and jelly." Brooks's expression fell, but he righted it posthaste with a cardboard grin. "Yum."

At his valiant effort to hide his distaste, she smiled. "Kidding."

He raised an eyebrow and set the milk on the counter.

"So, what's under here?" One hip against the counter, he lifted a corner of the foil covering a large platter.

"Meat loaf sandwiches. I used Clara's recipe."

"Now *that* genuinely sounds good."

At the reappearance of his grin, Amelia cast an anxious glance at the mudroom. "Where's the rest of the crew?"

"They're coming. We were looking at the neighbors' puppies. Just got a litter, and we're prime for a new cow-dog. You think Timmy's old enough for a puppy?"

"Depends. What kind of dog?"

"Border collie."

"Oh, what fun. Yes, they're well enough dispositioned to be good with kids." She nodded, then frowned. How could she remember insignificant trivia about missing luggage and dog breeds and not her own life?

"It'll come back," Brooks reassured, as if he knew the direction of her thoughts. "Give it time."

She nodded, but inside, her stomach tangled in knots. *What if she didn't* have *time?*

Chapter 6

"I'm afraid I've done something wrong," Amelia confided to Dr. Emma Andersson the next day. The psychiatrist had a knack for putting people at ease, getting them to open up. "Something illegal. I don't know what. Maybe a hundred unpaid parking tickets. Or a gambling debt? Or...worse." She worried her hands. "Something that would give me a reason to fear the police, to want to lay low."

"Mmm-hmm." Dr. Andersson scribbled something on her pad of paper. She looked to be around Jo's age, with straight, dark blond hair falling to her shoulders and gray-blue eyes behind stylish glasses. She wore a lavender sweater set and gray wool pants and sat on a chair beside Amelia as if they were having a casual conversation. "This is because of the policeman at the hospital?"

"Yes. I mean, the hospital made me nervous. I was on edge from the start, but *he's* what pushed me over."

More scribbling. "Tell me how you felt when you first saw him. Your very first reaction."

"Guilt. Again, like I'd done something wrong. I knew it, and he knew it, and it was going to be ugly if I didn't get out of there. Then it sort of escalated. I panicked."

"You were scared."

"Yes." She gave a blow-by-blow account of her panic attack. "What does this mean, Dr. Andersson? Am I nuts?"

"No, you aren't nuts. Quite the contrary. From what you've told me about your dreams and your panic attacks, I'd venture you're quite sane, and that your brain has shut down until it deems you're able to process some emotional trauma in your life."

"Psychogenic amnesia."

"You're familiar with the term."

Amelia nodded. "Dr. Jo mentioned it as a possibility. I've been wondering… If that's what's going on, if it's not just a bump on the head, can you hypnotize me or inject me with truth serum? Something to *jog* my memories?"

Dr. Andersson got up then and perched on the edge of her desk, taking off her glasses and setting them on her notepad at her side. "Medication and hypnosis *have* been used in cases of psychogenic amnesia, but I'd rather not go that route."

"But how am I supposed to *deal* with my trauma if I can't remember it?"

"By working *with* your mind's natural defenses, not against them."

She fought her frustration. "It seems like such a lengthy process. I wish there was some shortcut."

"Amelia, the human brain is a fascinating organ. It represses for good reason—survival. By working through the barriers, chances are you'll handle your repressed memories far better than if you force them to the surface."

She sighed. "Dr. Jo said something like that, too. Isn't there *anything* I can do, so I don't feel like I'm sitting around waiting for a lightning bolt to zap me?"

"Yes, as a matter of fact, there is. To start, I'd like you to keep a journal. Record your dreams and anything else that troubles you. Provide as many details as you can. Get everything down and bring your journal to our sessions."

"My dreams." She chewed her lip, not sure she wanted to document the direction some of her dreams had taken lately.

"You don't have to share anything you don't want to." Dr. Andersson smiled. "The important thing is to get you in touch with your psyche."

"Okay." She nodded. "I'll try it."

"Until next time then."

Amelia rose and shook hands with the doctor, thanking her for her session, then stopped at the appointment desk.

Brooks stood when he saw her, putting down the magazine he'd been flipping through. Judging from the stack piled beside him, he must have gone through a few waiting for her.

It was strange, but his waiting didn't bother her as she'd once expected. Rather, his presence comforted her.

"How'd it go?" he asked, helping her with her coat.

"Good. No earthshaking revelations, unfortunately." She tried to mask her disappointment by spending more time than necessary untucking her hair from her collar.

Brooks slid his hand behind her neck and scooped up the rest of her hair, then turned without a word and opened the door. Nodding toward the hallway, he stared somewhere over her head.

"Thanks." She walked out, ignoring the goose bumps on her nape where he'd touched her. "Sorry it took so long."

"Not a problem." He didn't press her to elaborate on her session, and she was grateful for that, but the tension between them stretched taut as they walked to the truck.

She felt badly she was taking up so much of his time,

that he'd had to chauffeur her everywhere. She would have driven herself today, felt fairly certain she remembered the mechanics of it, but until she located her driver's license, she was relegated to warming the passenger seat.

"If my ID doesn't show by Monday," she said once they were inside, "I'll go the replacement route."

He nodded, barely sparing her a glance as he released the emergency brake, popped the clutch and shifted the truck into Reverse, probably anxious to get home and unload her.

At the stop sign out of the parking lot, he cleared his throat. "You, ah, want to hit the mall while we're here?"

She frowned, certain she had heard wrong. "What?"

"The mall. Shopping. Chick stuff. There's a big one not far from here. I was planning to pay you next week, but I can swing an advance. You feeling up for it?"

Up for it? Just the *thought* of strolling past window displays and mannequins dressed in the season's finery made excitement bubble inside her. She pictured the sparkle and dazzle of colors, the din of muted voices and the smells of cinnamon, tobacco and perfume from various stores.

She turned, ready to express how much she would like to go when the admission died in her throat.

Brooks was watching her carefully, as if her response mattered a great deal to him. For some reason, the weight of his expectation struck a chord of caution in her.

"Is this a trick question?" she asked.

He frowned. "How would it be a trick question?"

She lifted her shoulder. She felt stupid saying it, but she didn't want to walk into a trap. "You could be testing me, making sure I'm not a spendthrift. I'm not," she said. "I know better than to spend money I don't have."

His frown deepened. "No, Amelia. I'm not testing you. I don't believe in *testing* people. Life's got tests enough, don't you think?'' He smiled then, a wry twitch of his lips, and she found herself smiling in return.

''Yeah, you're right.''

''So, what do you say?''

She wrinkled her nose. ''I think I like chick stuff. When you brought it up, my heart kind of did a jitterbug.''

''That's all I need to know.'' Brooks flicked on his turn signal and pulled onto the road.

It made a man feel good to know he could make a woman's heart dance. A little too good. Brooks told himself not to get used to it.

He returned from the cash machine to find Amelia at the makeup counter of the department store where he'd left her. They'd planned to meet up again in an hour, but since he'd run into her, he could go ahead and give her the money.

He'd suggested the mall in hopes of cheering her up. He could tell from the droop of her shoulders as they left Dr. Andersson's office the lack of progress was taking its toll on her. Jo always said when it came to cheering up, every woman responded to at least one of three things: chocolate, ice cream or shopping.

Chocolate worked for Clara. Ice cream worked for Jo. His mother had loved to shop.

''Champagne taste on a beer budget,'' the old man used to lash out in his drunken tirades. Whenever he hit the bottle earlier than usual, she'd pile them into the truck and head for town. With luck, he'd pass out before suppertime.

Once when they were on the highway, Mitch asked her why they didn't keep going all the way to Disneyland. She told him she would if she could, but she didn't have the money that day—maybe another day. And when that day came, Mitch insisted that's where she'd gone—without them.

Luke, he'd flat out refused to talk about her, as if she'd

never existed, while Brooks and Jo had held onto the hope of running into her in the mall one day, though the possibility seemed less likely as time went by.

To this day, malls still reminded Brooks of his mother, a woman he'd once thought the greatest in the world, a woman who could cheer up her kids better than chocolate, ice cream and shopping combined. And for a short time, he forgot all the ugliness and simply enjoyed that memory of her, a mother duck with her ducklings, parading along, like in the book he bought for Timmy, *Make Way for Ducklings,* the one he'd heard Amelia reading last night.

He straightened then and took in the sight of her at the makeup counter. The overhead lights picked up golden threads in her hair. She'd clipped it back before she left the truck, but a few strands slipped free around her face. She had a natural beauty—no fuss, no muss—that made her easy on the eyes. So easy it was hard to quit looking.

Smile, darlin'. Smile for me.

If shopping didn't do the trick, he'd try chocolate and ice cream next. He started for the counter where she stood, applying different lipsticks to the back of her hand while a heavily made-up saleswoman in a white jacket looked on.

"I have a sample of that color," the saleswoman said.

Amelia peered into a mirror, tilting her head as she angled streaks of lipstick up to her face. "That's okay."

"You sure? I know it's hard to tell on your hand."

She appeared to reconsider. "Well, if it wouldn't be too much trouble…"

"Not at all." The saleswoman sifted through a supply drawer and produced a tiny tube. Spotting another customer, she excused herself. "I'll check back on you in a minute."

"Thanks." Amelia smiled, her face in profile.

Brooks hung back, watching unobserved as she dabbed some color on her index finger and spread it across her upper lip. Slowly... Tracing the shape... Rubbing her lips together...

His breath stilled. His stomach dropped. He swallowed hard. *Oh, man...*

It wasn't like he'd never seen a woman put lipstick on. Hell, he'd grown up watching his sister do it multiple times per day. But as he'd figured out before, Amelia could wear his sister's clothes, sleep in his sister's bed and try on makeup just like his sister, but there was no way in hell Brooks could ever think of her as a sister.

Definitely not when the sight of her pursing her lips made his mouth go dry.

She turned the mirror for better light, and he sidestepped, so he, too, could see her face in the reflection.

The pale pink color was perfect for her—not too faint, not too dark. It made her lips look like dew-kissed rose petals and brought a glow to her face. More than that, it brought a sparkle to her eyes.

She liked what she saw.

And so did he.

Just then, she lifted her gaze, those bottomless, milk chocolate eyes locking on him. His gut pulled tight, and he tried to smile, but it probably looked like a leer. Right away, she reached for the tissue box on the counter. A few strokes, and she'd swabbed away all traces of color.

Brooks frowned.

Was she embarrassed he'd caught her trying on makeup? Hell, even nuns wore lipstick these days.

His frown deepened, and he stepped closer. "Amelia?"

"H-hi." She wadded the tissue in her fist, as if she meant to conceal it. "I didn't expect to see you so soon."

No, not embarrassment. Not even surprise. Anxiety.

The realization hit him square between the eyes, like a shovel plunged into the earth, turning up old, forgotten bones. Just like that, he was ten years old again....

His parents were going to a dance that night, and his mother had just finished getting ready. She came into the kitchen wearing a long denim skirt and a white blouse with pearly snaps. They'd all turned to look at her, and in that first instant, he remembered thinking she was the prettiest mom ever. He might have even started to say so. But then their father's chair had scraped across the floor, and he'd flown across the room in a rage.

Grabbing her face, he'd squeezed her cheeks between his fingers, so her lips puckered. "What the hell do you think you're wearing?" he had demanded, shaking her head back and forth. It was the lipstick. She'd chosen a shade of red, and he'd hurled a bunch of insults at her, accusing her of wanting to flirt with other men at the dance.

The second he released her, she'd grabbed a damp cloth and rubbed the offensive color from her lips.

At the memory, Brooks's blood ran cold. He didn't want to draw any parallels between now and then. He didn't want to, but...

Was a similar memory trapped in Amelia's subconscious?

The saleswoman chose that moment to return. "How are we doing over here?" She flashed a bright, eager smile.

Amelia smoothed her hair and shook her head. "I'm all set. Thanks for your time." She turned from the counter.

"Hold up." Brooks caught her elbow and returned the saleswoman's smile with a polite one of his own. "She's still deciding."

From practice, he let her go and stepped back, so he wasn't crowding her. "Not that you asked my opinion, but I think you deserve to splurge on something. It doesn't have to be big—just some kind of special treat for yourself. A book or a magazine? A giant cookie or a chocolate doughnut? One of those hair things or maybe...oh, I don't know…'' He rocked back on his boot heels. ''A lipstick of your choice?''

Amelia blinked. ''A lipstick…? Of my choice…?''

''Sure. You're the one who's going to wear it.''

She bit her lip and glanced at the tissue in her hand. ''Did you see the color I tried?''

The image flashed in his mind, and Brooks licked his lips before he could stop himself. ''Yeah, I saw.''

She lifted her shoulder. ''Did you think it was okay?''

Why did it sound as if she was asking his permission? ''Better than okay,'' he said.

''Really?''

''Really.'' He could hardly tell her that to his mind, everything looked better than okay on her lips. ''The real question's if *you* like it.'' He tapped his watch. ''You've got some time to think it over, though I suspect I know the answer.'' With a grin, he leaned down and whispered near her ear, ''I was peeping over your shoulder.''

Wide, brown eyes shot to his, and her hand fluttered to her throat.

He took said hand, deposited a wad of bills and winked. ''Have fun, lollipop. See you in an hour.''

For a long moment, Amelia stared at Brooks's back, then down at the money in her hand, before her vision blurred.

''Ma'am?'' The saleswoman's brows drew together. ''Are you okay?''

She bobbed her head. ''I just… I can't believe that man sometimes. What he just did… That was so…*nice*.''

''Ah, tears of joy.'' The woman smiled and handed Amelia a tissue.

''Thank you.'' She dabbed her eyes and tried to compose herself. But it was more than one incident. It was all of them. It was the uncanny way Brooks had of making her feel comfortable in her own skin. And though some of her earlier insecurities still taunted her, she pushed them aside.

Consciously. Firmly. Proudly.

A profound liberation engulfed her, as if she'd walked countless miles carrying bags of wet sand on her shoulders, never fully comprehending the weight until it lifted.

"I'd like that lipstick after all," she said, not for Brooks but for *herself,* forking over a bill from her small stash. "I've earned a reward."

"Good for you," the saleswoman said, taking her money. "And, honey, I'd hold onto that man with both hands." She tipped her head in the direction Brooks had disappeared.

"Oh, no. He isn't... I mean, we aren't..." Amelia shook her head. "He's seeing someone else."

The saleswoman turned from the cash register, arching a perfectly plucked eyebrow. "Not for long, judging from the way he looked at you when you were trying on that lipstick."

Amelia swallowed and tried to sound casual. "How long was he there?"

"The whole time."

"Oh." The heat of a blush crept up her neck.

The saleswoman laughed, handing her a bag along with her change. "Your receipt's in the bag. Good luck."

"Thanks." She gave a nervous smile, knowing she'd need far more than luck to fight her growing feelings for Brooks.

An hour later, Brooks found Amelia sitting on a bench in their designated spot. "Been waiting long?"

She shook her head. "Just got here."

He eyed her bag and grinned. He didn't ask what was in it. "Maybe you could bring Timmy down here a couple times a month. Bet you could both use a break from the isolation."

"Maybe. Malls are nice, don't get me wrong, but I prefer

the ranch. It doesn't feel isolated with all of you there. Plus, what you said about wide, open spaces... I'm beginning to understand. And I've barely ventured past the back porch.'' She smiled.

He stuck his hands into his pockets to keep from touching her face. ''We, ah, need to fix that. Whenever you're ready for a tour, just let me—''

''I'm ready.'' She straightened, her eyes lighting up.

''All right. Tomorrow, then. I'll take you around the range, give you an idea of what running cattle's all about.''

''Bright and early?''

''Early as you want. I'll be up before you.''

She crossed her arms. ''Oh, you think so, do you?''

''I know so, city girl.'' He grinned down at her. ''Come on. Let's hit the road.''

She stood with her bag. As they milled through the shoppers, he slipped his hand to the small of her back to guide their path. She smiled over her shoulder, and he tried to ignore the tightness in his chest.

Even before they came to the stand, Brooks smelled the fresh pretzels. ''Hang on.'' He caught her hand. ''Pit stop.'' Following his nose, he veered to the side, taking Amelia with him. ''This has always been the highlight of malls for me.''

''Pretzels?''

''Yeah.'' He realized he was still holding her hand and reluctantly let her go. ''Hart tradition. Our mom used to take us to town when we were kids. They'd just built this new mall, and pretzels were a huge treat. Later, when we were teenagers, Jo hounded Pete, then Luke and me after we got our licenses, to drive her places. Luke wouldn't step foot in a mall of his own free will, but me, I caved in for one reason and one reason only.''

''The pretzels.'' Her eyes danced with amusement.

Brooks grinned. ''With mustard.''

"I love mustard on pretzels," she said automatically, then gasped and covered her mouth. "Did you hear that?"

"I heard it."

"Oh, my." She bounced on the balls of her feet. "I had a memory. A real memory. It popped out of nowhere!"

He chuckled. "This day's getting better all the time."

"Yes. Yes, it is. We have to celebrate. My treat." She didn't even ask but sidled past him. "Two please."

"Hey, no fair. I was going to treat you."

"Please." She grimaced. "As if you haven't already. Numerous times."

"But—"

"No buts, dear." She patted his stomach, then made a shooing motion with her hand. "Why don't you get us some napkins?"

With any other woman, Brooks would have thought nothing of the casual endearment, the easy gestures, the simple request. But Amelia wasn't any other woman, and for her, this was major progress.

His gaze roved over her hand, her face, the crown of her head. He wanted to sweep her into his arms and swing her around, but he didn't budge, afraid to break the spell. Then she opened her mouth, and the apology he suspected on the tip of her tongue spurred him into motion.

He went for napkins, grumbling, "Three tyrant females," loud enough for her to hear. "Damned tragedy…" With a healthy dose of caution, he glanced up, unsure what he'd find. Catching Amelia's smiling and shaking her head, a leisurely grin stretched across his face.

They decided to stay a while longer, finding another vacant bench on which to sit and eat their pretzels. Soon, Brooks found himself sucked into a game of seeing who could make up the most outlandish stories about people walking by. They traded off, piggybacking on each other's ideas, arguing completely different scenarios, trying to one-up each other.

Before he knew it, a trip that started out as *his* effort to make *her* smile wound up with *her* cracking *him* up, at least as many times if not more.

"See, this chick stuff's not so bad." Amelia licked the salt off her fingers, then dabbed her mouth with her napkin.

He watched, fascinated. "Never said it was."

She laughed. "Give it up, Brooks. I'm on to you."

"You're...what?" He tore his gaze from her mouth.

The skin beside her eyes crinkled with her smile. "Next time you offer to take me to the mall, I'll know you're only in it for the pretzels."

"Yeah." He grinned. "The company sure sucked."

Her mouth dropped open, and she smacked his leg.

Brooks laughed and crumpled his napkin. But when she shifted to get her bag, her sweet, little rear end pressed against his thigh, and he shot off the wooden bench so fast, she must have thought he'd been hit with a cattle prod.

"I, uh..." He squinted at his watch.

"We should go," she said and stood, too.

He nodded and gestured for her to walk in front of him. Nope, not good manners at all. Just a slave to a good view.

Five more hours.

She wasn't jealous. Not the least little bit. Okay, maybe a tad. But she'd get over it. In time. Maybe. If she kept busy.

That evening after Brooks left for his date, Amelia and Timmy played in the nursery. Every time he gifted her with an ear-to-ear grin that showed off his new baby teeth, there was no doubt about it—the littlest Hart cowboy had lassoed her heart. The Blond Widow's loss was definitely her gain.

Please, don't let her come back, she selfishly hoped as she put Timmy down for the night. She left the nursery door ajar and took the baby monitor with her to the great room. She found Dean sprawled on the couch with a book. Tilting her head to read the spine, she murmured, "Cowboy Poetry."

Dean glanced up, his cheeks tinged with red. "I, uh, found it on the shelf."

Amelia didn't comment, though she suspected he had the soul of a poet. She wasn't sure he'd appreciate the compliment, or if he'd even take it as such. "I thought you were out checking cows."

"Nope. Mitch has it covered. He's a night owl anyway. I usually stick to days if I can."

"Well, let me know if there's anything I can do around the house to help out."

"Hmm…" Dean tapped his temple. "Maybe you could… I know." He snapped his fingers. "Take care of Timmy."

"Thanks, smarty-pants."

"You got that from Clara."

"Yes, I did. And I'm finding more and more occasion to use it. Imagine that."

Dean grinned, the devilish sparkle back in his eyes. A lady-killer in the making. Alongside the whole lot of them.

She muffled her sigh and glanced toward the desk. "I was going to leaf through some of the dude ranch brochures. Did you want to be alone in here?"

He shook his head. "I'm fine, unless… Did *you* want to be alone? I can take this up to my room."

"No, no. A little company's nice." She took a seat at the desk and started going through the various brochures, intent on keeping her mind occupied. That lasted a good minute. "So, has Brooks been dating Rachel a long time?"

"I wouldn't call it—uh, on and off for a few years."

"How is she with Timmy?"

"With Timmy?" At her nod, he frowned. "She's

never... Brooks doesn't... They, ah, haven't met." He raised the book higher, dubiously peering over the top as if to say, *Please don't ask me any more questions on this topic.*

She took pity on him and turned back to the brochures. She shouldn't have asked him anyway. Brooks's personal life really wasn't any of her business. Still, how important could this woman be to him if she'd never met his nephew?

Brochures. Dude ranches. Concentrate.

She drew a deep breath and forced herself to plunge in, reminding herself this was Timmy's future, too. Somewhere along the way, he'd become her motivation for everything.

Whatever worked.

She started skimming brochures, gradually separating them into different stacks and reaching for a legal pad to jot some notes. Soon, the notes filled several pages with cross-references to other notes.

"Hey, Dean?"

"Hmm?" He glanced over the top of his book.

"Sorry to interrupt, but may I use the computer?"

"Sure. Just don't ask me anything too advanced 'cause I'm hardly past the basics. Brooks has been teaching me to use the ranch management software he designed."

"He designed his own software?"

"Yeah. He checked out the ones on the market, but he wanted certain things his own way, so he made his own. He knows cattle ranching like nobody's business—the Triple H is one of the most successful family-run outfits its size. At least, it was. Before this loan. Now, I don't know...."

"You'll have to do something if you want to hold onto that claim," she said, and he nodded. Eager to help, she switched on the computer and monitor and found the programs she needed with ease. She must have picked up some computer skills along the way because she knew exactly which ones to use. Out of curiosity, she clicked on the icon for Ranch Management, not sure what to expect, but oddly pleased at the obvious bells and whistles she found.

Evidently Brooks had more than one hidden talent.

Though tempted to explore further, she closed out of the program before she could do any permanent damage and started the task of organizing her notes.

"Wow," Dean said, looking over her shoulder sometime later. "Do you moonlight as a business consultant?"

Amelia's head snapped up. An hour had passed without her noticing. "I was just fiddling around." She stacked her notes, feeling conspicuous as a bug under a microscope.

"Those tables look pretty fancy. What are they for?"

"A business plan," she said automatically, unsure where the answer came from but pretty confident about it. "I was comparing and contrasting—dude ranches for people who want working vacations and guest ranches for pampered getaways. Then there's price, region, activities, amenities, different things like that. I wanted to keep track of stuff popping out at me. And the next thing I knew... This came out."

"They teach *this* in Nanny School?"

She frowned as she looked at the screen. "It doesn't seem likely, does it?" It didn't *feel* likely, either. "I think I had another life—a different one with a different career— before I became a nanny." She shrugged. "I'm not sure. It's just a feeling I get sometimes." *Like there's more to me. Untapped... Dormant... Hibernating.*

"Well, I'm damned impressed."

"Well, thank you." She smiled. "Mind if I save and print this? I think I'm done for tonight."

"Sure thing. I even know how to turn on the printer."

"Um, Dean?" she asked when the pages started coming out. "Can you hold off on mentioning my plan to Brooks?"

Dean nodded. "He's not real keen on tourism, though he *is* the one who ordered these brochures. That means he's got to be at least considering the idea."

"He's considering it, and I understand his cold feet. That's why I want to put together something presentable."

With a nod, Dean handed her the sheaf of papers from the printer. "Mum's the word." He turned to leave, then looked back. "Hey, if *I* can do anything to help *you*, let me know. I can't make fancy tables, but I know dude ranches."

"You know, now that you mention it, there is one thing I was wondering... I haven't really seen all of the house."

"No one took you upstairs?"

"Well, I was kind of out of it when I got here. Brooks is taking me on a tour of the ranch tomorrow, but I wouldn't mind seeing the rest of the house tonight, if that's okay."

"Come on." He gestured for her to follow him. "I'll give you the nickel tour."

"Great." She swiveled out of the chair. "I'd like to make floor plans, figure out exactly what you have in terms of lodging space. A lot of the places in the brochures have one big, main house and some little cabins."

"Hmm. That might work for us. Plus, we've got those vacant houses."

"My thoughts exactly," she said, but before they could take another step, Timmy's whimper sounded from the monitor.

Their gazes locked on the device as if it allowed them to see as well as hear.

"Hang on." Amelia lifted her hand. "Sometimes, he goes back to sleep." At another whimper, she smiled and shook her head. "Not this time. Excuse me. Duty calls."

She stepped into the nursery just as Timmy's whimpers turned to full-fledged sobs. "Oh, sweetie. Come to ma—

Me,'' she caught herself. She lifted him out of his crib, rocking him as she applied the topical, painkilling gel. ''I know new teeth are no fun, but they're awfully cute when they come in.'' She prattled away as she rubbed his gums.

''Hey, look. What do we have here?'' She flipped the switch on the radio and turned the dial until she found a slow song. ''We'll pretend it's Sadie Hawkins, so the girls get to ask the boys. May I have this dance?'' She took one of Timmy's hands in hers. Humming softly, she swayed back and forth until finally, he fell back asleep. She pressed her lips to the downy softness of his hair, then eased him back into the crib, and covered him with his blanket.

''Good night, my sweet boy,'' she mouthed. Curling her fingers around the guardrail, she stared at his sleeping form, her heart full and content and proud. At a rustling noise, she glanced over her shoulder to see Dean in the doorway. With a shy smile, he ducked into the hallway. No sooner had she rejoined him than Mitch came bounding in.

''I need you, man. Damn cow's circling the corral.''

''Another one?'' Dean muttered an oath.

To Amelia, Mitch explained, ''The mother usually follows into the shed when we take her newborn calf to get warm and dry, but sometimes…'' He growled. ''So now she's going crazy looking for her baby, convinced it's still out there somewhere in the corral. Won't go anywhere near the shed. And I've got my hands full with other patients.''

''Be right there,'' Dean said, and Mitch tipped his hat to Amelia and headed back out. ''Sorry, Amelia. Feel free to take the nickel tour without me.''

''I might do that.''

''Just don't tell Clara about the dirty clothes on my floor. I was going to pick them up.''

She waved away his explanation. ''Go, go.''

''Going, going.'' He disappeared after his brother.

Just then the phone rang, and she rushed to answer it

before Timmy woke up. Even before the receiver reached her ear, she heard music and voices and knew it was Brooks.

"Everything okay?"

At the sound of his deep, husky voice, she closed her eyes and wrapped her fingers around the phone. *Come home.* She reassured him everything was fine. *I miss you.* "Just fine," she said for good measure. "You...enjoy yourself tonight." But as she hung up, her smile felt brittle.

Resolutely she crossed the kitchen and made herself some hot chocolate with an extra helping of whipped cream. Standing at the counter, she polished off every last drop, thought *who was she kidding?* and went for a double.

Damn lion tamers anyway.

Chapter 7

The booths at The Mint bar were made from the gnarled wood of trees, stripped of bark and shellacked to a high gloss of redwood, with twisting branches across the back.

Brooks sat across from Rachel Tanner, unable to keep from checking his watch every five minutes. He wanted to call home to check on Timmy again, but he didn't want to bother Amelia. He could tell she'd been distracted. He wondered what she was doing....

Rachel laid a hand on his wrist, catching him in the act of checking his watch again. She had reddish-blond hair, light green eyes, and a mouth that usually held his undivided attention. "Fatherhood's changed you, Brooks."

"That obvious?"

"Well, let's see." She began ticking off offenses on her fingers. "There's the constant monitoring of time. Your pool game's off. We've been here an hour, and you haven't made any noises about slipping out. Yeah, I'd venture there are some changes since the last time we met."

"What's it been? Six months?" Brooks rubbed the back of his neck.

"Give or take."

He nodded and took a long pull from his icy cold bottle of beer. "I've been told I have good manners." His gut tightened at the memory of liquid brown eyes staring up at him, satin-soft lips under his, and taste of cherry...

"Not that good." Rachel laughed, as if she'd read his mind. "So, do you have any pictures of the rug rat?"

"Do I have pictures?" he scoffed, as if she'd asked if Wyoming had wind. In one deft motion, he pulled his wallet from his back pocket and flipped open to the first of five photos.

"Aw, he's adorable."

"Yeah, Hart men aren't bad on the eyes."

"Modest, too."

He grinned. "We can't all have beauty and brains like you, counselor."

Rachel smiled raised her beer mug. "Now that's more like the Brooks I remember."

Under ordinary circumstances, Brooks would have taken her cue and suggested they continue their conversation in a nearby motel. But circumstances had changed—they were no longer ordinary. His body had a specific craving and would accept no substitutions. He didn't want Rachel. He wanted Amelia. And despite the fact the latter wasn't an option, no matter how hard he tried to psyche himself into carrying through on his initial mission, he couldn't seem to do it.

Stalling for time, he indicated the photograph in Rachel's hand. "So, do you ever think—"

"No," she said before he could finish. "Not everyone's suited to be a parent."

He nodded. "I didn't think I was."

"You didn't have a choice."

No, he didn't. And he didn't have to wonder what would have happened if Timmy hadn't come into his life. He would have been just like Rachel, exercising his choice not to reproduce, justifying his decision as ridding the world of the potential of one more bad parent.

He never would have experienced the wonder of the first time Timmy rested his head on his shoulder, or reached for him, or stopped crying at the sound of his voice. He never would have known such protectiveness over another human life, or the deep and abiding commitment to be the best he could be, or the profound sense of being part of something bigger than himself.

He never would have known what he was missing.

He looked at Rachel then—really looked at her—and saw in her eyes a reflection of the man he used to be, a man for whom meaningless sex seemed perfectly okay in a monogamous relationship between two consenting adults.

She was right. He wasn't the same. Timmy had changed him, made him want to live up to long-forgotten ideals and pass on a legacy of how it should have been.

Would have, could have, should have… It all suddenly mattered. And he realized in that moment whatever he and Rachel had shared, it was over.

She realized it, too. Probably before he did. Handing back his wallet, she said, "I know you'll do right by him."

"Thanks. I appreciate the vote of confidence." He eyed the door and wondered what he should say next.

As if she'd read his mind, Rachel patted his hand. "The beauty of knowing someone a long time is not having to say the obvious." She reached for her coat and purse and slid from the booth. "You take care, Brooks."

"You, too, Rachel." He stood and helped her with her coat, then pecked her cheek and watched her leave.

Amelia hesitated outside the door of Brooks's bedroom, the final room in her nickel tour of the first and second floors. The third-floor attic had been too cold for her bare feet, so she opted to save it for later. Maybe she could wait on Brooks's room, too. Maybe he had a thing about people in his bedroom. Maybe she should ask before—

"Oh, get over it already," she muttered, knowing full well he wouldn't care, that she was simply stalling.

Though she'd seen Mitch's and Dean's bedrooms, there was something more intimate about Brooks's. Her feelings for him were unlike those for his brothers. She didn't want to face the futility of her attraction any more than she wanted to face the fact she was jealous of his girlfriend. But sooner or later she'd have to come to terms with both, and Brooks's bedroom was by far the lesser of the evils.

Squaring her shoulders, she pushed open the door and stopped short. Whereas Mitch's and Dean's bedrooms had a notable, tornado-like consistency—furniture arranged more for convenience than appearance, unmade beds, clothes and clutter everywhere—Brooks's did not.

A king-size, pine sleigh bed dominated the room, its quilt and pillows arranged with military precision. The dresser top boasted a few framed photos. Two chairs sat with a chest in between, positioned in front of a large window that faced east, the direction of endless rolling hills. Under her feet, a thick, sand colored rug left a wide perimeter of uncovered, polished hardwood.

As she stepped further inside, the warmth of the room wrapped around her like a cocoon. She spun around, taking in walls painted moss-green with crisp, white trim. She crossed to the bed and ran her fingers over the handmade quilt, wondering whose painstaking efforts had resulted in such a beautiful creation.

Clean, simple and comfortable, this was a bedroom that invited sweet dreams at the end of a hard day. She allowed herself the quiet luxury of standing there, taking it in for a few moments longer, then got busy, repeating the procedure she'd done with the upstairs rooms.

In. Out. No big deal. No need to linger over the photos on the dresser, wondering who was whom and what they meant to Brooks. No need to look longer than necessary at the bed. No need to imagine Brooks moving casually around the room, emptying his pockets, undressing each night.

Pushing away such thoughts, she used the tape measure she'd found in a kitchen drawer and noted the dimensions of the room on her paper.

She knew the precise moment she wasn't alone, as if sensing a shift in the air molecules. Whirling, she saw Brooks in the doorway, one shoulder propped against the door frame, brows knitted.

Her gaze flew to the digital clock on his nightstand. Nine o'clock. Why was he home so early?

He wore a denim jacket, the same hue as the jeans that encased his impossibly long legs. She imagined muscles hard as rock beneath soft, faded material and wiggled her fingers to stop their sudden tingling.

Get over it.

Clutching her notes to her chest, she rose on the balls of her feet, then lowered herself. "I, um, know what you're thinking. You're wondering what I'm doing traipsing through your drawers."

He tilted his head as if to say, "And?"

"I—I wasn't actually *in* your drawers. I was just..."

"I'd know if you were in my drawers, Amelia."

"Oh. I would never..." she started, then stopped. He was teasing. She knew that. Good. He couldn't be too mad then. She exhaled, then bit her lip, trying to formulate the right words before she blurted out any more nonsense.

"I have a good explanation," she said, opting for the

direct approach. "I just don't want to tell you yet. It's nothing dishonest. I don't want you to think—"

"Okay." Brooks unfolded his hulking frame from the doorway and stepped into his bedroom, slinging his jacket over the back of a chair as he passed.

The once-large room felt much smaller now. She blinked and shook her head to clear it. "Okay?"

"Yeah. Whatever." He pulled the tails of his shirt from his jeans, sat on the edge of the bed and dragged the bootjack over with his foot. "Did Timmy wake up again?"

That was it? No third degree? He'd just take her word she had good reason to be snooping around in his bedroom?

"No. No, he didn't," she stammered. "Just the once. Haven't heard a peep since. I checked on him about an—"

"I'm sure he's down for the night."

She stared at him in stunned silence, the realization sinking in that to some degree, this man trusted her—alone in his house, in his bedroom, with his baby nephew.

His faith humbled her. He was a good man, an honorable man. And she wanted him.

Her heart pounded whenever he was around, whenever he so much as glanced in her direction with those beautiful sapphire eyes, whenever he spoke in that deep, sexy timbre.

"You'd better go," he said. "Don't want to offend you by changing into my jammies."

What she wouldn't have given to see his jammies. She shivered, rubbing her arms. "Do you...do you have horsies like Timmy?" her voice came out scratchy and hoarse.

"No." His jaw set in a hard line. "No horsies."

"Of course not." What an unbelievably stupid thing to ask. She ducked her head and made tracks for the door, but in her haste, a few papers slipped free. Stooping to gather them, she glanced up, an apology on the tip of her tongue. Glimpsing Brooks's unguarded expression, her mouth went dry.

He looked like a wounded soldier returning from battle. She noted dark smudges beneath his eyes, recalled how he usually took off his boots in the mudroom and wondered...

Was it just fatigue? Or was it something more?

Whatever it was, it was none of her business. Brooks Hart was off limits for a multitude of reasons, and he didn't need her poking around his head any more than his drawers. She rose and scurried for the door. It was a bad idea coming into his room tonight. She should have known her jumbled emotions couldn't withstand such temptation.

"Amelia?" His voice came behind her, the quiet rumble like the ocean at low tide, its subdued power rippling over her senses, its warmth lapping at her ankles, teasing and tempting and promising so much more.

Don't do this to me. Don't tilt my world any more out of whack. Don't make me want you more than I already do.

"Yes?" She rubbed her temples, not trusting herself to turn around.

"About Rachel..."

"Don't. Please, don't." Whatever it was, she didn't want to hear it. Not now. Not here. Not when he was so close and yet so far. "You don't owe me any explanations."

The weight of his gaze bored between her shoulder blades. A long pause and then, "'Night, Amelia."

"'Night." She got halfway out the door before she caught the door frame and gritted her teeth. "I meant to tell you...a cow was circling the corral looking for her calf earlier." She told him what she knew. "Dean hasn't come back yet."

A weary sigh. The scuff of boots. "I'll go check."

"Brooks?"

"Yeah?"

She turned, her concern outweighing her caution. "Is everything okay?" she forced the words past her lips, unable to shake the feeling this was more than exhaustion and cows.

"Yeah. Why?" The tightness around his mouth told her otherwise, but she didn't pry.

"No reason. Just…try to get some sleep later, okay? You don't look so hot."

He gave her a wry smile. "Thanks."

"I didn't mean—"

"I know what you meant, lollipop. I appreciate it."

"Okay then. Good night."

"Good night."

Brooks arrived on the scene to find Dean smearing balm on a cow's sunburned bag while Mitch bottle-fed her starving calf. Dean had maneuvered the frantic cow Amelia mentioned into the shed to reunite with her calf, and the new mama was now licking it bright and humming. Brooks offered to finish night duty for Mitch, but Mitch said no, he had things under control, so Brooks turned back for the house.

He was halfway up the hill when Dean hollered for him to wait up. He slowed, walking backward. "Uh-oh. What'd you do now? You got that confession look on your face."

From the time he was a kid, Dean had never been one to cover up his mistakes. "I, uh, mighta stuck my foot in it earlier with Amelia," he said. "She asked about Rachel."

"Oh, did she?" Brooks couldn't help but smile. *Not so uninterested after all.* He hooked his thumbs into his pockets and listened to Dean's account of their conversation, after which he clapped his brother on the shoulder. "Don't sweat it. No harm done." But when he started back for the house, Dean didn't fall in step. He turned and studied him in the moonlight. "What?"

Dean shrugged. "I really like her."

"*Like,* like. As in a crush?"

"Hell, no." He screwed up his face like he'd sucked a lemon. "That's like asking if I got a crush on Jo. Gross."

Brooks gave a rueful chuckle, wishing he could echo his brother's sentiments. It sure would simplify things.

"I just like *having her* here, is all. Takes a while to get to know her, but she's real smart. Funny, too. 'Course Timmy loves her. You should have seen her dancing with him in the nursery, twirling around."

He could just imagine. "Okay, Dean. I got that you're Amelia's new fan club president. Is this going somewhere? You want me to give her a raise? Double her salary? What?"

"Well…" More shuffling. "I was hoping you'd maybe give some thought to, ah, making her a permanent part of the family."

"You want to adopt her?"

"I want you to marry her."

"*Marry her?*" Brooks straightened to his full height. "You bang your head wrestling that cow into the shed?" He purposefully searched his brother's eyes. "The lights are on, but no one's home."

"Ah, hell, I don't mean tomorrow. She's got *amnesia* after all." Dean blew out an exasperated breath. "It's just something to think about since you and Rachel aren't ever gonna take it to another level…."

Damn. He was actually serious. "Read my lips, Dean. *No way. Never. Not gonna happen.*"

Dean dropped his gaze. "What if the Blond Widow comes back?" he asked quietly, the raw fear in his voice cutting Brooks to the quick, slicing the defensiveness out of him.

"Is that what this is really about?"

Dean looked up, and the moonlight caught the sheen in his eyes. "I love that kid. I don't want to lose him."

Brooks didn't hesitate. He slung an arm around his brother and hugged him hard, then pulled back and grasped his shoulders, looking him in the eye. "Neither do I. And I promise you *if* it becomes an issue, I'll do everything humanly possible to keep him. But until then... We can't live our lives afraid of things that might never happen."

Dean nodded and dabbed at his eyes. "You're right." He threw off his brother's hands and shoved him in the gut for good measure. "You're a hypocrite, but you're right."

"Hey." Brooks caught him in a headlock and mussed his hair before pushing him away. "Watch your mouth, son."

Dean chuckled. "You sound like Pete. I feel a lecture on the birds and the bees coming up."

"Well, now that you brought up the subject..."

"I...what? Ah, hell." He kicked the ground. "When am I gonna learn to keep my trap shut?"

"Ain't your trap I'm worried about. What do you know about condoms, junior?"

"Aw, Brooks. I'm twenty-five, not fifteen."

"Good, then you should have all the answers."

"But we already had this conversation *back then*."

"Think of it as renewing your driver's license."

They lingered on the porch and had their man-to-man, after which Brooks was sure Dean understood the physical precautions necessary with intimacy. Unfortunately Dean turned a deaf ear to Brooks's counsel not to risk his heart on a girl who would never stay in the Cowboy State past tourist season.

"You don't want my dating advice," Dean said. "And I sure as hell don't want yours."

"All right," Brooks said. "Fair's fair. But will you at least be honest with me about significant women in your life? I don't want to learn you got married after the fact, or find a birth announcement in-person on my doorstep."

"Don't worry, I promise not to pull a Luke on you," Dean said, cutting to the heart of Brooks's fear.

"Thanks." He opened the back door. "Ready to hit the showers?"

"Thought you'd never ask." Dean slid off the railing.

The big, old house was silent as Brooks walked barefoot down the hall. He eyed Amelia's closed door and checked on Timmy, then headed for the shower.

Five minutes under the hot spray, and he thought he'd dissolve down the drain along with the soap. Exhausted, he fell naked into bed, dropping his wet towel on the floor.

It was only ten o'clock, but he felt as if he'd pulled an all-nighter, five nights in a row. His eyes burned, and his muscles felt like lead weights, but despite his fatigue, he didn't sleep.

It was the same every night, had been for almost three weeks with no sign of letting up. No matter how dog-tired, he lay in bed and stared at the ceiling.

He couldn't go on like this much longer, suspended in some perpetual state of denial, going through the motions of his new life and pretending he was dealing just fine, while in truth he was avoiding entirely.

Avoiding Luke's boxes in the attic. Avoiding the pain of finding out his brother's secrets. Avoiding letting go.

The boxes would reconcile the stranger who'd shown up on the porch with the brother he'd once known. He dreaded those boxes like he'd dreaded nothing in his life, and the longer he waited, the harder it got. He knew there was no getting around it.

Grief, like death, demanded payment in full.

With a succinct oath he hadn't voiced in a long time, he rolled out of bed and rubbed both hands over his face. Then he took a deep breath, threw on a pair of jeans and headed for the third floor.

* * *

Amelia tossed and turned and finally gave up. She sat up and clicked on the lamp, took her business plan from the drawer of her bedside table and went back to work.

She'd definitely done this before—she was sure of it. Using a ruler, she drew scaled floor plans of the first and second floors. Excited by how everything fell into place, she climbed out of bed and changed into a pair of sweats. With the tape measure and Timmy's baby monitor, she crept through the silent house to the third floor to finish the last of her measurements.

When she got there, the attic door was open. In the dim yellow light, she saw Brooks sitting slumped over on a box, arms braced on his legs, another, smaller box open by his feet. He wore only jeans, low on his hips, every inch of his body muscled from hard physical labor. If he had an ounce of fat on him, she didn't know where he kept it. She held her breath and inched back, hoping to sneak out, but a floorboard creaked beneath her feet.

Brooks lifted his head. Across the room, their gazes met and locked as if bound by an invisible force. At the raw, naked pain in his eyes, her heart constricted.

Luke's boxes, she realized. Brooks was going through his possessions, all that remained of the brother he loved.

"Not much left," he said, raking his fingers through his hair. "We arranged an estate sale for his furniture. This is just…personal stuff."

Amelia didn't think but merely acted, crossing the room on the impulse to return even a small amount of the comfort he'd given her in her time of need at the hospital.

Recognition flickered in his eyes, as if he understood her intent. He held up his hand, shuttering those gorgeous, blue windows to his soul, and turned his back.

"Don't," he said. "I'm fine. I'll be…fine." His voice sounded heavy with strain, as if he'd wrenched each word free with Herculean effort.

She ignored his protest, placed the tape measure and baby monitor on a shelf and bent to wrap her arms around him. His shoulders were so broad she looped one arm over his shoulder, the other around his neck. His skin was so hot she half expected to see steam wafting into the cold attic.

At her touch, his back went straight as a beam in the rafters overhead. "Amel— *God.*" He made a low, wretched sound and reached for her arms as if to remove them. "You shouldn't be here."

"Well, I am. And I'm not leaving. So don't even try to tell me to go." At the moan of pure agony that rumbled from his chest, she tightened her hold and realized he was shaking. "Shh. It's okay," she whispered, knowing full well he could overpower her if he wanted. But he didn't. Instead he held onto her as a drowning man gripped a life preserver. Gently she lowered her cheek to his hair and repeated the words he'd said to her at the hospital, "Just rest for a minute. Lean against me and catch your breath."

For long moments, they remained like that, until she wasn't sure who was giving whom the comfort. Beneath her palms, his heart pounded a steady tempo. He smelled nice, like spring rain in the mountains, clean soap and shampoo and the natural, earthy smell of a red-blooded male. Her breath caught, and she shivered.

The shiver seemed to pass from her body into his, and he shuddered. His chest expanded and contracted in choppy jags. Still, she made no move to leave.

"Everyone hurts sometimes," she said, her voice thick, raspy. "You aren't alone."

With the deep, tortured growl of a wounded animal, he turned, framing her face in his large hands. "*You* are *not* going to hurt again. Not under this roof."

A hard lump of emotion closed her throat, his words like

a salve on a wound she didn't realize she had. But this wasn't about her. It was about him. *His* suffering.

Amelia didn't utter another word—not one syllable—simply folded herself into his arms, holding onto his big, warm body in the chilly stillness of the attic. Her name tore from his lips on a ragged groan, and he stiffened at first. But she laid her cheek against his chest, and his arms wrapped around her, holding her loosely, but holding her nonetheless.

Her hands rubbed up and down his bare back, wanting nothing more than to soothe him as he'd soothed her. He moved his own hand to the back of her head, stroking her hair as he would a kitten.

But when he lowered his head, her heart skipped a beat and started pounding double-time. If she moved a fraction of an inch, their cheeks would touch. Another, their lips. If she stood...

From nowhere came the image of his face nuzzled in the valley of her breasts, her fingers tangled in the silk of his hair. Darts of heat launched straight to her stomach and spiraled outward, until every nerve ending pulsed to the beat of her erratic heart, her breathing rapid and shallow.

She had to move. She couldn't stay like this. He was too close. And she wanted him much closer.

Swallowing hard, she ignored the mounting ache inside her and untangled herself from him, easing away. But the rush of cool air only intensified her need. Her need for him. And when she noticed the loss of her body heat had raised goose bumps on his skin, it took every ounce of her willpower to *stay* away.

She took his hands in hers, squeezed once, then with great effort, let him go, forcing her gaze to an open box.

It held photo albums, the first of which lay open on top of the others. She recognized the younger versions of Brooks and Jo and a boy who must have been Luke.

They wore cowboy hats as they sat atop bales of hay in the bed of a pickup, but it wasn't their camera-ready smiles that caught her attention. It was their eyes—the sadness in Brooks's and Jo's, the anger in their brother's, and an age-old worry in all three that had no business being there.

"How old were you in that photo?"

"Eight." His jaw worked mechanically. "Our mother bought us new hats that day. Luke warned her she shouldn't, that the old man would chew her out and there'd be hell to pay, but she insisted we needed them, and he'd understand." He closed his eyes shut and pinched the bridge of his nose, as if the memory was too painful to bear. "He didn't."

"Oh, Brooks…"

"God, I hated him," he said. "It was so pure, what I felt. I didn't know what it was like to love someone and hate them at the same time. I didn't know what *she* felt." He flexed his hand on his thigh. "Until Luke died."

Tears sprung to her eyes, emotion clogging her throat. She didn't know why she should feel his pain on a soul-deep level, but she did. "I know that feeling," she said. "I know it in here." She covered her heart, the place where she felt the grief of lost opportunities and unresolved turmoil and words left unspoken, as if they were her own.

"Ah, lollipop." He gave her a sad smile. "I wish to hell you didn't know a thing about it."

Something nagged her. A question that had floated in the back of her mind surfaced. "Brooks? How did he die?"

He covered his eyes and shook his head. "I can't…"

"Can't…what?" She bit her lip. "What is it? What happened?"

He lowered his hand and looked at her—really looked at her—with so much pain and guilt and remorse in his eyes she didn't have to ask again.

The answer quivered through her as if by a sixth sense.

Starting as intuition, growing to a mental picture. Blood. So much blood. Spattered. Everywhere. On walls. On the carpet. Bile rose in her throat. Her hands trembled, and the single word escaped her lips: "Suicide."

At his anguished sob, her heart tripped and fell. She couldn't stay away. She launched herself at him. Her body collided with his, and she held him as tightly as she could, a flood of her own, hot tears gushing nonstop down her face. He closed his arms around her, gathering her close as if to absorb her into him. Salty tears mingled, his silent, hers ragged, both ripped from the depths of their wounded souls.

"If only I'd known," Brooks said. "I should have done something. I should have *been there* to stop him."

"No. Look at me. *Look.*" She caught his tear-dampened face between her palms. "You can't help someone who doesn't want to be helped. You can't…" She shook her head, her eyes beseeching him as she slid her thumbs over his cheeks.

His gaze lowered to her mouth, and his eyes darkened. For a single instant, she thought he was going to kiss her, then he swore, low and coarse, and jerked away, rubbing his face with his hand. "This is wrong."

"Brooks?"

"No. Don't." He turned his back. "No more. Please. You need to go now. I can't…*take* any more sympathy from you. *I'm* the one who should be giving it."

"You've given, believe me. You've given me so much. It's my turn. I want—"

"No," he gritted out. "Not like this. Not at all." He put his head in his hands.

"Brooks." She fought her rising panic. "You aren't making any sense. I don't understand—"

"You have amnesia."

"No kidding." She gave a nervous laugh, but when she

laid her hand on his shoulder, he shrugged it off, holding up his own hand to ward off further contact.

"Please. Go. Now."

She shook her head. "Look, you're really worrying me. I don't want to leave you alone like this. Do you want me to get Mitch or Dean?"

"No."

"Then you're stuck with me. What can *I* do for you? And don't tell me nothing. There has to be *something*."

With a self-derisive oath, he turned and let her look at him. It was all there in his eyes, the raw, primitive hunger he'd tried to conceal. And when her gaze slipped lower, to his faded jeans, the evidence was unmistakable.

"Oh." Breath whooshed out of her lungs. Her pulse leaped. Blood hummed in her veins. Then just as quickly, reality encroached.

Rachel. It's Rachel he wants. Not you.

Her throat locked, and she tugged at the hem of her sweatshirt, feeling frumpy and inadequate and way out-of-her-league. "You could call her."

"Who?"

"Your girlfriend." She winced, ashamed at how much the mere word stung.

His jaw set in a hard line. "She's not my girlfriend." He sounded like Dean, denying the obvious. "She never was. And whatever we had, it's over. We broke it off tonight."

"You broke it off…?"

"I tried to tell you earlier."

Her pulse kicked up again. Was it possible? Could it be? *"Why?"*

"A hundred reasons, not the least of which is that I'm seeing every woman as a damn substitute now." He lifted his shoulder in an offhand shrug, contradicted by the hard line of his jaw. "Probably will for a while. Hell, maybe longer. I'm not real sure which end's up anymore. So do us both a favor and get out of here, lollipop. Please. I can't take much more of this.''

At the familiar endearment, her heart squeezed tight. She didn't move. She couldn't. ''A…substitute?''

He drew a breath and tipped his head back, staring at the rafters. ''I can't stop thinking about you,'' he said, his voice rough with strain. ''In ways I shouldn't. Even *now*.'' He shook his head in disgust. ''That's why you need to go. Understand? You can't keep touching me. I can't keep pretending I don't feel anything.''

Her? He wanted *her*? Amelia covered her mouth, hardly able to believe what she was hearing.

''We need to go back to how it was before,'' he said, as if he'd told her nothing of consequence. ''You caught me at a bad time…a low moment, that's all.'' Only the agony in his voice told her it was more than that—so much more.

''Brooks—''

''I shouldn't have said anything.''

She felt something infinitely precious about to slip from her fingers and lunged to grab it by instinct. ''No. No, don't say that. What you told me… What you feel—''

''It doesn't matter. None of it matters.''

She was bent over a cliff, holding on with both hands. ''It matters. You matter. To me.''

''Damn it, woman. You don't understand. I am the *last* man on earth who should matter to you.''

''Why would you say that?'' Her voice shook. ''You have to be the most incredible man I've ever known.''

He gave a short hiss and mumbled something about her basis for comparison. She would have been insulted, but the anguish in his eyes told her he didn't mean to insult. He braced his weight on his knees and stood, gazing none-too-subtly at the door.

"I'm not leaving, Brooks." She stood her ground. "Not after what you just said. You can't expect me to forget—"

He swore softly, his frustration edging his voice. "I can't *act* on this."

Amelia drew a shaky breath. This was her one chance. Now or never. Her choice: mousy nanny or gutsy lion tamer. What was it going to be?

Watching him carefully, she reached for the hem of her sweatshirt and pulled it over her head. "*I* can."

Chapter 8

The air hissed out of Brooks's lungs, and his jaw went slack. She was so beautiful standing there before him, her small, high breasts bare, her hair framing her angelic face.

How could *anyone* hurt her?

And then before he could formulate another thought, she was in his arms, all that incredible, soft skin against his, the rush of pleasure beyond anything he'd ever felt. The sounds that ripped from their chests barely sounded human. Hungry mouths sought and found. They clung to each other, kissing like lovers reuniting after a painful separation, their passion fueled by needs they'd fought for so long.

But no longer...

Warning bells went off all through his body. She wasn't in the right frame of mind. She was vulnerable. He'd be taking advantage of her.

"Brooks." She gasped and stretched up, curving her arms around his neck. The tips of her nipples rubbed against his chest, making him burn from the inside out.

"Amelia." He ran his hands along her body—the sides of her breasts, the dip of her waist, the swell of her hips.

He wanted her. God, how he wanted her. All this time, he'd dreamed about her. But this was wrong. No matter how right it felt. No matter how much he wanted her. No matter how much she *thought* she wanted him.

"Amelia." He tore his mouth away. "We have to stop."

"No." Her muted whimper nearly undid him.

"Honey, please. Don't make this any harder…" He cradled her head with infinite care as something too delicate for his work-roughened hands. "We can't do this."

"Why not?" Her eyes searched his, begging him to give her one good reason. Her guileless expression stole his breath, made him ache to hold her close and never let go.

"Because." Hell, he couldn't even give her an answer, had to wait out the amnesia, let her remember on her own.

He didn't *want* her to remember. He would have done anything to take the awful memories away, to undo all the hurt, take back the pain that had been inflicted on her.

With a shudder, he buried his face in her soft hair and inhaled deeply, trying to regain his senses. But his senses were otherwise occupied, drowning in everything about her. "You smell so good. You taste so good. You feel so good."

"Ditto, ditto, ditto." She reached up and kissed him. Once. Twice. Three times, and he went under, pulling her to him as he kissed her tenderly. "See, we can," she said, her fingers gliding down his neck and chest. "Everything you said before… I feel it, too. About you. All of it. I can't stop thinking about you, either. Wanting you…"

Dear God. In all his life, had anyone looked at him the way she was? The irony of the trust on her face felt like a low blow—the woman with *least* reason to trust him, and here she was.

Here she was.…

Damn, he wasn't this strong. Not enough for both of them... He closed his mouth over hers, capturing her sigh. Just one more kiss. One more, and he'd let go. He took his time, tracing his hands along her bare shoulders, her spine and the curve of her back, kissing her with the bittersweet reverence of a man on death row smoking his last cigarette.

"Tell me when to stop. Just say the word, and—"

"I don't want you to stop." She lifted her face, her eyes heavy-lidded but her gaze steady, determined. "No one's ever made me feel like this, Brooks. Somehow, I know that. My body knows it. I've felt it ever since that day at the hospital. When you held me. It wasn't like this before. My life. This is better. Better than anything."

Brooks closed his eyes. She had no idea what she was doing to him.

She laid her petal-soft fingers against his lips. "You asked me what I wanted. You said tell you, and it was mine. Did you really mean it? Or were you just saying that?"

"I meant it," he said roughly, kissing her fingertips, needing her to believe *he* would never lie to her.

"Then don't stop. Please, don't stop. I want...your skin against mine. I want to feel you...everywhere."

A harsh, guttural sound ripped from his chest. God, he needed this woman. More than air. He knew what it cost her to be so bold, to go after what *she* wanted. But he was torn between wanting to grant her heart's desire and knowing he was the last person who had that right.

He wasn't the man for her. Not in the long run.

"Brooks...?" She was killing him slowly.

He was afraid to give in, afraid not to. Would she hate him when her memory came back? Would she hate him now, if he didn't?

This could be his last chance to touch her, to show her how she deserved to be loved, how she'd deserved all along... Could he deny her that? Could he deny himself?

He lowered his gaze to the bump on her nose, tracing it lightly with his fingertip. Then he bent his head to drop a kiss where his finger had been, caressing her with his lips. When she sighed, he felt his own surrender. "Do you know I could still taste you? All week long... I must've brushed my teeth a dozen times, and I still couldn't get the taste of cherry out of my mouth. The shirt I wore that day, it still smells like you. I couldn't bring myself to wash it."

Her eyes softened, and she lifted a hand to his cheek.

He covered her hand with his own, turned his face and kissed her palm. "I don't want to add tonight to your list of regrets when you get your memory back."

"I'll never regret this. *Never*." She rose on her toes to meet his lips, and he groaned, deep in his throat as he kissed her. His hands slipped to her waist, anchoring her to him. He wanted to bottle her kisses, to keep them on his bedside table, to take every night before he went to sleep.

But when he would have picked her up, he dropped to his knees in front of her. Circling her hips with his arms, he crushed his lips to her womb.

"I'm sorry," he whispered, knowing there were no words that could ever atone for another man's sins.

A sob tore from her lips. "I know you are. I know." Her fingers wound into his hair. "Just don't be sorry too long, because life's for the living...."

And the rhythmic pounding of their pulses told him how very alive they both were.

He looked up then, saw her beautiful brown eyes gazing down at him and let himself feast on the sight of her. "I wondered what you'd look like underneath that ugly flannel." His let his eyes devour her small, firm breasts, his hands unsteady as he cupped the soft mounds. His thumbs grazed her hardened nipples, smiling at the catch of her breath. "I knew you'd be beautiful. I didn't know how beautiful."

"Oh, Brooks." Her stomach quivered with her short, ragged breaths. "You make me hot and shivery everywhere."

"Hot and shivery's good. Hot and shivery's real good."

"Do you know you're so handsome it hurts to look at you sometimes?" She grazed his cheek with the back of her hand. "The way your eyes darken... The way you touch me... You make me feel...real."

"Honey, you are real. Come closer and let me show you how real you arc." As he rose, she wrapped her arms around him, and her breasts grazed his chest, cranking up the heat under his already-boiling desire.

He picked her up and kissed her thoroughly, loving the way she felt against him, the way she fit in his arms, the noises she made in the back of her throat as if she couldn't get enough. Easing her down, he bent to kiss the hollow of her throat, then feathered moist heat across her collarbone.

Her skin smelled like baby powder and something all hers...the scent that had lingered on his shirt, driving him crazy. He lowered his head and closed his mouth over one taut nipple, sucking hard, then lightly flicking his tongue.

She gasped and arched, the sound of his name on her lips making blood rush in his cars and pound through his veins. He took her mouth again as her hands traced the sides of his rib cage, his back and the curve of his spine.

When her nipples, hard and wet from his mouth, rubbed against his chest, he gritted his teeth, every inch of him hard as a rock and throbbing in earnest.

Her fingers pressed the small of his back, then slid under the denim of his jeans driving him mad. He wanted to lift her up, to sink into her and feel her heat around him. He wanted to touch her and taste her and make her moan in pleasure. He gripped her arms and pulled her against him.

Her sharp, indrawn breath pierced through his desire. It wasn't the normal sound. It was the other one... He glanced down and saw from her expression she was in that place again, the place she went when she felt threatened.

"It's okay." She shook her head, and he knew she was fighting it. "It'll pass. Please, just let go of my arms."

He did as she asked, realizing at once, "That's what happened before." At her nod, nausea roiled in his chest. Had the bastard, even once, made her feel good? Or had it all been take, take, take—pure dominance and submission?

He bit back a vicious oath and reached instead for her sweatshirt, his body still hard and aching for her. "No one or nothing's going to hurt you again." *Especially me.* "I swear it." His voice was gruff, but his hands were gentle as he helped her back into her sweatshirt. "It's all right. Everything's all right. We're going to stop. You're safe."

Tears streamed down her face as she pried open her eyes, her gaze searching his. Ever so slowly, she reached out and took his hand. He saw in her slight wince what the effort cost her, and a heaviness settled in his chest.

He held his breath as she traced each of his fingers, then held her own palm up against his. "It's just your size and strength. Sometimes, it overwhelms me. That's crazy—"

"No, it's not."

"But it's nothing you've done. It's…"

"My potential."

Her gaze flew to his, clearly surprised. "Yes," she said. "You're so much bigger than I am." The difference in their hands—hers smooth and delicate, his rough and tough— drove home her point. "So much stronger."

The big and strong stuff didn't flatter him anymore. Not when she meant it to show his unfair, physical advantage over her. "I am," he said. "But you've got a power all your own. You can level me with a single word or a look."

She gave him a hopeful smile. "I can?"

His throat tightened. Where before, he would have put up every last barrier known to man, die before he let a soul in on any weakness, he said simply, "You can. And you do."

She drew her brows together and looked again at their hands. Biting her lip, she laced her fingers with his and drew his hand to her lips, kissing his banged-up knuckles. "Don't give up on me, Brooks. Please, don't give up."

His eyes stung. God, when she remembered...

She rubbed his hand against her face. "I didn't want to stop. I don't..." She shook her head. "Please, can we try again?" The mixture of desire and vulnerability in her eyes made it impossible for him to let her believe for even an instant he would reject her.

"Anything you want." The words tumbled from his lips.

"Anything...?" At his nod, she hesitated, then placed his hands on her breasts and met his gaze. "I want to make love to you. I want to get past this. Help me?"

Longing stampeded over him, kicking him in the head, the heart and below the belt.

He'd imagined her body wrapped in his, imagined how she'd look wearing nothing but a satisfied smile with those red high heels.

Damn, how he wanted to be the man who put that smile on her face. How he *needed* to be that man, to show her that it didn't have to be bad, that it could be so very good.

With a groan, he picked her up, lifting her into his arms. He glanced at the old mattress in the corner. But when he looked down into those bottomless brown eyes, her trust stole his breath. And he knew in that moment, there was only one place he could love her the way she deserved.

With quiet stealth, he carried her through the big, dark house.

The first and last woman he'd take to his bedroom.

Like a child on a haunted river ride at an amusement park, Amelia clutched Brooks's neck in the darkness. At the foot of the stairs, he dropped a kiss on her forehead, and she sighed and let her head fall against his shoulder.

In his bedroom, pale moonlight spilled through the open curtains, illuminating familiar shapes. Closing the door with his hip, he took the baby monitor and placed it on the bureau, then laid her down on the bed, ever so gently.

But at the sight of his large, looming body in the shadows, she fought the instinct to scramble back.

Right away, he retreated, rounding the foot of the bed to the other side. He read her so well, knew exactly what she needed. Though relief flooded through her, shame came fast on its heels.

"I'm sorry," she said automatically.

"For what?"

"My Academy-award winning imitation of an old-fashioned sink with two faucets, hot and cold."

He shrugged. "Nothing wrong with that. I'd worry if the hot wasn't working." Casually, as if preparing for bed on any given night, he turned his back and unzipped his jeans.

Tingles raced up her arms. Denim fell to the ground. Her eyes widened. Captivated, she stared at the gorgeous, sleek lines of his bared body, bathed in the ethereal glow of moonlight. Oh, yes—the hot was working just fine. Her fingers curled, bunching up the quilt.

"A little maneuvering…" His voice came low, intimate and seductive as a caress as he kicked off one leg of his jeans then the other… "And we'll find warm."

Desire flowed through her, warm and intoxicating, and she let herself drown in the heady rush of the moment, for in that moment she was a woman overcome with the dizzying need to see and touch and taste everything about a man.

This man.

Brooks's movements were slow and easy as he crossed

to the closet and took a box of condoms from a brown paper bag.

"My mall purchase," he said, dropping a few packets on the bedside table. But before she could jump to the next, logical conclusion, he cut her off at the pass. "I was thinking of you, lollipop." His deep, quiet voice rolled over her like a rumble of thunder chasing the wind. "All this time, it's been you in my dreams. No one else."

Her lips parted on a sigh. She stared at him, at his amazing body, one hundred percent male and fully aroused. And she knew whatever happened tonight, it would be worth it.

"Brooks..." But before she could open her arms in invitation, he pulled back the bedding and climbed inside.

In one deft move he reached for her, lifting her with minimal effort. She landed against him, straddling his hips over the covers. Through the sheets and her sweatpants, the evidence of his desire pressed intimately against her.

"Easy, honey." He shifted and guided her hips as if she'd mounted a horse and needed help with the saddle, then laced his fingers behind his head and turned over the reins. "You're calling the shots. I'm just going to lie here and let you get comfortable. You can do whatever you want. I promise not to do anything without permission."

She didn't move for a full minute, simply absorbed the sensation of his big, hard body beneath hers. She felt both incredibly turned-on and terribly nervous. She was dressed, and he was naked. "I...I don't want to disappoint you..."

"Ah, lollipop." His voice was like warm peach brandy, smooth and intoxicating. "It's our first rodeo. You know how that goes? You fall down, you get back up. Next time, you know a little more, you stay a little longer, you ride a little better. But we all start somewhere."

"Our first rodeo." She smiled. "I like that."

"Good."

"Help me, Brooks."

"Anything."

"Tell me what *you* want…"

"What I want…" He swore softly, as if he would have infinitely preferred showing her. But then, the words came, husky on his lips, "I want you, hot and shivery like before, only more. I want to feel your naked body against mine, and love you like you've never been loved before. Until morning light streams in the window, and we're too tired to lick our lips. Until we forget about yesterday and tomorrow…" His voice grew hoarse. "Until the hurt goes away."

Something inside her crumbled then. She didn't know whose pain he meant, hers or his. It didn't matter. She closed her eyes and dipped her head, slowly kissing the hollow of his throat, tasting him, inhaling his scent. Flexing her thighs, she marveled at the power harnessed beneath her, imagined the thrill of riding, the beauty and grace of a tamed beast, the exhilaration of strength that didn't work at cross-purposes but in harmony.

One hand came untucked from behind his head. "Honey?" He was asking permission. At her nod, he grasped her hip, moving her back and forth against him just once, as if he couldn't take more than one tempting stroke, one shattering taste of how it would be between them. Then he stroked her cheek with the back of his finger. "So damned beautiful…"

At the image of this strong, gentle man making love to her—making her feel in ways she'd never dreamed possible—she broke free of the prison that held her captive through her fear of failure. She bent and kissed his eyebrow, his eyelid, his cheekbone, before settling her mouth over his. And then the ride wasn't slow at all. But fast and bumpy.

"Oh, Brooks." Her thighs flexed harder. "Brooks…"

He murmured endearments between kisses, his tongue

stroking hers, his hand slipping inside her sweatshirt. Deftly he whisked her away on a riptide of pleasure, transporting her to a faraway kingdom where knights slew dragons, and maidens had nothing to fear, no reason to run.

Beneath her palms, she felt his limbs ripple and flex with restraint, while inside, her own heat intensified, building to a fiery pitch. Their breathing labored, their bodies arching toward each other through the barriers of sheets and clothing that proved both safe and confining.

In the light of silvery moonbeams, her hands skimmed the planes of his body, growing more bold as his whispers went from gentle and soothing to sexy and provocative.

Touching him, hearing and feeling his responses, her passion mounted until it flowed freely, until she found herself reaching for the hem of her sweatshirt again and pulling it over her head.

At Brooks's sharp, indrawn breath, she smiled. It was her first rodeo, but she was learning. She leaned forward, the tips of her breasts grazing his chest, earthy sounds of pleasure like a low, bluesy melody. Brooks lifted his head from the pillow, his dark, hungry gaze making no secret of what he wanted.

"Yes," she whispered. "Please."

In one smooth motion, he rose onto his elbows and captured a tight, straining nipple in his mouth. He knew exactly how much pressure to apply as he expertly suckled and nibbled and blew softly until she writhed against him, until fierce, urgent desire pooled between her thighs. She loosened her death-grip on his shoulders and shifted so she could trail her hands down his abdomen to close around him.

His body jerked in reflex, and a low, strangled groan vibrated through him. She felt it, absorbed it, and ached to have him even closer. "Brooks," she cried. "I want…"

"What? Tell me what." He took her mouth and kissed

her long and deep, until her loins quivered with longing, and a hollow ache intensified between her legs.

"You. Now. Inside me. Please."

At once, his hips lurched against her. "Damn, woman. Talk dirty to me, and the ride's gonna be over before it starts." He growled his pleasure, and her toes curled.

"Can we…? Can you…? I can't wait much longer."

"Yes, and yes," his voice was thick with promise. "But one of us has too many clothes on." He was smiling at her—the intimate smile of lovers who shared inside jokes with a mere glance—and she found herself smiling back.

It surprised her it could be like this between a man and a woman, that the act of lovemaking could be so *natural*. As she rolled onto her back and lifted her hips to shed the remainder of her clothes, Brooks levered onto an elbow, his heated gaze making her light-headed. "Beautiful," he said again, and she trembled, opening her arms to him, prepared to give him whatever he needed, knowing he had never been anything but gentle with her and hoping he might ease the ache inside her just a bit before he finished.

But he didn't instantly climb on top of her as she'd expected. Instead he rained hot, moist kisses over her shoulder and the sensitive skin of her inner arm, raising delicious goose bumps. "Come inside, honey." He scooted over, making room for her, and turned back the covers.

Skin slid against skin, and he nuzzled her neck, the scrape of late-night stubble intimate and erotic, sending electric current dancing along her nerve endings.

She sighed. "This feels good."

Brooks kissed her lips. "This is only the beginning." He trailed his hand down her flat belly to rest on her thigh. "Let me really touch you," he whispered near her ear. "Open for me?"

When she did, he found her ready for him—oh, so ready. He told himself to go slow, to set an easy pace, to satisfy her completely. When she remembered this night, he wanted her to remember her pleasure was foremost in his mind.

"Brooks, what…? What are we doing?" Her hips lifted to meet his long, leisurely strokes. She was on her back. He was still beside her, the hard length of him pressed to her side.

"*We* are doing what *you* said you wanted."

"But why aren't you…?"

"Do you want me to stop?"

"No. No, don't stop."

"Good. Hold that thought." And then he was moving ever so slowly down her body, his mouth joining his hand. And soon she was gasping and writhing on the sheets, trying to muffle the sounds of her pleasure with the pillow. And Brooks was sure he'd never been so turned on in his life.

But it was more than lust as he held her hips and she bucked against him. More than an itch he needed to scratch as her knees fell limp onto the mattress and he stretched his body over hers. More as he folded her into his arms, kissed her collarbone and gave her some time to regroup.

"More," he said then, gently easing her up the next mountain.

"Oh, Brooks…" She lifted her trembling fingers to his cheek. "I don't think I can—"

"Think again, honey." His mouth closed over one taut nipple, and he kindled her flames once again. She moaned softly, her hands clamping on his head, holding him to her breast. When her hips rose and fell, satisfaction coursed through him, and he groaned, matching her tempo.

Her passion reignited, she gripped his shoulders, her muscles quivering. But it was her face when he glanced up—her beautiful face contorted in desire—that drove him mad. "Damn, if you aren't the sexiest woman I've ever known…"

"Brooks… It's happening… Again… I think…"

He flicked his tongue over the hardened peak of her nipple, nibbled gently, then pulled hard. She arched off the bed, convulsing around him, his name a soft cry on her lips before she toppled back onto the pillows, boneless.

He smiled down at her, a bead of sweat trickling from his brow onto hers.

She smiled, too, a satisfied smile, and reached up to take his face in her hands, her fingers threading into the damp hair at his temples. "Where did you come from?" She didn't even try to hide the effect he had on her. It was all there, shimmering in her eyes… Her confusion. Her passion. Her bliss.

He was humbled.

Her fingers trailed down his neck to caress his chest. "All of you, Brooks," she whispered, shifting beneath him, so the most intimate parts of their bodies rubbed together. "I want to feel all of you. Now. Please."

"Yes…" His voice came out in a hiss. He grabbed a foil packet from the bedside table, ripped it open with his teeth and readied himself. Hovering for an endless moment poised above her, he feasted his eyes on her desire-slick body, aware that she was doing the same to him. He wanted to memorize everything about her, this woman who was everything he'd ever wanted, everything he would never have again.

Once she regained her memory…

Her hands moved to touch him, to stroke him, to close around him. "Come inside, Brooks." She urged him forward. "Let me really touch you."

He couldn't have held back another second if his life depended on it. His gaze locked with hers, he inched into her moist, awaiting heat, their bodies rocking together as he slid ever deeper until finally, she had all of him, and he had all of her.

Amelia didn't think she had the energy to move. She found it. She wrapped her legs around his hips, restless hands clinging to his broad shoulders, tracing the muscles of his back and gripping his bottom. And again he stoked the embers of her desire, whispering hot, carnal words of longing and sweet, tender encouragement.

A fuse spread within her, exploding into brilliant colors, like fireworks on the Fourth of July. On and on, she catapulted Brooks over the edge with her. He cried out his release against her neck, his body pulsing inside her. Fingers interlocked. Held tight. Tremors zinged between them like currents in a live wire.

When at last Amelia caught her breath, she couldn't keep the amazement from her voice. "I don't think I've ever... I can't believe I..."

"Three times." Brooks rolled onto his side, taking her with him, their bodies still joined.

"Notches in your bedpost?" she asked, only half joking.

"No." He wound his fingers in the strands of her hair, his thumb caressing the side of her face. "Not at all."

She pressed her lips to his palm. "Thank you."

"For what?"

"For treating me like something...someone special."

His voice lowered, husky near her ear, as if whispering a deep, dark confession, "You are, lollipop."

A knot of emotion welled in her chest. "You are, too," she said and closed her eyes, unwilling to tarnish the night with worries over what the morning would bring.

Chapter 9

"Hey, Brooks? You up yet? Rise and shine, cowpoke."

As his bedroom door started to open, Brooks rolled over and hauled the quilt over Amelia's naked body. They'd dozed on and off, waking to make love twice more, before Amelia declared his mission accomplished and crashed on top of him.

"Man, does your timing stink. New calves are waiting." Dean stuck his head inside, still rambling, "Catch up on your sleep—" At the sight of Amelia in his brother's bed, his eyes popped wide-open. His jaw went slack. "Later."

Brooks raised a finger to his lips, cautious of waking her and wary of what he was going to say to his brothers.

After Dean's initial shock passed, a wide grin spread across his face. He flashed a thumbs-up and made a hasty retreat, closing the door behind him.

Brooks blew out a breath and sank onto the pillows, staring at the ceiling for long moments before he turned his gaze to the sweet curve of a bare shoulder exposed from the quilt. He traced it with his finger, rose onto an elbow and cupped it with his hand. Closing his eyes, he bent and brushed his lips over the delicate skin, inhaling deeply.

He was hard in an instant.

He'd never woken up with a woman on the other side of the bed, never mind *his* bed. Like a wino with the drunken shakes, his body craved a nip before breakfast to get him through what he knew would be a trying day.

Was this how it started, an unhealthy obsession?

Brooks didn't want to find out. He pulled away. He needed space. Needed to be alone. To breathe his own supply of air. He rolled out of bed, careful not to shift the mattress too much, and rubbed his hands over his face.

There was *no* chance Dean would keep this under his hat. He'd probably tripped over his feet, running to tell Mitch.

Damn.

Brooks hated to give his brothers false hope. They had no idea what had happened to Amelia, what was at stake, how complicated it was. He couldn't begin to tell them, even if he wanted. Hell, he didn't know the half of it himself.

Who the hell was this abuser to her? An ex-boyfriend? An ex-husband? Was her past in the past, or was he still a threat to her? And the big one. Did she still love him?

At the thought, Brooks broke into a cold sweat. He pulled on his jeans, grabbed some clean clothes and slipped out of the room without a sound. Just as he closed the door, the phone rang. He dashed to the kitchen, hoping to get it before Timmy woke up, and answered midring.

"Hey, Brooks. It's Jo. Listen, I'm in the car. I've got an emergency at the hospital. Could you do me a favor? There's some mix-up at the nanny agency," she said without pause. "Zach erased a couple of messages this week, and I feel like an idiot with these people calling to follow-up. Like, 'Why haven't you returned my call?' Anyway, someone forgot to cross our name off the waiting list for a nanny. So, can you buzz the good people, and tell them we're set? I think they're open a few hours today. Otherwise, you'll have to wait until Monday.''

''Yeah, sure. I'll take care of it.'' He hunted for a pen that worked and jotted a note to call the nanny agency.

''Thanks, I appreciate it. How's it going with Amelia? You two getting along?''

Silence.

''Brooks? You there?''

''Yeah. I'm here.'' Barely. ''Amelia's… We, um… We're getting along.''

''See. What'd I tell you?'' Static crackled the line. ''All right, I'm gonna lose you soon. Better say bye now. See you at supper tomorrow.''

''See you.'' Brooks hung the receiver in the cradle. Well, Jo would know soon, too. Nothing stayed secret at Sunday supper. Great. He started down the hall when he heard footsteps.

''Hey, Brooks?'' Dean's voice came behind him. ''Does this mean…? What we were talking about last night…?''

''No.'' He kept walking, flicked on the bathroom light and dropped off his clothes on his way to the nursery.

''So it was just sex.''

Brooks spun in the doorway, coming nose to nose with Dean. ''Don't start with me.''

''Too late.'' Dean set his jaw. ''I've seen what I've seen, and Amelia's no buckle chaser. You can't treat her like your other—''

''I am *not* discussing this with you.''

''Fine.'' He stepped back, nostrils flaring. ''But if you hurt her, I'll personally kick your ass to Montana—I don't care if you *are* my big brother.''

If he hurt her…

Bile rose in the back of his throat. Acrid. Burning. As Dean stormed off, Brooks swallowed hard and braced a hand on the wall. Damn if he wasn't proud of his little brother. At the same time, never in his entire life had he felt more between the proverbial rock and a hard place.

He opened the nursery door and crossed to Timmy's crib. Bathed in the soft yellow of his Cat in the Hat night-light, sprawled on his back with his arms straight up, rosy cheeks and blond hair damp with baby sweat, slept the tiny person who had changed Brooks's entire life.

Their littlest cowboy.

A fierce protectiveness filled his chest. He adjusted the blanket and placed a hand on Timmy's tummy as he'd done on so many nights after he first arrived, reassured by the deep, even pattern of his breathing. He'd never left Timmy's side that first week. He bundled him up and took him in the pickup for morning chores. He pulled the rocker beside his crib at night, so he'd get to him at slightest sign of trouble. And he slept with one hand on resting listlessly on Timmy's tummy, whether for Timmy or himself he wasn't sure.

Neither of them had slept much in the beginning. Then came the night Timmy stopped crying at the sound of Brooks's voice. At the memory, and each one after it, his throat closed, and his chest tightened, every breath like a razor to his lungs.

What if Dean was right? About Amelia *and* about Timmy. What if all the love he had to give wasn't enough? What if Timmy needed a mother?

Could Brooks do it—risk everything—for Timmy?

His hand shook as he smoothed the hair from Timmy's forehead and touched his cheek. "I love you, chief," he whispered. "God help me, I only want the best for you."

At the sound of Brooks's baritone coming from the baby monitor, Amelia stirred awake, her lips curving as his words penetrated her sleepy haze. Languidly she raised her arms over her head and stretched, then opened her eyes, taking inventory of her surroundings. It was a short list.

The sun had barely crested the horizon. She was alone. Not wearing a stitch of clothing. In Brooks's big bed. An indentation in his pillow marked the spot where she'd last seen him, the tenderness between her legs providing further evidence it hadn't been a dream.

At remembered images and sensations, her body flushed, and she hugged his pillow, her smile bittersweet.

She didn't know how much experience she had with these awkward morning-afters, but she doubted it was very much, or she might have had a clue as to how she was supposed to act.

What did a woman say to a man to let him know she had neither regrets, nor future expectations of him?

Thank you for undoubtedly one of the best nights of my life. Could you pass the OJ?

She pulled the covers over her head, wishing she could blank out all unpleasantness as easily.

And in that moment, hiding in the protective cocoon of Brooks's soft quilt, she had a flash of realization. *This is what I do. This is how I cope. I pull the covers over my head and shut down.* Then she asked herself: *Is this how it's going to be? Is this how you want to live your life?*

She closed her eyes and drew a deep breath. Cautiously she poked one arm out, then the other, biting her lip as the early-morning chill turned her skin to gooseflesh. Yes, it was warmer under the covers. Yes, it was safer. But the whole world was out there, not in here, and she wanted to reclaim her place in it. Undeterred, she lowered her arms.

Cool, brisk air swirled around her head, clearing away some of the cobwebs, as if for the first time. Golden-pink rays of sunlight streaked through the windowpane, spilling across the quilt. She held out her hand, turned it this way and that, then pulled herself upright to embrace the day.

Whatever awkwardness she felt, she would deal with it. Pulling the covers over her head wasn't dealing. It was avoiding. *Running*. Both of which she'd done far too long.

She showered quickly, her timing impeccable as Timmy woke up when she'd finished dressing and drying her hair.

Hair sticking out every which way, he stood up in his crib, holding onto the railing and bouncing as he cried.

"Hi there, sweetheart." Seeing her, his cries turned to whimpers. He plopped down on his bottom, stuck out his lower lip and raised his arms. At his pouty portrait, she chuckled. "Come here, you lady-killer." She picked him up and kissed his temple, his whimpers stopping. "Aw, that's my good boy. Did Timmy sleep well? Hmm?" She wiped his tears and rubbed his cheek with her finger. "Let's see a winning Hart smile…"

Timmy obliged and gave her a toothy grin, then reached for a handful of her hair and stuffed it in his mouth along with his fist. Her heart brimming with love, she kissed his nose, then got him cleaned up for breakfast. They found Clara in the kitchen, standing at the stove with an apron tied around her waist, the smell of chili making her mouth water, and it wasn't even seven o'clock in the morning yet.

"Good morning," Amelia said.

"Morning, you two." Clara smiled. "I'm taking Pete into town for physical therapy later on, so I thought I'd pop over and whip up some grub while I got the time."

"From the smell of it, that grub's not going to last until suppertime. See, Timmy. Grandma Clara's trying to tempt our tummies, isn't she?" She put Timmy down on the counter and tickled his stomach, coaxing a belly laugh, before reaching for his baby food warmer from the cabinet.

When she turned around, she caught Clara dabbing the corners of her eyes with the apron. "Clara? You okay?"

"Fine. Fine. Darned onions." She sniffled, but there wasn't a raw onion in sight.

Amelia put Timmy in his high chair with an assortment of colorful plastic cups. "It's what I called you, isn't it? I'm sorry. It slipped—"

Clara held up a hand and shook her head. "I just never heard it before. Jo's kids call me Miss Clara. That's what she and the boys used to call me a long time ago. They grew out of it—kinda like Mommy and Daddy become Mom and Dad—so it brings back fond, old memories. But Grandma Clara… It sounds nice."

"Well, I certainly can't speak for Brooks, but I have a feeling he'll go for it. You're the mother of his heart, you know." When she looked up in surprise, Amelia nodded. "It was my expression, but he agreed."

Just then, Mitch came bounding in, his freshly washed hair damp and slicked back. Typically he stayed up later and woke up later than everyone, requiring less sleep than the others. "Hey, good-lookin'." He pecked Clara's cheek. "Whatcha got cookin'?" He tried without success to stick a finger in the chili pot, but Clara swatted his hand.

"Mitchell, I swear. You ain't changed a lick in twenty years." The warmth in her eyes offset her stern reproach.

"Ma'am." He grinned, unabashed. "Hey, chief. Hey, Amelia." He swiped a carrot from the cutting board and popped it into his mouth. "Brooks said you're coming out with us later. I take it you're up for Ranching 101—the crash, intro course."

"That's right." She practiced drawing deep, calming breaths, knowing a confrontation was unavoidable. The sooner they got past it, the sooner the tightness in her chest would loosen. "My lay of the land's been limited to a hospital and a mall so far. Not exactly what you write home on your Wyoming picture postcard."

"Just leave it to my big brother to take care of that."

He hooked his thumbs into his pockets, striking a casual pose, though he kept glancing at her from the corner of his eye.

"As long as it's not on horseback right off the bat..." she mulled aloud.

"Yeah, I can see where you might not want to, uh..." His lips twitched, and he rubbed a hand over his face as if he'd remembered some private joke he didn't want to share. "Yeah, that makes sense."

"What's going on, Mitch?" Clara asked from the stove.

"Nothing, why?"

"You're hemming and hawing like Dean when he's bursting at the seams." She lifted an eyebrow. "What'd you do? You gonna confess to something?"

"Nope. Not me. No confessions here." Mitch leaned against the counter, crossing one ankle over the other and inspecting his fingernails. "You seen Brooks this morning?"

Amelia flushed, her gaze skittering away.

"No, why?" Clara whacked the wooden spoon against the pot a few times.

"Geez. Can't a guy ask a simple question?"

"Don't know. You ain't asked one yet."

"Why, Clara." He faked a wounded look. "Whatever do you mean, darlin'?"

She narrowed her gaze and brandished the spoon at him. "You know darn well where to find your brother, which tells me you got an ulterior motive for asking."

"Is it warm in here?" He turned to Amelia with a grin.

"Oh, no." Amelia held up her hands. "Leave me out of it."

"All right. All right." He straightened away from the counter. "I'm outta here." He paused by Timmy's high chair. "You come visit Uncle Mitch later on." He rumpled Timmy's hair, and Amelia smiled, noticing all three of the brothers made the same affectionate gesture with the baby. "I sure have missed you helping us on feed runs. Oh, for me?" He grinned as Timmy handed him a bright blue, plastic cup and pretended to drink from it. "Yum-my."

"Mmmm-eeee," Timmy tried to parrot back.

"Close." Mitch laughed. "Real close." Then he turned to Amelia. "You mind if I take him to the neighbors' after dinner, either today or tomorrow?"

"Oh, the ones with the puppies?"

"Yeah. I'll be careful."

At his automatic reassurance, she smiled. "I know you will."

"Is that yes?"

"Of course. You don't need my permission."

"Sure I do. Plus, I don't want to mess up your schedule or anything."

"All right then." She smiled and stirred the selection of baby food she'd warmed up and took a bib from the drawer. "Consider your permission slip signed. I'm sure Timmy would love to spend some quality time with his uncle Mitch."

"Hear that?" Mitch said to Timmy who was methodically tossing his cups to the floor one by one, craning his head over the side to watch them fall. Squatting, Mitch picked them up and gave them back to Timmy, widening his eyes and mouth in exaggerated excitement. "The boss said yes. We're on. Puppies. You and me."

The boss. At the easy expression, Amelia's heart pulled tight. The way they all treated her made her feel important, like she belonged. She didn't want that to change because of one night. One wonderful, incredible, unforgettable night.

Yes, the sooner she and Brooks got this morning-after business behind them, the better. "We'll head down to the barn after breakfast," she told Mitch. "If you could tell—"

"I'll tell him." His lips started to twitch again, but Timmy enthusiastically babbled some nonsense, stuck a cup into his mouth and bounced another off his uncle's head. "Ouch. On that note, I'm *really* outta here. Bye, all."

After he left, Amelia snapped Timmy's bib around his neck and stroked his hair. "Everyone's so good with him. He's so happy here. He even has a happy baby glow."

"Mmm-hmm." But Clara's eyes were on her, not Timmy. "He's not the only one glowing this morning, come to notice."

Heat crept up her neck, into her cheeks. "I, um, like it here, too."

"Mmm-hmm." She looked at the mudroom door and nodded, as if to herself. "I keep telling 'em, ain't no substitute for a good woman."

"As evidenced by you." She sat down to feed Timmy.

Clara laughed. "You been listening, huh?"

"Well, it's plain to see you raised them well."

"Oh, yeah?" She picked up the wooden spoon again. "You mean the way they're always trying to get away with whatever they can, pull the wool over my eyes? Think I won't notice." She clucked. "Boys will be boys, I suppose."

"*Your boys* love and respect you a great deal, and that respect obviously extends to the way they treat others…the way they treat other women. That's quite an accomplishment."

Clara beamed as she stirred the chili. "They do me proud, that's for sure. Them and their sister. Like my own kids. Everyone but Luke…" Her expression turned pensive. "Never had much time with him. And the time we had…" She shook her head. "He was already a man by then, with his own ideas about the world. You know that saying… Get 'em young, train 'em early. It gets harder as they get older."

Amelia nodded. "And when you're repairing damage…"

Clara looked up in surprise. "Brooks told you?"

She shrugged. "Just enough that I figured out Ma and Pa Hart didn't have an ideal marriage."

"Not by any stretch." Clara's eyes grew distant as if seeing long-lost memories. "She was too fragile from the get-go. Wimpy little thing, not cut out for ranch life, or anything else that takes a backbone. *He* was one prickly son of a gun. Jealous. Possessive. Controlling. Add to that his bottle tipping, and it was ugly. Often. Mostly he stuck to wife-beating. The kids got emotional scars.

"Luke, the worst. Then Brooks. Then Jo. The other two were young enough—Mitch barely remembers, Dean don't remember at all. But you can see how those early years shaped the older ones. Brooks nurtures life. Jo fixes what's broken. Luke…" She shook her head. "Like Cain and Abel, him and Brooks. We thought he'd found an outlet for his anger hunting down bad guys. Turned out, the only way he stopped his pain was to pass it along. In the end, to the people closest to him."

A shiver crawled up Amelia's spine, raising the tiny hairs on the back of her neck. "Do you think she drove him to it? The, um, the Blond Widow." The name was thick on her tongue. She'd never liked it, right from the start.

"Laura's a convenient target. They blame her. They blame themselves. Blame, guilt, they're natural parts of grief, of healing. They'll work through it, come to see ain't none of us responsible for someone else's actions."

At the matter-of-fact pearls of wisdom, something loosened in Amelia's chest. "Now I see why you're the mother of their hearts. Brooks was right—you *are* the best."

Clara laughed and wagged her finger. "Okay, missy. You done made an old lady tear up once. Now, cut it out."

She smiled. "I'm really glad they had you and Pete—

four out of five, anyway. You've made a warm, nurturing family *this* little guy's lucky to be part of.'' She made funny faces at Timmy as she gave him another spoonful of strained carrots.

''Say, Amelia?'' Clara crooked her head. ''How'd you like to learn to make apple pie?''

''Are you serious? Your secret recipe?''

''I reckon it's time. Past time.''

''I'd be honored. Thank you.'' Amelia felt light on her feet as she got up and crossed to the sink to dampen a cloth to mop up Timmy's face. There, her gaze happened to land on a note in Brooks's handwriting. Dated today, the message was like a pin popping the balloon of her happiness.

Call agency re: Amelia.

Chapter 10

"**D**amn it, Mitch. Get the hell out of my way." Tired of his brother's comical attempts to block his path, Brooks shoved past him, wiping the blood from his cheek where the barbed wire had snagged him while he was out mending fence.

"Oh, sure." Mitch grinned from ear to ear. "Like it's *my* fault your mind's somewhere else this morning."

Brooks ignored him, going to the sink in the barn and washing his scrape.

"You know," Mitch drawled, hooking his thumbs into his belt loops and rocking back on his heels. "You're awful uptight for a guy who just got lucky. Where's your dumb, happy grin?"

"Shut up, Mitch. I'm not in the mood."

"What? Performance problems?" he coughed under his breath. "Maybe Amelia—"

In three brisk moves, Brooks grabbed his brother by the collar and pinned him against the wall. "You say *one* crass word about her—whether she's around or not—and I'm gonna shove your tongue down your throat. Got it?''

The humor faded from Mitch's eyes. He nodded once.

Brooks let him go and brushed him off.

''Sorry, man,'' Mitch said, walking with him to the hay truck.

Brooks popped the hood to check the oil. ''Forget it.''

Dean, who had watched the exchange in silence up to this point, chose to jump in then. ''Ain't *his* fault, you know.''

''Dean,'' Brooks said in a warning tone.

''What? You're the one sending mixed signals. Excuse us all to hell for trying to act like you want Mr. All-I-Want's-A-Roll-in-the-Hay. *No way, never, not gonna happen.* Maybe if you spelled out your intentions.''

His *intentions?* Cripes.

''Fine.'' He faced them both. ''I *intend* to keep this between Amelia and me until *we* figure things out. And I expect *you* to butt the hell out until then. How's that?''

At that moment, Mitch cleared his throat and socked him in the arm. He looked up to see Amelia standing there, with a bright-eyed Timmy strapped piggyback in his baby carrier.

One look at Madonna and child, and Brooks's heart damn near stopped beating.

Until that moment, he'd half convinced himself she couldn't have been as pretty, as sexy as he'd thought. In his experience, women never looked as good as they did in the heat of the moment. ''Warm afterglow'' was just a sugarcoated term for ''serious buzz kill.''

Until now.

One look at Amelia Rigsby's milk chocolate eyes, her shimmering hair and clear, smooth skin, and Brooks's buzz was nowhere near killed.

She was stunning. More beautiful in the light of day than

she'd been last night. More beautiful to him *because* of what they'd shared last night. And the simple fact made him alternately want to drop to his knees *and* run like hell.

"Morning." Her voice held false cheer.

How long had she been there? Had she overheard them?

Mitch and Dean sprung to action before he could open his mouth. "Hey, Amelia. How's it going? Watch your step. You look awful pretty today. Sure you're up to slopping around? You don't have to if you don't want. Is the chief too heavy on your back? Need a hand with that diaper bag? Here, take my arm." They fawned over a red-faced Amelia.

"I'm fine, guys. Thanks." Anxious eyes cut to him. "Brooks? Could I speak to you?"

His brothers narrowed their gazes, managing both to spur him on and glare in caution.

"Over here." He tipped his head toward the office and held out his arm, guiding them as they went inside.

"They know, don't they?" she asked the minute he closed the door.

He didn't try to tiptoe around it. "Dean delivered my wake-up call in person this morning."

She raised a hand to cover her eyes. "Oh, no."

Without thinking, he stepped closer and tucked her hair behind her ears. Surprised and annoyed by the easy, natural gesture, he dropped his hand, his voice gruff. "Nothing to be embarrassed about."

She opened her mouth, but whatever she was about to say got cut off at the pass as her brows drew together. She reached up and took his chin, gently turning his head a fraction. "What happened to your cheek?" Her tenderness caught him off guard, freezing his diaphragm.

Gentle and tender were *not* common handling instructions for a cowboy. Especially not a burly, six-foot-two cowboy. Not even when his injuries warranted major plaster.

Brooks swallowed against the stupid locking of his throat and stepped back, his voice rusty with emotions he fought to keep in check. "Barbed wire. I'll live."

She nodded and folded her arms, taking a deep breath. "I...saw your note. In the kitchen. To call the agency. A-about me." Her voice dropped. "You want another nanny."

"*No*. God, no. Amelia..." It was his turn to take her chin. He lifted it with the curve of his finger, his heart pounding as he met her gaze. "I don't want anyone but you, honey." Mercy, that was the truth. "I swear it."

Tears welled in her eyes. "But the note..."

"It's nothing." He told her what Jo had said. "I'll straighten it out in two seconds."

"That...that's it?"

"That's it."

She expelled her breath in a rush. "I thought..."

"I know what you thought."

With a relieved laugh, she pushed her hair from her forehead. "Nothing like a good scare to put things into perspective." She stepped back, and he let his hand fall away. "Brooks, about last night..." she said, obviously uncomfortable with the subject but braving it head-on. "I know I caught you at a low moment. You were grieving and understandably upset."

She was giving him an out. An invitation to chalk it up to one reckless night.

"I'm glad I could be there for you." She swayed back and forth, rocking Timmy who had started to squirm in his carrier. "Settle down, sweetie. We'll go outside in a sec." But Timmy was having none of that. Having expended his patience, he kicked and grunted, gearing up for a wail.

"You're boiling in that coat and hat, aren't you?" She grimaced over her shoulder. "All right, we'll go out—"

"Here." Brooks gestured to a small side room. It had two cots and a bedside table with a lamp and an alarm clock in between. In the corner sat a folded playpen, a toy chest and a space heater.

"What's this? A mini bunkhouse?"

"Nah, just a place to crash. Comes in handy when we're working 'round the clock."

"Looks like Timmy's broken the place in." She sat on a cot, eased the baby off her back and out of his carrier, and unzipped his coat while Brooks took his hat.

"There're few places on this ranch he hasn't touched." He unfolded the playpen and crouched by the chest to pull out an armload of toys. "Check it out, chief. All your favorites." He rattled plastic keys on a ring and tossed them into the playpen, grinning as Timmy's eyes widened in anticipation of an all-you-can-eat buffet.

But it was Brooks whose mouth watered when Amelia leaned over the playpen, her coat riding up over her shapely little rear. A fist of desire nailed him below the belt, slamming home the fact one night was nowhere near enough.

He itched to pull her hips against him, to unzip her jeans and find his way back to the promised land. He wanted to make her burn until she melted in a rush of pleasure so intense the thought of her leaving would never cross *either* of their minds.

Good God. What was happening to him?

He turned his back and gulped large quantities of air, rubbing a hand over his face.

"Are you going to play on your own, little one? Yeah? Not going to be Mr. Clingy? Good boy." She rustled behind him. "Brooks, I… Oh… I remember now…"

She remembered.

Brooks went still, his heart paralyzed in an iron fist. A

trickle of sweat dripped between his shoulder blades, his mouth as dry as dirt.

"This is part where the guy goes cold and distant, and the girl wants to talk, right?"

His head swam, and he nearly doubled-over from relief. He took off his hat and wiped his brow with the back of his hand. He didn't know how much time they had, but it wasn't up yet.

"This isn't easy for either of us," she said.

"No, it's not." He straightened and faced her, still holding his Stetson, his neck muscles aching with strain.

"Maybe we could keep it short, sweet and to the point?" At his curt nod, she clasped her hands together. "As I was saying… About last night…"

"It was incredible."

Her eyes softened, and she drew her lower lip between her teeth. "Help me out, Brooks. Tell me where we go from here." She lifted her shoulder as if it was no big deal, but the way she worried her lip told him otherwise. "I don't have expectations. I just need to know where I stand."

She didn't have expectations. How many times in his past would such a declaration have made him whoop with joy? Countless. So why did it tick him off to hear it from her?

Because it was a sorry reflection of a woman's self-worth, that's why, and he wouldn't stand for it. A woman comes along and bends a guy's mind and body into a pretzel—she ought to know she's got some leverage, damn it.

Brooks wrestled with a lifetime's defenses. He'd never stepped out from behind his walls, opened up enough to let a woman be special to him. He'd never wanted to this badly. He thought of Timmy. "Where do you *want* to stand, honey?"

She blinked as if no one had ever put the question back to her. "I—I don't know."

"Well, then." He dragged a hand through his hair and stuck his hat back on. "I suppose you better think it over and get back to me." With that, he stooped to get Timmy's coat and hat from the cot. "We should get going—"

"Wait a minute. Not so fast. Are you saying *you* don't have a preference?" At her belligerent tone, his gaze shot up. She was giving him the evil eye, one hand on her hip, her foot tapping her impatience.

And just like that, something loosened in his chest, making him suddenly, absurdly happy.

A week ago, she never would have talked to him like that, never would have lasted two minutes cooped up in a small room with him blocking the only door.

She felt free around him.

Maybe not completely. But enough. Enough to speak her mind. Enough that she didn't see him as a physical threat.

Brooks felt his face breaking into the dumb, happy grin his brother had expected. "Yeah, I've got a preference." He wanted to kiss her, wanted to lock the door and take off her clothes and have his way with her on the cot. He clamped down on his jaw and clutched Timmy's coat and hat tighter to keep from doing just that. "I *prefer* to give you what you want." His voice was thick, hoarse with the strain of his suppressed needs. "Whatever you want."

Her eyes searched his, suspicion warring with hope, as if she couldn't believe he didn't have something hidden up his sleeve. "I don't know how to play this game, Brooks."

"It's no game, honey. It's the way you deserve to be treated. You…have a right to certain expectations." At the words he'd never spoken before, Brooks braced for some natural disaster. But there was no flood, no hurricane, no tornado. The sky didn't fall. The earth didn't move. He exhaled a breath he didn't realize he'd been holding. "Now we can stand around and analyze this to death, or I can show you the range and let nature run its course. Your choice.''

She blinked. ''Gee, when you put it like that...'' She turned toward the playpen but not before he caught a flash of hurt she tried to hide. ''Come on, Timmy. Uncle Brooks is going to—''

''One more thing.''

''What?''

He waited for her to look at him, then opened his arms. ''Come here,'' he said gruffly, a muscle pulsing in his jaw.

Her stiff upper lip gave way, and she launched herself at him. He heard a tiny catch in the back of her throat as he caught her, sucking in his own breath at the feel of her soft body against his again. Dropping Timmy's coat and hat on the cot, he held her tighter.

''Damn women.'' He kissed her forehead. ''Always wanting to talk everything into the ground.'' He closed his eyes and buried his face in her hair, inhaling the clean smell of her shampoo. ''I'm no good at this, lollipop.''

''Yes, you are.'' *This* was what she'd needed, what she'd been waiting for—to be held in his arms again, a place that had fast become her favorite in the world. All the pretty words meant nothing if they weren't backed up with action. ''I'm not ready to move. Can we stay like this all day?''

''I don't know.'' He brushed his cheek against her hair. ''I was thinking those cots never looked this appealing...''

She laughed against his chest, then turned her head and listened to the steady beat of his heart. When he moved his hand to her hair, she sighed and let her eyelids slide shut.

''Are you sore?''

''A little.''

''Anything...I can kiss and make better?'' His voice was deep, rich, intoxicating with promise.

Liquid heat spilled through her body. ''C-careful, that sounds like an offer.''

"Take it any way you want." At the sexy smile in his voice, her breasts grew heavy, her limbs weak, a familiar, hollow ache throbbing inside her.

All the right words. All the right gestures. Why did it feel so strange, so foreign to her?

She drew back and lifted her face, peering up at him through hooded eyelids. "You could spoil a girl this way, Brooks Hart."

His eyes darkened as he dusted a fingertip along her nose from the bridge to the tip, then dipped his head and brushed his lips over hers. "That's the plan."

She rose on her toes, seeking his mouth again, but he groaned and pulled away.

"That's it, honey. I can't take much more temptation. I wasn't kidding about the cots." He crooked a rueful grin, straightened his arms and set her away.

At the loss of his body heat, she shivered and eyed the cots with longing. "Maybe if we didn't have an audience…"

He groaned again. "Hold that thought. The kid's gotta sleep sometime."

Her eyes cut to his. Where was this going? Where did she want it to go? How could she even begin to contemplate having a relationship when she didn't have her memory?

How could she not?

No one had ever made her feel like this. She was sure of it. Her body wouldn't forget. This was something new.

New and exciting. Exhilarating and terrifying.

And yet, it was like walking a tightrope *knowing* she had a safety net. She could actually let herself go and bask in the adrenaline rush without fear of physical harm.

"So." Brooks shifted. "You gonna take that ranch tour, or bail on me?"

She was too fragile from the get-go. Wimpy little thing,

not cut out for ranch life, or anything else that takes a backbone.

For some reason, Clara's description of Brooks's mother had struck a nerve, made her want to prove herself different.

She smiled. "A woman would be crazy to bail on you."

Was that vulnerability that tempered the heat in his eyes before he averted his gaze and brushed past her?

"All right, chief. Up and at 'em. Time to show Amelia how we check calves." He hoisted Timmy onto the cot, bundled him up again and planted him on his shoulders, to which the baby squealed with glee and drummed his hands on Brooks's hat. "Hey, buckaroo. What's the first lesson we learned about hats? That's right—if it ain't yours, don't touch." He laughed and plunked his Stetson on Timmy's head.

It engulfed him, settling well past his eyes. With one chubby fist, Timmy pushed up the brim, his tongue lolling to the side with his happy, toothy grin.

"Wait! The door!"

"Relax, lollipop. I'm an old hand at this." He bent his knees and covered Timmy's head with his hand, clearing the door frame without incident.

She blew out a breath. "Okay, I'm impressed."

"You ain't seen nothin' yet, city girl." He winked, and her stomach turned over.

They buckled Timmy into his car seat, went out the gate Mitch was kind enough to open and close for them and started up one of the ranch roads. Amelia was glad to have Timmy as their chaperone. The cab was intimate enough before. After last night, the effect only multiplied. Every glance, every sound, every body part had new meaning.

She found herself greedily cataloging small details about Brooks—the scars on his hands, the lines on his face, the shape of his earlobes. All the places she'd touched. Places that had touched her.

Places she wanted to know again.

She looked at him, and she no longer saw just the outer trappings of a drop-dead gorgeous cowboy in faded jeans and a Stetson. She saw him naked—physically and emotionally. She saw a man who, when stripped bare, possessed a deep, intense passion surpassed only by his gentle soul, his boundless patience and rare generosity. A warm glow of excitement hummed in her veins, the idea of a day in his company making her giddy as a teenager on her first date.

"So, where are we going?" she asked.

"North pasture," Brooks said as they crested a hill and started down into a valley. "We move cow and calf pairs out here after the calves are a week old. Before then, we keep them in corrals closer to the barn, so if there's a problem, they're easy to get in and help." He bent and reached under the seat, pulled out a clipboard with pages of computer printouts and handed it to her. "Hang onto this for me?"

"Sure." She scanned the top page. "What is this?"

"Calving log. Every calf's got a number and tag. Every morning, we ride through and check them off."

"*All* of them?"

"It goes quickly."

Not too quickly, she hoped, smothering the unease that never completely left but lingered below the surface. The feeling she was somehow living on borrowed time, that sooner or later, the black hole of her repressed memories would open up and claim her.

She smoothed Timmy's hair, and in the short time it took to look up again, she'd lost all sense of direction. The house and the red-and-white buildings had disappeared from view. All around them, an endless, white blanket of pasture stretched to the bottom of a cornflower blue sky.

"This is amazing," she whispered in awe.

"Yeah, it is." He smiled and shook his head. "I swear sometimes it seems like yesterday I was sitting where you are, Pete was driving, and this car seat held Mitch or Dean. So much has changed, yet this view… It's timeless."

God's country. The thought whispered through her mind.

Soon, they were driving through a herd of grazing cows. The hay appeared a startling green against the bright, white snow, and steam billowed from the cows' noses and mouths.

Amelia wondered what it would be like to live here, day after day, year after year beneath the big, open sky on this unspoiled, remote land where the animals outnumbered people. Would the novelty wear off? Would the incessant wind blow loneliness into her soul, or would the mysteries of Mother Nature continue to captivate her? What kind of a backbone did ranch life require, and did she have it?

"This is a good time to check calves," Brooks said. "The cows are busy stuffing their faces, so they aren't too concerned with the calves. See there." He pointed out her window where calves bucked, charged, frolicked about, often colliding into one another.

"They're like kids at recess," she said as four calves in a row ran by, playing follow-the-leader.

"You remember coming out here, chief?" Brooks rubbed Timmy's tummy. To her, he said, "He was a regular hand the first month since we were on the waiting list for a nanny. He's helped mend fence, chip ice from windmills, feed and water the herd, tag and check calves…" He animated his voice for Timmy's benefit as he rattled off ranch chores.

Timmy chortled and kicked up a storm. Happy feet.

She smiled. "Looks like another born cowboy, huh?"

Something flashed in his eyes then, something fierce and proud. He left one hand on Timmy's tummy, taking it away only to shift gears, steering with the other. "This land's his legacy. I want him to grow up to have the same choice the rest of us had—whether or not he wants to stay and raise his family here."

Timmy latched onto his uncle's fingers with both hands, trying without success to get them into his mouth. Watching their interactions, Amelia's heart crowded her lungs. She swallowed. "He really loves it here. He…loves you."

Brooks cast her a sidelong glance, a muscle pulsing in his jaw. "I, uh… It's mutual." At the rugged, handsome profile of this tough yet tender cowboy, an inner peace settled over her. They rolled to a stop, and he got out. "Back in ten. Fifteen tops."

She gave him the clipboard and soon heard clunking in the bed of the truck as he armed himself with whatever he needed. She craned her neck to catch some of the action, but he was hidden behind the herd. Oh, well. Maybe next time.

Around them, wind whipped snow across the pasture, and the pickup rocked from side to side. She reached for the radio dial and turned it on low, leaving the station where she found it. By the time Brooks returned—twelve minutes later—she was humming and tapping her foot.

He smiled. "Glad you can tolerate my music."

"I like all kinds of music." The words rolled off her tongue so easily her gaze darted around in suspicion. "Wow, don't ask where that came from."

"A memory?"

"Nothing that concrete." She shrugged, then noted his mouth had set in a grim line. "Everything okay out there?"

"Yeah. Fine. Is this too boring? I can take you—"

"I'm not bored. Unless we're…*I'm* cramping your—"

"You're not."

"Okay, then. Let's keep going."

With a nod, he scribbled something on the calving log, and she took the clipboard when he finished. "Thanks," he said and started driving again.

"How about that one?" She pointed to a calf who was lying down, its head on the ground. "How come she's not playing like the others?"

"Good eye." Brooks turned the truck in that direction. "That's why we check them every day. You just figured out a way we spot sick or weak ones—they aren't up and about."

Amelia preened. "Hear that, Timmy? Score one for the city girl." But when she looked at the baby, she saw he'd fallen asleep ahead of schedule. "Oh, sweetie. It's still early for your morning nap. Was it something I said?"

Brooks grinned. "Get him inside a moving vehicle, and his snoozing's fit to last an hour." He cut the engine and put on the emergency brake. "Be right back." He stuck out his hand for the clipboard.

She didn't give it to him this time, but took off her seat belt, opened her door and climbed down.

His grin slipped into a scowl. "What are you doing?"

"Helping you," she said brightly and closed the door as gently as possible, so she wouldn't wake Timmy.

Brooks rounded to the back, put down the tailgate and opened the lid of a big, plastic toolbox strapped to the bed. "I don't need help."

"I'm sure you don't. You can probably do this blindfolded with one hand tied behind your back. But I thought maybe I could—"

"Watch."

She closed her mouth, her attention drawn to what he was doing.

He inserted a narrow, two-inch pill into a foot-long, plastic cylinder, readied a syringe and stuck both into his pocket as he snuck up on the sick calf. The instant he grabbed its hind leg, the calf sprung up, bawling and trying to wiggle free.

She could see Brooks's lips moving, imagine his deep voice gentled as he slowly but surely worked his way up the calf's leg to its flank, hand over hand like a game of tug-of-war, then on to its neck until he'd straddled the calf, securing its head between his knees.

In minutes, he'd opened its mouth, slipped the cylinder in and out, then administered a shot in the neck and marked the calf with an orange paint strip.

"That's it, baldy." He released the calf with a pat on the flank. "Go rat on me to Mama."

The calf bellowed and scurried toward the grazing herd. Nestling between its mother's legs, it looked back at Brooks as if to say: *Hey, Mom! He grabbed me!*

When Brooks walked back to her without a word, she got the distinct feeling she'd done something to displease him. She cleared her throat and tried to sound carefree. "Is it okay to ask what you did, or would you rather I not talk?"

His nostrils flared, emotion swirling in the blue of his eyes. As he popped open an industrial-size box of disposable, antibacterial wipes and cleaned his hands, he explained the pill was for scours, the shot was a general antibiotic to fight anything else the calf might have, and they used paint to mark the calves they doctored. "Sorry if I was a jerk. I just…" He took an unsteady breath, then blew it out. "Cowboying isn't in your job description."

She frowned. "Neither was last night."

"That's the point."

"*What's* the point?"

"I don't want to take advantage of you."

"You're not."

He averted his gaze and reached for the clipboard, but

she sidestepped him. "Honey, am I gonna have to use my shepherd's crook to get that clipboard?" He took an inch-thick, aluminum pipe from the toolbox, extending it to show her a question mark shaped hook. "Catches the calf's leg just above the hoof."

She didn't feel like blowing off the subject. "You know, it's not like you've got a gun to my head, Brooks. I'm exercising free will here."

He didn't say anything.

"Do you doubt my competence?"

"No."

"Do you think a woman's place is barefoot and pregnant in the kitchen?"

"Hell, no."

"Do you want these thousands of acres—" she swung her arm in a wide arc "—all to yourself right now?"

He caught her hand midair. One flick of his wrist and she was standing in between his rock-hard thighs. His hands gripped her hips, his eyes as blue as flame. His voice came low, tortured. "The only thing I want all to myself right now is *you*. I want you to stay, Amelia. And I'm afraid you're gonna change your mind about this place. About me. I don't know what I'm going to do if…when… I've tried not to get attached, but I…" He closed his eyes. "It's too late."

"Oh, Brooks." She tugged down his head, rising onto her toes to kiss him. "I want you to get attached. It's only fair since I'm attached, too."

He groaned and kissed her back, his taste, his scent, the feel of him seeping into her, an arrow straight to her heart. The clipboard clattered onto the bed behind him as she wound her fingers into the hair at his nape, leaning into him. He widened his stance and cupped her bottom, pulling her closer, letting her feel the hard ridge of his desire as he kissed her, and kissed her, and kissed her.

She was somersaulting, like tumbleweed on the wind, happy and dizzy and free. *Free*. Every fiber of her being cried out in joy. Here she was in Brooks's embrace, and she didn't feel trapped but free. She wanted to stretch out her arms, lift her face to the sky and twirl around and around.

When at last they broke for air, puffs of steam wafted from their noses and mouths. She gazed up into his heavy-lidded eyes and saw a reflection of her own desire.

"This is what I want," she said. "A life where I can walk beside my mate. Not in front. Not behind. *Beside*."

A myriad of emotions flickered in his eyes. He raised a finger to the bridge of her nose, tracing over the small bump so reverently, he brought a lump to her throat. "Tell me that when your memory comes back. Tell me then…" He bent and kissed her softly, sweetly.

"I'll tell you, Brooks Hart." She playfully nipped at his chin. "But *only* if you teach me how to doctor calves."

He laughed and hugged her hard, then set her away and rubbed a hand over his face in the familiar gesture she now recognized as his way of reining in his emotions. "Okay, fork over that clipboard, woman." He plucked it out of her hands and moved so they stood hip to hip leaning against the tailgate while he explained the calving log. "Get it?"

"Got it."

"Good." He smiled and dropped a kiss on her forehead. "Let's go."

Once they'd climbed back into the cab, she pulled one of her legs up onto the seat and angled her body to face him and Timmy. In that moment, she felt more comfortable than ever—with Brooks, with Timmy, with *herself*. "I meant to tell you earlier, you're like Quick Draw McGraw with that syringe. Needles obviously aren't on your list of fears."

"Nope. Not afraid of needles." Of course a card-carrying Red Cross donor wouldn't be afraid of needles. "You want to try it next time?"

"Me? You mean…stick…the needle?"

"I was thinking the paint—"

"Oh, paint's good. I'll do the paint." She bobbed her head in enthusiasm. "I can prep that pill gun thingy, too."

"Okay, you're on paint and pill gun thingy duty."

"Great." She beamed as if he'd just deputized her.

They combed the north pasture, checking and doctoring as needed. With Brooks's encouragement, she tried her hand at the easier tasks, reveling in the sense of accomplishment and warmed by the respect in Brooks's eyes. When she made mistakes, he didn't criticize but coaxed her to try again. So she did. And succeeded.

Somewhere along the way, the last of their awkwardness and overpoliteness evaporated. Often, their gazes met and held in the intimate connection of lovers who could exchange thoughts with a single look. They chatted as casually as old friends about everything and nothing, then let golden silence stretch between them just as companionably. When Timmy woke up, Brooks changed him and Amelia gave him a bottle to tide him over until dinner.

"Does it ever bother you…?" She pursed her lips and tried to find a tactful way to ask her question, but Brooks understood what she was getting at.

"Raising hamburger, you mean?" At her nod, he stared out the windshield, at the cow and calf pairs spread over acres of rolling hills. "The food chain *is* what it *is*."

"But what about *you,* personally?"

"Me, personally?" He tipped his head in reflection. "Living on the land, you see the cycle of life up close and personal. Everything has its season, and each season leads to the next… From life comes death. From death comes life. It's endless, unbreakable. Awesome." He smiled. "*Personally,* working the land and the cows reminds me to be grateful for every day, make the best of the time I have.''

Her gaze swept over the wide expanse, the endless sky, before returning to the cab, to the baby beside her and the man on the other side. She, too, felt grateful, alive in a way she doubted she had ever experienced before this ranch.

Before this baby.

Before this man.

She studied his profile. "What *are* you afraid of? Or is that too personal a question?"

He slanted her a look that said: *After last night, you have to add that disclaimer?*

And she shot one back that said: *Well, you know... You could be touchy...*

He flexed his hand on the steering wheel. "Everyone's got something."

"And you...?"

"No exception."

"Snakes? Spiders? Small spaces? Heights? Death?"

"None of the above."

"Don't tell me you're afraid of the dark."

He shook his head.

"What, then? Don't keep me in suspense."

"Myself," he said quietly.

She frowned. "You're afraid of *yourself?*"

He shrugged. "You asked."

"But why?"

"Bad blood. I'm the kin of an alcoholic wife-beater."

That didn't mean anything. Not for this man. She'd know. She would see the danger signs.

But would she pay attention? Or would she deny the obvious, make excuses...pull the covers over her head?

A shiver crawled up the back of her neck again. What was it? Something...just out of reach.

"Amelia?" Brooks raised an eyebrow. "You okay?"

She nodded and rubbed her arms. "There's a piece of trivia I can recall. I get these odd insights sometimes. While most alcoholics and abusers come from alcoholic and abusive families, the reverse doesn't hold—the majority of those who grew up in alcoholic and abusive families do *not* become alcoholics and abusers. And not that you asked for it, but I'm going to give you my two cents... I think your awareness—your *heightened* awareness—says a lot. Add to that how much you value life—not just yours, but *all* life— and I don't see *you* as someone who deliberately takes your pain out on someone else. For what it's worth."

An unfathomable look chased across his face. He opened his mouth, on the verge of saying something, then closed it.

"What? Tell me."

He gave her a curious glance. "How is it possible to barely know anything about someone yet feel like you've known them your whole life? I don't know where you were born, what happened to your folks, why you chose to come here." His throat worked. "Sometimes, I want to know everything. Other times..." His nostrils flared, and his voice came gritty. "You strip these *facts* away, and all that's left is what's real. What's true. What matters."

She mattered to him. In his own roundabout, master-of-the-understated, cowboy way, that was what he meant. Tears pooled in her eyes, and she dabbed them with one of Timmy's cloth diapers.

"Ah, hell. Now I've upset you. I shouldn't have—"

She shook her head. "You didn't upset me. You...did what you always do." She lifted her shoulder and smiled. "You show me the glass is half-full instead of half-empty."

"Look who's talking."

"Maybe we're both closet optimists?"

"Maybe." His eyes softened, and he reached for Timmy's discarded milk bottle. "Don't think you're done yet, chief. No way your tummy can be full. Let's try again.'' He lifted the nipple to Timmy's mouth, testing whether he'd drink some more, and sure enough, the baby latched right on.

"Here, sweetie. You tired of holding it?'' She brushed Brooks's fingers as she took over for him, smoothing Timmy's hair from his forehead. "That's better, huh? You've been such a good boy today. No wonder Uncle Brooks likes to take you with him.'' She leaned down and kissed his head. "Where to now, Uncle Brooks?'' she asked as they crested a hill, and the barn and corrals came back into view.

"Now, I drop you two off and go check on that cow.'' He pointed to a lone, black cow who had wandered from the herd.

"Why? What's wrong with her?''

"She's about to calve.''

Amelia squinted. "How can you tell from here?''

"Actually it's easy looking down on the corral. See, cows like to be together, close, until they're calving. Then they want to be by themselves. So we look for the loners, the drifters, cows with kinked tails, cows lying down—all possible signs.''

"This is going to be an adventure.'' She smiled and laced her fingers together. Letting her head fall back against the rest, she turned her gaze out the window in newfound appreciation for the stark beauty of the land.

When they returned, she eased Timmy from his car seat and into her arms, then accepted Brooks's hand climbing down. "Thanks,'' she said, but he made no move to let go. Neither did she. Their fingers laced together as he walked her out. The wind kicked up, swirling her hair. "I had a great time.''

"Yeah, you're not half-bad with the pill gun thingy.''

"Hey.'' She dropped his hand to rap the brim of his hat

with a finger, knocking it over his eyes. "Don't be stingy with the praise, cowboy. I *kicked butt* with the pill gun thingy. I saved you a *ton* of prep time." On a roll, she barely registered his slow grin as he tipped back his hat. "Why, you'd still be in the north pasture if not for—"

Gently he put a finger over her lip. "You're a woman of many talents," he said, and then she did notice his grin, because it had a bittersweet sadness tugging down a corner.

She kissed his finger. "What is it, Brooks? Why are you sad underneath that smile?"

"I'm not—" His gaze shifted between her and Timmy, and something raw and powerful surfaced in the depths of his eyes before he blinked it away. "It was strange having you with me today. I've never... No one's ever... I liked it."

Emotion crowded her lungs. "Is that bad?"

"Could be, lollipop. Could be." His voice was gruff, his lips tender as he lowered his head and kissed her. "I don't want to hurt you. Not ever..."

"Then don't," she said simply and deepened the kiss.

Chapter 11

Brooks didn't return until eight that night. When he poked his head into the nursery, Amelia looked up from the bed-time story she was reading Timmy. She could tell he was worn-out, but his face brightened as he took in the two of them nestled in the rocker, Timmy nodding off on her lap.

"Welcome home." She smiled, jiggling the bottle in Timmy's mouth to get him to suck a little more. "How was your day?"

"It just got a whole lot better. You?"

"Good." She'd played with Timmy, worked some more on her plan during his nap, then helped Clara with supper, all the while trying in vain not to watch the clock. "We, um, missed you."

The corner of his mouth lifted in a slow, easy grin. "I missed you, too." The words, like so many of his others, touched her even more because she suspected he didn't say them often, if ever.

"Are you hungry?"

"Starving."

"Want me to warm a plate for you?"

Though his eyes told her the offer sounded good, he shook his head and said, "You don't have to wait on me."

"I know, but... You can pay me back. In other ways." She peered up at him through lowered lashes, hardly able to believe she was flirting.

His laughter came low and intimate, her meaning clear. "All right. I'm a stinkin' mess, though, so I'm gonna hit the shower first, okay?"

She nodded. "See you in a bit."

"The, ah, sooner the better." On that suggestive note, he rapped the door frame twice and headed down the hall.

Amelia found herself racing through the bedtime story, her body tingling with anticipation. But by the time she put Timmy down, the shower had turned on and off.

Darn he took fast showers.

She closed the nursery door behind her and noticed the bathroom door open the barest crack. Should she? Shouldn't she? She stood there, paralyzed with indecision for a full minute as the scent of soap and shampoo and Brooks drifted out, wrapping around her senses. Unbearably tempted, she edged forward and peeked through the tiny opening. Nope, not even a flash of skin.

Double darn.

She swallowed hard, realizing she really *wanted* to see him, and nudged the door just the tiniest little bit. But it was enough of a nudge that the door swung open, and she stopped short, her eyes wide, her pulse scrambling.

Brooks stood at the sink, a navy towel slung low around his waist, a razor in hand. Shaving cream lathered half his face. Golden skin stretched taut over sleek, hard muscles. He looked big and strong and sexy beyond belief. The way blood rushed in her veins, she couldn't imagine being more attracted to a man. Any man. As though her body had been expressly created with a homing device to recognize his, to respond to and fit his, and only his.

This is it. This is where you belong. Home, at last.

At the surge of cool air, Brooks turned his head. Seeing her, he smiled, sending her insides to quivering and clenching as had become the norm around him.

"Gonna stand there and let out all the steam or come in so I can get a decent shave?" he asked, clearly indicating his preference with a welcoming flick of his wrist.

For once, she didn't apologize but stepped inside and closed the door, greedily drinking in the sight of him.

"Damn." He growled, raking his own gaze over her. "On second thought, I'm liable to slit my throat with you here."

She smiled and took a step closer. "Can't have that."

"Hell, no." He turned on the faucet, rinsed his razor and reached for a washcloth. "Who needs a complete shave?"

She caught his arm, her smile widening. "Kiss me."

"Now?" His eyes sparkled with mischief. "Like this?" At her nod, he warned, "You asked for it." He lowered his head, and she laughed when shaving cream transferred to her face. But when he fused his mouth to hers, all humor fled, replaced by an urgent need that made her tremble with its intensity. His tongue traced along the seam of her lips, and she opened eagerly, gripping his shoulders.

"I've been waiting all day," she murmured.

"Me, too." He slipped his hands to her nape and angled her head. "It's damn uncomfortable trying to work when I've got you on my mind."

"Did you…?"

"What do you think?"

"Tell me."

"I can't get enough of you."

"Good."

As he kissed her senseless, she wound her arms around

him, pulling him even closer, shifting to cradle the hard length of him. Restless hands kneaded his shoulder blades, traced his spine to the small of his back, before settling on his perfect, tight butt.

"Brooks?"

"Yeah, honey?"

"We're in the bathroom."

"Yeah, I know."

She broke away to gaze up at him, her breathing ragged. "*I'm* in the bathroom *with you,* and the door's shut."

Understanding dawned on him. Abruptly he let her go, shoving a hand through his hair. "Sorry. I got carried—"

"No, it's okay." She reached for him. "*I'm* okay."

"You're...?" His brilliant, blue eyes searched hers, sparkling like polished gemstones. "Really?"

"Really." She let her fingers drift over his cheek, the strong column of his throat and the rock-hard planes of his chest. Gently she took the razor from his hand, wiped off her face and neck with the washcloth and slid her fanny onto the counter. "May I...finish?" She held up the razor.

At the glint of the shiny blade, apprehension flickered in his eyes. "This is trust, you know."

"I know." She was in the bathroom. Alone with a man. The door closed. And she was okay. Because it was Brooks. And she knew—in her head and in her heart—it was the way nature had intended.

She had nothing to fear.

She laid her hand against the side of his shaven face, her fingers caressing his cheekbone. "Has anyone ever told you just how handsome you are?"

He drew an unsteady breath and eased it out with a colorful oath. "This is an exercise in restraint, right?"

She trailed her hand over his lips, his jaw and down his throat. "You are *unbelievably* handsome, Brooks Hart."

"Damn, woman. I get hard at the sight of you in that

god-awful flannel nightgown. You're killing me here. You might as well put me out of my misery with that razor.''

"Brooks, I…'' *I, what? It's more than skin-deep? I'm falling for you? I never thought it was possible to feel this way? I was so scared before, but now I'm not? For the first time, I'm not.* She swallowed and lifted the blade. "Hold still.''

His nostrils flared. "You sure you know what you're doing?''

"No, but I'll be careful.'' She said each word slowly, "I would never deliberately hurt you. Please, know that.''

His eyes darkened. He reached up and grazed her cheek with his knuckles. "I do.''

"Good.'' She turned into his touch and rubbed her face against him, then straightened. "Feel free to give me some direction.''

"Smooth, upward strokes.'' His gaze fixed on her mouth.

She swallowed, remembering smooth, upward strokes of an entirely different nature. "Direction. Not distraction.''

He grinned but didn't say anything more. She'd made it halfway through the task without incident when his voice came low and intimate. "Would it distract you very much if I told you I wanted to be inside you right this second?''

She slipped.

He winced.

"Sorry.''

"My fault.''

She executed one last stroke, then wiped his face with the warm washcloth. They stared at each other for the space of a heartbeat—one short, erratic heartbeat—then reached out at the same time.

"Ah, lollipop.'' Brooks caught her face in his hands and kissed her long and deep. "I keep telling myself you can't possibly taste this good, that it's all in my head, but it's not. It just gets better…'' His hands drifted down her neck, along her collarbone to cup her shoulders. His open mouth roved over her face, coaxing a broken sigh.

"Yes. Oh, yes…"

He groaned and pressed closer. His heat against hers. No mistaking their desire. Her head fell back, a soft moan escaping her lips. She hooked her ankles around his waist. Holding back nothing, she kissed him with all her pent-up longing, and he matched her with devastating thoroughness.

And then his towel was tumbling to the floor, her clothes following one by one. Soon, they were naked, two overheated bodies renewing their acquaintance, grasping for each other, delighting in remembered tastes and textures.

She inched down, reveling in the earthy sounds he made as her breasts glided over his swollen flesh, and her hair brushed his chest, his belly and lower. When she reached for him, touching him as intimately as he had touched her, his hips lurched, and he swore, gritting his teeth.

She jerked away. "I—I did something wrong—"

"Yeah," he choked out. "You stopped. Please *don't.*"

She didn't. She let instinct guide her, all her senses focused on him, attune to his every sound, every movement—signs that told her she was pleasing him. His eyes closed. His breaths slowed, thickened. His fingers plunged into her hair, low growls rumbling in his throat. But when his body started to quake, he tugged her away, breathing hard again.

"Okay. Enough."

"But—"

He shook his head and hooked his hands under her arms, lifting her up to him. "I'm taking you with me." His mouth found hers, strong arms like a security blanket around her.

A muffled whimper escaped her. He felt so good—*so very good*—against her, and her body moved instinctively, seeking completion.

"Not yet." A bead of sweat trickled down his temple,

his biceps flexing with his restraint. "Essentials in the bedroom."

"Then why are we still in here?" In one fluid motion, she bent and snatched up her clothes and his towel, thrust it into his stomach and whispered, "Hurry."

They fumbled with the barest necessities of clothing before making a run for his room, where everything hit the floor at warp speed. Bathed in silvery moonlight, Brooks peeled back the quilt and followed her down onto the bed. She wrapped her limbs around him, cradling his head to her breast, threading her fingers into the silk of his hair as his tongue and teeth streaked white heat through her body, slowly driving her mad.

"Brooks..." She twisted on the sheets as he blazed a fiery trail of kisses down her belly, parted her legs and showed her without words how very much she meant to him.

"Okay. Enough." She gasped, every nerve ending aglow. She tugged him up, scrambled for a foil packet from the bedside drawer and tore it open. "I'm taking you with me."

Brooks held his breath as she readied him, then eased her onto the pillows and smoothed the hair back from her face, so he could see her eyes. His gaze locked with hers, he slid into her, filling her completely. Tasting heaven. They made love with a fierce tenderness that brought tears to her eyes and an ache to his heart.

Her once-shy hands freely explored his body, learning exactly how to touch him, exactly what he liked. And he matched her in a rhythm as old as time, yet as unique as only their combination of mind, body and spirit could be.

As the tremors of her release started, he stared into her eyes, watching the fog roll in, thinking: *I did that. I brought her this pleasure. For this moment, she's mine.*

All mine.

"Brooks…" She lifted her trembling hands to his face, a sleepy smile of satisfaction on her face. "Feel this. Join me."

He didn't want it to end. Wanted to keep her his for as long as he could. Mine, he thought. *Mine, mine, mine.* But when she touched him, a mounting roar filled his ears. His vision grayed, and he was lost. Lost in her.

The climax shuddered through him, not the lightning quick thrusts of the night before but one endless riptide after another. He plunged long and deep, as if pouring his very soul into her, and she sighed and wrapped her legs around him, hugging him tightly.

"Don't go anywhere. Stay right there."

"I'm too heavy—"

"No, you're perfect. Perfect for me."

His throat closed as he gathered her close, kissing her nose, her cheek, her temple. He didn't know what to say. *I didn't know I could want so much, need so much? I can't let you go… Not now. Not ever.*

Spent, they clung to each other, a tangle of boneless limbs and slick, sweat-dampened skin.

After a time, Amelia reached up and traced his brow. "It's never been like this before. My body knows it. I feel it." She lowered her fingers to her heart. "In here."

The softly spoken words and open, honest gesture were his undoing. It hit him then, like the ground rising up and smacking him in the face, knocking the wind from his lungs.

He had known. The moment he'd seen her in the kitchen window, Brooks had *known* this woman was dangerous to him in a way unlike any other. She was the one. The *only* one who could cut through the barbed wire fenced around his heart. Make camp in his soul. And knowing that, it was no real surprise he'd ended up exactly where he'd always feared.

Addicted.

To her.

Brooks Hart was in love with the amnesiac nanny.

Amelia smiled at Timmy banging away on the over-turned bottom of a pan with a wooden spoon. "I know—your uncles are going to kill me for teaching you this." She finished outlining the necessities of her plan for converting the Triple H into a dude/guest ranch when the doorbell rang.

"Hmm." She glanced at the clock over the door. Four-thirty. "Now who could that be? Maybe Aunt Jo?" Leaving her plan on the table, she picked Timmy up and took him with her to peek out the front window. "Nope. Not Aunt Jo..."

But at the sight of a red pickup in the driveway, her pulse gave a sudden leap and started drumming in her ears. She eyed the company name and logo painted in black on the side: J&B Towing. She knew that name and logo. She knew...

Dear God. Could it be? She threw open the front door, already anticipating...

Yes! Sweet heaven, yes!

A short, stocky man with a potbelly stood with his hat tucked under his arm. He had kind brown eyes and a salt-and-pepper mustache that matched what was left of his hair.

"I remember you!" She shifted Timmy to her hip and nearly bounced up and down in delight. "I remember you!"

He blinked in surprise at her warm welcome and glanced over his shoulder as if to make sure she was talking to him. Though he shifted awkwardly, his smile was genuine. "Howdy, ma'am. Uh, good to see you, too."

"You brought me here. In that truck. It was cold and damp...freezing rain! And you...you gave me...coffee!"

"Yes, ma'am."

"Oh my God. I remember all that. This is wonderful!" She covered her mouth with her hand. "You see, I lost my memory, and I haven't been able to remember a thing. Until now. Until you. I have *you* to thank!" She hooked an arm around him in a quick hug, practically smushing Timmy, who looked around as if trying to figure out the reason for all the excitement. "Thank you, thank you, thank you."

"Well, shucks." The man's round, pudgy cheeks colored. "Ain't every day customers thank me quite like that. You're certainly welcome, though I didn't do much. Just gave you a ride and towed your car to my shop."

"My car...?"

His expression turned apologetic, as if to prepare her to receive some bad news.

She braced herself. "Go ahead. Lay it on me."

"You banged it up pretty good," he said. "Roads were icy that day."

"It wasn't a dream..." she whispered.

"Don't know how you walked away without a scratch."

"I...I bumped my head." Dazed, she raised a hand to her forehead. "Please, won't you come in? Have a cup of coffee and something to eat." She stepped back.

But he shook his head. "You're mighty nice to offer, and I'd take you up, except I gotta get back to the diner on account of we're shorthanded today. It's a diner/service station," he said. "You walked there. A mile in the freezing rain. You were soaked to the bone. We thought you'd catch the death of pneumonia if you didn't get into some dry clothes, so my wife lent you some of her things."

She nodded, remembering these things. "She was tall, and she wore a pink uniform. Kind eyes. Blue eye shadow."

"That's her."

"Please, thank her for me and let her know I'll return everything. You're sure you can't stay?"

He nodded. "Thanks anyway. Had to run an errand up here and thought I'd save you a trip to get these."

It was then she noticed the handle of a medium-size suitcase in his hand and a brown-and-cream leather purse slung over his shoulder.

Her luggage! She remembered each piece!

Tears stung her eyes. "This must be my lucky day."

"Got one more out in the truck." As he put down the suitcase and held out the purse, she felt the wonder and excitement of a child on Christmas morning.

"A green duffel bag?" At his nod, she took the purse with reverence, unable to stop the wild fluttering of her heart. Finally a break. It was all coming back! "I've been waiting, all this time… I can't even begin to tell you…" She shook her head. "Thank you. So much."

The corners of his mouth twitched as he put on his hat. "Makes me feel kinda guilty charging you for repairs."

"No, no. Don't feel guilty. We've all got to make a living, and you've already been more than generous, coming out here twice now. I really appreciate it."

"Pleasure, ma'am." He went back to the truck to get her duffel, then pulled a slip of paper from his breast pocket. "This here's the estimate. Didn't want to do nothin' without your okay."

"Thanks."

"Number's on there, so give us a ring and let us know what all you want done."

"I'll do that." She glanced at the invoice. And did a double-take. Not at the dollar figure but at the customer name. Written in big, block letters. Her heart lurched, jamming in her throat. Sweat broke across her upper lip. "There must be some mistake. This isn't… I'm not…" She swallowed, unable to finish the protest. "Wh-where did you get this name?"

"Sorry to paw through your wallet, but I was hoping to find a phone number. Got your name from your license." His voice seemed to come from a great distance. "I'd better get going. A speedy recover to you." He tipped the brim of his hat and turned for the truck.

Outside, the wind kicked up, its anguished moan filling her ears. The world started to spin, faster and faster, a top out of control. She put Timmy down before she dropped him, closed the door and leaned against it, fighting to pull oxygen into her lungs, to keep her vision from tunneling.

Hands trembling, she unzipped the purse, found a wallet and unsnapped it. There it was, plain as day. In paralyzed bewilderment, she gaped at the Nevada driver's license. *Her* face, *her* vitals and *her* real name: Laura Hart.

"Oh God!" She cried out in shock and horror, clamping a hand over her mouth, as it all came back to her in a rush.

She was the Blond Widow.

Chapter 12

Her stomach swam. Spots danced before her eyes. The wallet slipped from her hands. With a clatter, it bounced on the hardwood and landed open to a plastic-covered photo of a baby. A very familiar baby.

Hers.

"Timmy." She fell to her knees, gasping for breath.

At the sound of his name, Timmy looked up and gave a huge grin, crawling toward her. "Mamamamama."

"Yes..." Air rushed from her lungs. "Yes, I *am* your mama." She caught Timmy in her arms. "Oh, my sweet baby. How could I forget you? How *could* I?" Her fingers stroked the downy thatch of fine, blond hair she knew so well. Hot, salty tears gushed down her face as she rocked him back and forth. "I was so worried about you. I didn't know where he took you. I looked everywhere. And then they told me..."

The police had found Luke—dead—with no sign of Timmy, and she had lost it. She'd spent two weeks in a psych ward before the news of Timmy's location penetrated her brain.

"Amelia?" Mitch called to her. "You out there?"

Hastily she wiped the moisture from her face. "Yes," she said, hoping he wasn't headed their way but bracing all the same.

He couldn't know yet. No one could. They all hated her. They'd think she deliberately deceived them. Faked her amnesia. Pretended to be the nanny when all along...

Laura hung Luke out to dry before she headed for the hills...

No, that wasn't what happened! They had to believe her. She had to make them believe. It wasn't her fault!

Man...if she ever shows her face around here...

She shuddered. They blamed her for their brother's suicide. And why not? She had blamed herself, too.

She's probably moved on to her next victim...

Fresh tears stung her eyes. Would they even give her the chance to explain? What on earth was she going to do?

"Hey." Mitch came around the corner. "Who was that? I didn't recognize the truck. Ran up to see if you needed anything."

"No. No, I don't need anything." Except a miracle— did he have one handy? "My luggage showed up." She made a lame gesture toward the bags, trying to downplay the event.

"Great. What happened?"

"Car accident."

"*That's* how you bumped your head. One mystery solved."

All of them, actually. But as Mitch moved toward her suitcase, her gaze fixed on a luggage tag. With lightning speed, she scrambled up off the floor and blocked his path. "Slow day at the office, dear?" She forced an easy smile.

He chuckled. "No such thing—I need to get back soon." He glanced over her shoulder. "I'll take those bags in—"

"I've got them, thanks." Moving to block his vision, she made a dismissive gesture and nonchalantly crossed her arms. "Is Brooks still down at Pete and Clara's?"

"Yeah. Clara's Sunday honey-do list takes a good part of the day. Don't think we'll see him until supper. Hey, chief. Whatcha got there? Uh-oh." He hunkered down on his haunches. "You chomping on Amelia's wallet for dessert?"

Timmy cooed and reached for Mitch's nose. Thankfully the wallet was snapped shut, but the incriminating evidence was too close for comfort. The wild clamor of her heartbeat filled her ears. Throbbed in her head. Even the walls appeared to pulse in rhythm. Like Poe's *Telltale Heart*.

With a nervous laugh, she reached for Timmy. "Come here, baby." She lifted him into her arms and held him close. Her baby. Her happy, healthy reward for surviving hell. She bit back an anguished sob and closed her eyes.

"Amelia? You all right?"

The horror of her dilemma dried her mouth. "F-fine."

"You look kinda pale."

"Headache." She rubbed her temple. "I have a slight headache."

"Want me to get you some aspirin?"

"Yes, please." She latched onto an excuse to make him go away. "I—I'm going to lie down. Try to nap with Timmy."

"Good idea. I'll get your—"

"No!"

But he moved too fast this time. "You take the kid. I'll take the bags." Ignoring her protest, he hefted the suitcase and duffel bag.

She bit her lip and tasted blood. They would never believe her. Never in a million years. And Brooks...

What if his mother wants him back?
Over my dead body.

Dear God, what if they tried to declare her an unfit mother? It was true she had suffered a nervous breakdown.

Agonizing pain sliced through her gut, and she laid a hand over her stomach, afraid at any second she would lose the contents.

Mitch dropped the luggage and flew to her side. In a flash, he hooked one strong arm around her waist. "Amelia, what's wrong?"

I'm not Amelia. I'm Laura. You know me as the Blond Widow, but you see, I'm neither a blonde nor a widow, nor the vile, despicable person Luke made me out to be.

"Heartburn," she whispered. "I'll be okay."

"I can call Jo—"

"No. Thank you."

He nodded but didn't look convinced as he picked up the bags again. She forced herself to take one step after the other, as a prisoner walking to the guillotine, anticipating the imminent fall of the blade. But Mitch deposited the bags on her bed without comment, and she gave silent thanks for the temporary reprieve.

"Be right back with your aspirin."

"You know what? I've, um, got some. Right here in my purse—I forgot."

"Want me to take Timmy for you? I can put him down."

She shook her head. She couldn't bear the thought of letting Timmy out of her arms for even a second and prayed Mitch wouldn't force the issue.

He didn't, but his eyes told her he was still trying to figure what was off. "You'd tell me if something was really wrong, wouldn't you?"

The lie stuck in her throat. "I promise to holler if I need anything."

"Okay." He glanced at his wristwatch. "Remember we're having supper at Pete and Clara's tonight."

She nodded and clutched her child and her wallet to her traitorous heart. As soon as he left, her tears overflowed, blurring her vision.

Not wanting Timmy to pick up on her stress, she kissed his forehead and put him down on the carpet. Unzipping the green duffel bag, she put it in front of him. One by one, he took out each of his favorite toys.

"I remember..." she whispered, then covered her mouth. "Oh, baby. Mommy's in a world of trouble."

"You've been holding out on me." Brooks looked up from the business plan he'd spent the last hour poring over.

Amelia stood in the doorway, Timmy on her hip.

He'd come home to find a note from Mitch telling him she had a headache, and she and Timmy were napping. He'd showered and changed without disturbing them, sat down at the kitchen table to do some paperwork before supper, and came across her plan.

When she hovered in the doorway, he raised an eyebrow. "How's the headache?"

"Better, thanks."

"So, when were you planning on telling me about this?" He lifted the papers. "And how much are you going to bill me?" He grinned. "This is professional work. I've never seen anything like it. I was just gonna peek. Then skim. Ended up reading the whole thing start to finish."

"I wanted to help, to do something for you, after all you've done for me. You...really like it?" Her voice was barely a whisper.

"What's not to like? You put structure around the uncertainties, spelled everything out in black and white, even worst-case scenarios. And you gave me options." He couldn't stop grinning he was so impressed. "Guest ranch.

Dude ranch. Refinance. Don't. Here's what it all means. Here's what I need to find out. You were damn thorough.''

Her chin wobbled, and two big, fat tears rolled down her cheeks.

In a flash, he was up and out of his chair, but she shook her head and held up a hand. At the wary, haunted look in her eyes, he froze. "Something's wrong."

She nodded and covered her mouth.

"Okay. All right." He held up his hands. "Is it another panic attack?"

She shook her head. "Nothing that simple."

Brooks wrestled down a wave of his own panic and steadied his nerves. With the distinct feeling he was talking her down from a mental ledge, he gently coaxed, "Whatever it is, we'll get through it." He held out his hand, but that only opened the floodgates.

She burst into tears, shaking her head and waving to keep him at bay. Timmy started to fuss, and she rubbed a hand over his back. "Have you seen Mitch?"

"He's down at Pete and Clara's with the others."

"Could you see if he'll come and get Timmy? I don't want him upset. He picks up on tension."

"I can take him—"

"You and I have to talk. Alone."

In that second, Brooks knew. He read it in her eyes.

She remembered.

A sense of impending doom wrapped around him like a cold, damp parka. He fought off a shiver and braced his hands on the table. "I'll call Mitch."

It wasn't her fault, she repeated to herself. It had taken a while for her to believe that after Luke first hit her. Less the second time. But then there was the shame.

And the fear.

She'd lived in fear so long, she'd forgotten what it was

like to live without it. She had forgotten until she came to the Triple H. And fell in love with her abuser's family.

Now, as she sat across the kitchen table from Brooks, she knew no matter how angry she made him, he'd never raise his hand to her. And that gave her the courage she needed.

"What I'm about to tell you…it's going to change the way you look at me, and I…I'm not sure you'll ever see me the same again." Tears pricked her eyelids, but she fought to hold them back. If she started crying again, she'd never stop this time, never get through everything she had to say. "Just know one thing. There's never been anyone like you. Not ever." Her voice wavered, but she forced the words out. "What I felt, what I *feel*… It's real. It hasn't changed because I have my memory back."

Brooks closed his eyes and pinched the bridge of his nose, then looked up and met her gaze directly. "What do you remember, honey?"

Honey. She was still his honey. But she wouldn't be in another minute. Oh God. She *was* going to cry. "I—I grew up in the southwest. My mother died when I was in high school. I never knew my father. I spent a few years living with a distant aunt who didn't want me but had no choice. I didn't have any other family.

"When…this man…came along and took an interest in me, I thought he was my knight in shining armor, come to rescue me. But he wasn't…" Her voice dropped to a whisper. "He was the fire-breathing dragon. And by the time I figured out my mistake, I was a newlywed."

She closed her eyes, not wanting to tell him Luke had beaten her. Not for shame, not for protecting Luke, because she was over both of those. But because she knew how hard, how *personal* a blow it would be if he believed her, and as much as she wanted to set the record straight, it broke her heart to heap more pain on a family that had known enough.

"I know what he did to you," Brooks said thickly, and her head shot up. His eyes clouded. He braced his elbows on the table and rubbed a hand over his face. "I... We... At the hospital, Jo took a bone scan."

She went still, recalling Jo's reaction to her X rays. Afterward, Jo had asked her to sign a release form, so she could talk to Brooks.

"When I found out..." His mouth set in a tight, grim line. Big hands clenched and unclenched on the table. "I wanted to snap the bastard's neck." The lethal edge in his voice would have terrified her before. It didn't now.

"Oh, Brooks." Her eyes searched his, remembering the reverent way he had touched the bump of her nose, the way he'd kissed other broken body parts. "All this time...?"

"I've known. Jo swore me to secrecy. Even from you. I'm sorry."

"No. Don't be. I understand now—why they wanted me to remember on my own. I needed to come to terms with..." She pressed her lips together. "There's so much more..."

There was no question now that he would believe her. But in place of any relief came only a soul-deep sorrow. She would have given anything not to hurt him this way.

Brooks reached over the table, took her hands in his and squeezed. "Talk to me, lollipop. Tell me everything. I won't let anything happen to you. I swear it."

Emotion clogged her throat, threatening to choke her.

Once upon a time, she wouldn't have believed a woman like her deserved men like Brooks. Her aunt had reminded her countless times she was lucky to get what she could—beggars couldn't be choosers. So her husband knocked her around every now and then. Be grateful she *had* a husband, accept that no marriage was perfect, take the bad with the good… This, her aunt's counsel when she'd refused Laura refuge in her home, even temporarily.

How she had sold herself short. To believe for an instant an abusive marriage was better than no marriage.

She blinked and took back her hands, folding them in her lap. "He…had control issues. Alcohol and gambling added fuel to the fire. I left him twice before…before the final time. There was no hiding from him. He always tracked me down. His job gave him connections everywhere. He'd come after me. It was the same pattern every time.

"First, he'd grovel. Apologize. Profess his love. Beg me to forgive him, to go back. Swear on a stack of Bibles things would be different. When sugar didn't work, he used acid. He'd threaten…to hurt himself, to hurt me. He said he couldn't live without me—and he wouldn't let me live without him. I…always caved in. Until the baby."

"Baby," he breathed. "You were right. It wasn't just a dream."

She shook her head, lifting a shaky hand to shield her eyes, not wanting him to see the truth just yet, unable to look at him without blurting it out. "Th-things got really ugly when I became pregnant. He…was already caught up in a vicious cycle. Stress drove him to drink more, to gamble more. But the costs of drinking and gambling led to more stress. So did the idea of having another mouth to feed.

"I took a part-time job waitressing to try to make up for his lost wages. I was already working full-time to pay my way through college, slowly but steadily. He…resented the time and money spent on my 'selfish' pursuits. Hotel management." She gave a weak smile and ran her fingers through her hair, staring at a spot on the wall just over Brooks's shoulder. "That's my field…my degree…how I know what goes into a business plan."

"A woman of many talents," he said softly. "*All* of them admirable."

A sob locked in her throat. How different they were, Luke and Brooks. Like Cain and Abel, Clara had said, and she was right.

Laura swallowed hard. She couldn't lose it. Not now. Not until she finished. She thanked him and forced herself to continue. "For a graduation present, I received a trip to the emergency room. I almost lost the baby, born a month premature, and I thought *no more*." She hugged her stomach. "It wasn't just *my* safety—I had a child to protect. So I pushed for a divorce, which he granted in his usual period of remorse. Of course, it didn't last. It *never* lasted....

"But I had landed a dream job in Colorado. Assistant manager at a ski resort. I packed up and got the hell out while I could. My ex obviously didn't take the move well. Soon enough, he was back to his old ways, trying to get me to go back to him. His drinking and gambling spiraled out of control. He owed loan sharks. He was fired from work. He said it was my fault. Said again and again he couldn't live without me, wouldn't let me live without him. But I refused to listen. Refused to go back to him. I *couldn't*. I was a mother. Then one day, clear out of the blue, he took my eight-month-old from day care and disappeared."

Brooks fought the anger burning in his veins, beading sweat on his brow, making his heart pound. It was all he could do to sit there and hear how the woman he loved had been terrorized, to keep his mind from veering down dark corridors, fantasizing about loading his rifle, going on a manhunt. Anger was easy, seductive. Keeping a cool head was pure hell. He wished he knew what to say, what to do, how to fix it, make it better. God, he wanted to make it better for her.

"Amelia..." He reached for her hands, fisted on the table, but she drew back with a jerky shake of her head.

"Eight months old, Brooks." Her eyes watered, and his throat closed. Tears caught in her lashes, and like them, he, too, felt close to falling over the edge. "A baby boy..."

A shiver stole up his back, as if someone had walked over his grave. His neck prickled with sudden foreboding.

She looked at him then. Looked right into his eyes. "His name is Timmy."

Brooks blinked. She couldn't have said... Couldn't have meant...

Eight months old.

A baby boy.

Timmy.

His heart stopped. Blood drained from his head. The red-hot heat of his anger went arctic cold and poured down his spine.

"No." He shook his head, searched her eyes, waiting, expecting her to go on, explain further. She didn't. And that could *only* mean... "*No,*" he said again. "Not Luke..." When she closed her eyes, he jackknifed to his feet, the chair falling backward. She didn't flinch but opened her eyes, and in them, he saw a world of pain. "Oh, God." He shoved a rough hand through his hair. He was shaking from head to toe. "You *can't* be—"

"Laura," she whispered, and somewhere in the distance, came the low, tortured howl of a wounded animal.

Vaguely he registered it came from him—the sound of his heart being cut out and his soul dropping into a black hole, devoid of all thought, all emotion.

He didn't remember stumbling out to the back porch. Didn't know how long he stood, gripping the rail. Didn't feel the slap of frigid air as slowly, fury boiled inside him again. He whirled and kicked the side of the house.

"Damn you, Luke." He swore savagely. "Damn you!"

Lies. All *lies!* Like father, like son.

He punched the wall and split the skin on his knuckle. He didn't care. He turned, slumped against the sandstone, slid to the ground and put his head in his hands.

His own brother.

How could he? How could Luke hurt her? How could he kidnap Timmy, swindle his own blood kin, *knowingly* destroy the people who loved him most? His father had been cruel. But not even *he* was this cruel.

Laura.

Good God, that's why the nanny agency called, why they were still on the waiting list. Something must have fallen through at the last minute. The woman in his house, his life, his heart wasn't Amelia Rigsby, the best nanny in the agency, but Timmy's mother. His worst nightmare. Only she wasn't... She had no easy tag, no peel-and-stick-on label.

Timmy.

No wonder he'd taken to her on sight. He'd known what the rest of them had not. And given a choice, he chose her every time.

Panic reared its head. The day Brooks had dreaded was here, and he didn't know if he had the strength to face it. To do the right thing. Hell, he didn't know which way was *up* anymore.

"Brooks, come inside." Amel— Laura crouched in front of him. He hadn't heard her footsteps. "Come on," she said again, taking his hands. "You'll freeze to death out here."

But he was already frozen. From the inside out. And he wasn't sure he'd ever thaw. Wordlessly he let her lead him into the house, stood at the kitchen sink beside her as she washed his hands, smeared ointment on his knuckles and wrapped them with gauze, then sank into the chair she held out for him. There was a mug of hot chocolate on the table. Gently she took his hands and placed one on either side.

"I can't tell you how sorry I am." She took the chair

next to him, sitting sideways, her knees touching his thigh. "I didn't want to hurt you. I *don't*." She pressed her lips together.

How many times had he kissed those lips? Not enough. Not even close.

"He was your brother—"

"He was your *husband*. He had no right, *no right* to do what he did to you. *No one* has that right." He closed his eyes. "If I could take it back…"

"But you did," she whispered. "Our time together…"

His heart constricted. Any second, he was going to crack, cry like a baby.

"I blamed myself for Luke's death."

"No." He shook his head. "It wasn't your fault."

Her eyes softened. Her voice trembled. "Thank you. I…know that now. But I didn't before. I lost my way, Brooks. I checked out of my own mind. But I came back, stronger than ever, able to face reality, because of *you*. You showed me the way home."

"*You* showed *me*." Emotion splintered his voice. "You and Timmy."

Tears sprung to her eyes, spilled down her face. She didn't bother to wipe them.

Around them, the silence amplified. The creaking and settling of the big, old house. The soft moan of the wind. The rattle of the windowpanes. The tick, tick, ticking of the clock over the door.

"I… We… We can't stay, Brooks. I'm sorry. I'm so…"

He didn't hear the rest. The earth tilted, jerking the ground from under him. He was falling…down, down… His hands braced on the table. His stomach roiled. Desperation clawed free.

The room spun madly. Colors bled. Sounds garbled.

"It's not you… It's me… I have a job, a life in Colorado… Went to hell and back… To rebuild… Stand on my own two feet… No more Cinderella complex… Don't need saving… We can visit… You can visit… After a while…''

Bits and pieces of information penetrated the fog of his brain. He felt numb. Detached. Empty. Until slowly, pain seeped into his bones like acid. The pain of knowing beyond a shadow of a doubt she was going to walk out of his life and take Timmy with her, and there wasn't a damn thing he could do to stop her.

''I'm sorry,'' she said again, decimating him.

No! The roar echoed in his head like a battle cry. He felt like a soldier with a bullet in his heart. His life, recent events, flashed in rapid sequence before his eyes.

Luke showing up with Timmy. Luke telling him about the Blond Widow. Timmy pulling every book from his bookshelf in the nursery. Timmy falling asleep on his chest as he rocked him. Amelia—his Amelia—on the couch in the den and in his arms. His lollipop…sharing his bed, his work, his life.

Don't go, he wanted to beg. Screw pride. He wanted to get down on his knees, do anything, say anything to keep the woman and child he loved. *Stay here. Stay with me. I love you. I need you. I'm lost without you.*

But he said none of those things. Because she had heard them all before, and he would not—could not—repeat the sins of his brother and force her into something she didn't want.

His eyes burned, and his throat was raw. But through the dark haze of misery and despair, Brooks saw clear to hang his hat on one true thing. ''I want you to be happy,'' he said. ''Whatever makes you happy, that's what I want.'' If it wasn't him, then it wasn't. He had to accept her decision, respect her wishes and pray in time it wouldn't feel like his heart had been hacked into pieces with his shepherd's crook.

Because that was how he felt right now.

''Brooks, I—''

"I have to go." He shoved back from the table before she could say she was sorry again. He knew she was sorry. He was sorry, too. And if he didn't get the hell out of there—fast—she was going to see just how sorry he was.

He turned his back and covered his eyes. "I'll...tell the others." Every breath splintered his throat, his lungs, his heart. "You...want me to bring Timmy back now?"

"Please. I don't want him to pick up on your tension." Her voice was as raw, aching as his. "We won't leave for a few days. You'll have time..."

Time to say goodbye.

The unsaid words hung in the air, thick and oppressive.

Brooks grabbed his keys from the nail on the wall and bolted from the house, not bothering with his coat or hat. He cleared the back porch but didn't make it as far as the pickup.

In the muddy driveway, his legs gave out, and he fell to his knees.

"But why?" Dean kept repeating through his tears. "Why can't she stay? Did you tell her we love her, we want her here? She's a part of this family as much as Timmy. We don't care if she's not Amelia. Did you tell her any of that?" He covered his eyes with the heels of his hands. "And what about the dude ranch plans? What about riding lessons?"

"Puppies," Mitch choked out. "We were going to pick out a new puppy."

"Thank God it wasn't *murder*-suicide." Jo closed her eyes. "Luke could have taken Laura with him. That's what usually happens."

"Wasn't mercy." Dean scowled. "He buried her alive instead. Kidnapped her child, fed us a bunch of lies to guarantee we'd hate her on sight, made her lose her mind. The gift that keeps on giving."

Mitch shook his head. "Damn, I'm going to miss them."

Clara held Pete's hand and dabbed the corners of her eyes with his handkerchief. "We'll *all* miss them, but your sister's right. It's a tragedy—no way around that—but we got plenty of reasons to give thanks. For the chance to get to know them. For them to know us. If we knew up-front she was Laura, instead of believing she was Amelia, it would've been impossible for any of us to connect like we did." She turned a sympathetic eye to Brooks.

He sat in the corner, thankful for his family during what had to be the most trying time of his life. "It's not like we're never going to see them again," he said, trying his damnedest to pull himself together. "They'll...visit. Amel— *Laura*—" he was still trying to wrap his mouth around her name "—said we can visit them, too." It wouldn't be easy. Ranch life didn't lend itself to vacations. Couldn't leave the herd with a neighbor. Still. "Colorado's not that far—a day trip."

"No way." Dean bounded to his feet and swiped his nose with the back of his hand.

Brooks lifted his head. "Where are you going?"

"To the house. If you won't make her stay, I will."

"Don't even think about it," he warned, low and intent.

"Yeah? Watch me."

Mitch unfolded his tall frame from against the wall and grabbed his younger brother by the arm. "Sit down, Dean."

But Dean shook him off. "Up yours."

"Hey." Brooks stood. "I know it doesn't look like it, but I know what I'm doing—"

Dean reeled around and jabbed an accusing finger, tears of frustration streaming down his face. "You know *squat,* if this is your idea of *everything humanly possible*—"

"James Dean Hart." Pete's normally mellow voice boomed in the room. Grasping his cane with both hands, he levered off the couch. "Act your age, son. I know you're hurtin'. Take a look around this room. You ain't the only one."

"But—" Dean gestured lamely to Brooks.

Pete narrowed his gaze. "But nothin'."

As Brooks sat down, the older man crossed to his side and clasped one firm, weathered hand on his shoulder. And just like that, the years slipped away, and he was fifteen again, Jo thirteen, Mitch and Dean nine and seven. Before them stood the man half-responsible for instilling in the foursome a code of honor and respect by which they'd lived and loved going on two decades now.

"If you think for one second," Pete said, resuming his usual laid-back, no-nonsense tone, "this ain't eatin' your brother alive, then you don't know him very well, and I take back all the times I said Clara and I didn't raise no fools, 'cause one musta slipped out the gate."

Deflated, Dean closed his eyes and slumped into a chair. "Brooks, I didn't mean—"

But Brooks shook his head and waved away his brother's apology. "I know you didn't. *I know.*" He leaned forward, bracing his weight on his elbows as he met Dean's gaze. "I wanted to tell her," he admitted. "Everything you said. More. But she's been down that road, Dean. It was ugly."

"This ain't the same—"

"Damn straight." Brooks set his jaw. "I know that, and you know that. But unless *she* knows…" He rubbed a hand over his face. God help him, he didn't know how he'd get through this, only knew somehow, he had to find a way. "We can't keep her in our lives if she doesn't want to be here. No ring, no promises, no threats can chain her soul. She's got to want it—*want us*—on her own, all by herself." He closed his eyes. "We have to let her go."

Chapter 13

Laura had never felt so alone in all her life as she did when Brooks loaded the last bag into her newly repaired car, gave Timmy a hug and a kiss, and closed the door. The baby had skipped his morning nap in all the hustle-bustle, so he was fast nodding off with his bottle.

She was glad to have exchanged goodbyes with the others inside—that was difficult enough. Now only one remained—the most difficult of all.

"See you, chief," Brooks mumbled under his breath, one finger against the window. In the reflection of the glass, she saw him mouth, "I love you."

The knife plunged and twisted, guilt stabbing at her heart. She laid a hand on her chest and drew her resolve around her like a cloak for Timmy's sake.

She was doing the right thing returning to Colorado, returning to the life she'd painstakingly forged for herself and her child. There was a time when she wouldn't have had the strength to face an uncertain future on her own. When she would have chosen the status quo over rocking the boat.

But that time was not now.

Squaring her shoulders, she rounded to the driver's side door. Brooks followed, coming to stand beside her, hands in his pockets. Though a good two feet separated them, she could feel his body heat. His eyes, shaded under the brim of his black Stetson, stayed carefully neutral.

"I...don't know how to thank you," she said. "For taking such good care of my baby. For everything..."

Tension bracketed his mouth when he smiled. "Wasn't a chore."

She looked back at the house, then at him. She hadn't forgotten anything. There was no reason to dawdle. "I...I guess this is goodbye, then."

He gave a curt nod and shifted his weight from one boot to the other as if he didn't know what to do next.

She didn't, either. She wanted to hug him, to at least give him a proper goodbye. But everything was still so raw, her feelings for him too close to the surface. If she felt the beat of his heart against hers again... Awkwardly she stuck out her hand.

He looked at it for a long moment before he took it, engulfing it in his, and she knew he was thinking all the same things she was—remembering everything they'd shared. Blissful in their ignorance.

"Goodbye, Brooks," she whispered, hating the catch in her voice.

"Later, lollipop," he said, his own voice strung taut.

Tears stung her eyes, and her resolve weakened. But he didn't ask her not to leave. Not once had he tried to convince her to stay. He just clasped her hand and let his gaze rove over her face, as if memorizing her features.

Maybe it hadn't fully hit him yet. Maybe it would later. When the shock wore off. Maybe he'd change his mind. Come after her. Not with malice. She knew that.

But she was taking Timmy. A piece of his heart. Sooner or later, he would want it back. Wouldn't he?

And then what?

She looked again at the big, stone house. Remembered the one she had shared with Luke. Her prison. She didn't want to be kept. Not again. Not by anyone. And yet, her gaze lingered on the house where she'd discovered a part of herself that had been missing, on the man who had shown her the way, helped her believe in herself.

Oh God. The weight of her decision pressed down on her chest. And then, just when she thought the hell with it, she wasn't this strong, Brooks let go of her hand and opened the car door.

"Drive carefully," he said.

She blinked, snapping out of her momentary lapse, and climbed into the car. "Thank you," she said one last time, then forced herself to drive away.

But the image in the rearview mirror stayed with her the whole way. A tall, proud cowboy with his black Stetson tipped low, one hand raised in parting, moisture glistening on his cheeks.

He didn't come after her. In the weeks that followed, Laura kept expecting a knock at the door, a phone call, or a letter. But there was nothing.

Day by day, she and Timmy settled back into their routines. In the mornings, she took him to the day care center at the resort where she worked. Around noon, she picked him up for lunch—picnics outdoors if the weather allowed—then took him back for the afternoon.

Single parenthood had more than its fill of challenges, but her job came with a lot of perks—on-site day care being the biggest—that made it easier for a working mother. Her work was demanding, but she enjoyed it—applying herself, making a difference, taking pride in her accomplishments.

In the evenings, she and Timmy returned to their rented two-bedroom town house. It was comfortable and homey, and in the fenced-in backyard, the landlords let Laura start a small garden.

For the first time, she didn't have to worry about a dangerous ex-husband hunting her down. She had nothing to run from, nothing to fear but fear itself. And bit by bit, she learned she could do it, could put one foot after the other and find peace within herself.

She didn't need anyone to take care of her. She could take care of herself. But that didn't mean she didn't miss them. Because she did. Every day.

Especially Brooks.

Every day, she took a photo of Timmy and wrote a letter with his update, a daily "log" of her own. Once a week, she put an envelope in the mail to Wyoming.

At first, the lack of response was almost a relief—comforting because she needed time and space to resume her life. But as weeks turned to months, she couldn't help worrying. Was everything okay at the Triple H? Had Pete taken another spill? Had anything happened to Clara?

Brooks. What was he doing? Did he think of her, not just Timmy? Did he have regrets?

And then one day, a week before Timmy's first birthday, a box arrived packed with festive confetti. She sat cross-legged with Timmy on the floor of the living room, "helping" him open his presents.

First came a scroll of cream paper tied with red yarn. Laura's eyes stung when she tugged the bow and unrolled the paper to see Dean's neat print. Titled *The Littlest Cowboy*, it was a poem telling a story of a little boy who helped his three bumbling uncles with ranch chores. She found herself laughing even as she blinked back tears.

She pulled Timmy onto her lap and read it to him, along

with the message scrawled on a sticky note, "Got more in the works. Will send when done."

So that was why Dean was reading cowboy poetry. She smiled as she rolled the poem back up and retied the yarn bow. She thought he wanted to write a love poem for the girlfriend-who-wasn't-a-girlfriend. Of course, that was probably in the works, too.

The next present was a plush, stuffed animal—a border collie puppy. She turned her head to read the tag to Timmy. "Dakota the Cowdog. From Uncle Mitch."

Timmy cooed and lunged for the puppy's black, plastic nose.

As she took out the third present—a tiny, black Stetson—her heart constricted, and she could barely breathe. The note read: "This is the smallest I could find, but he still needs to grow into it." From Brooks.

"Look, Timmy. Your first cowboy hat." Emotion clogged her voice as she settled it on his head, fingering the brim.

But it was the fourth and final item that brought her off the floor and sent her running toward the phone in the kitchen.

Nestled in a small box marked For Laura, was a house key. The note—Brooks's handwriting—read: "To come and go as you please."

Her fingers trembled as she dialed. She didn't know what to say, only knew she had to call. To connect. Tingling with anticipation and apprehension, she wiped her clammy palms on her jeans. But when Dean answered on the third ring, she couldn't contain the bubbles of excitement that spilled from her voice. "Dean! How are you? It's—"

"Laura!" he said. "Man, is it ever great to hear your voice!"

She thanked him for the gifts, and they proceeded to chatter nonstop for the next fifteen minutes. He thanked her for the updates on Timmy, asked about her job, what she did, how she liked it. He told her about spring roundup when they'd moved cow and calf pairs to summer pasture.

He started to say something more when instead he cleared his throat. "We, uh, miss you. *Both* of you."

"Dean." The low, warning tone of an achingly familiar voice came in the background, and she pictured Brooks at the kitchen table, making a slashing motion across his throat.

Her hand tightened on the receiver. "Is that Brooks?"

"Uh, yeah. He, um, can't come to the phone," Dean said before she could ask.

"That's okay. I'm sure he's busy." She tried to keep her voice light and casual, but had to ask, "How is he?"

"Fine. Same. I, ah, should probably let you go now."

She nodded, though he couldn't see her. "It was so good to catch up. Please, give the others my best."

"I will. And, Laura?"

"Yeah?"

"Don't be a stranger. We're *your* family, too."

An ache tightened in her chest. He couldn't have known how much those words meant to her, a woman who used to dream of belonging in a family like theirs.

Once upon a time, she'd sacrificed her self-esteem for a chance at those dreams, learned the hard way that kind of sacrifice meant it was time to get new dreams. So she had.

She'd dreamed of independence and self-reliance. Made those dreams come true.

She looked down at the key on her palm.

To come and go as you please...

"Thanks, Dean." She dropped the receiver back in its cradle and closed her eyes, missing Wyoming more than ever. Missing all of them.

Missing Brooks.

Her hand closed over the key, clasping it to her heart.

Then she went to her supply drawer, found some scissors and yarn, and hung the key like a charm around her neck.

For the past few months, she had repeated to herself she didn't need him—didn't need any man—in order to be happy. But time had given her a chance to reflect. And distance had given her perspective.

She was right. She didn't need him. But that didn't mean she didn't want him.

Touching the key, a slow glimmer of realization seeped into her heart... How truly different Brooks was from Luke on every level...

She had walked out on him, and he hadn't tried to lure her back with threats or empty promises. Never once had he ever criticized her or put her down in any way. He made no noises that made her feel as though she couldn't survive on her own, or that *he* couldn't survive without *her*.

There was nothing to block out, or let slide, or deny.

If she let it, every memory they'd made would play in her mind not as a horror flick but an old, favorite movie. Brooks rocking Timmy and reading to him from the *Farmer's Almanac*...making her hot chocolate...getting her through her panic attack at the hospital...giving her pep talks when she needed them most...taking her shopping to cheer her up...the way he touched her.

While one brother had nearly destroyed her, the other had brought her back to life.

Yes, time and distance had given her the objectivity to connect the dots, to see the pattern that had been there all along: From the first moment they met, Brooks Hart had given her everything of value he had to give. Ultimately he gave her Timmy—his heart, the most precious thing in his entire world—without a fight.

I just want you to be happy. Whatever makes you happy, that's what I want.

Dear God. It finally hit her full force. She'd ripped his heart from his chest, and he'd done nothing to stop her.

He'd given up his heart *for her*.

A Wyoming-size boulder dropped in Laura's gut.

He loved her. Brooks really, truly loved her.

Laura lowered her window, and both she and Timmy perked up at the musky-mint scent of sage, lifting their faces to inhale the freshness of spring in all its glory, poised to burst into summer.

In their absence, the vast landscape had undergone a complete facelift. Gone was the endless blanket of white, replaced by a sea of emerald-green grass that swished and rippled in the wind, its symphony like the soft clapping of a thousand hands. Cottonwood trees grew lush and bountiful, dancing and swaying in the breeze as the sun descended, spilling golden amber like magic pixie dust.

Along the ribbon of the two-lane road that led to the Triple H, drivers of oncoming pickups lifted their hands in greeting, and Laura did the same. Soon, they crested a hill and caught sight of the first familiar windmill, its silvery arms stretched to the wide, open sky. As she followed the fence lines, the rambling ranch house and barns appeared.

Laura's heart swelled, and she smiled. "We made it, Timmy." She stroked her son's cheek and coaxed a giggle.

In the late afternoon, she found the house deserted as expected and took a few minutes to savor the familiarity on her own. It was just as she remembered. Heaven on earth.

The back door was unlocked, and the mouthwatering aroma of Clara's chocolate chip cookies drifted into the mudroom. She must have baked them after dinner, figuring no one would be around to steal any from the cooling rack.

Wrong.

Laura broke off a piece for Timmy, noticing a dozen of

his photos on the refrigerator. There were more, scattered throughout the house. Some framed, others pinned, all of them on public display. Including the ones with her.

Just then, a door slammed, followed by Clara's excited voice. "Laura? Is it really you?"

"It's us," she called back, suddenly nervous as she carried Timmy into the kitchen. But then, one look at the unmasked joy on Clara's face, and she didn't hesitate but gave the mother of *her* heart a big hug. "Look, sweetie. Who's this? Is it Grandma Clara? Yeah?"

Timmy grinned and held his arms out to Clara.

Tears sprung to Clara's eyes as she took him, then she swiped a dishcloth from the counter and swatted Laura's arm. "What'd I tell you about making an old lady cry? I swear, Laura, you ain't changed a lick."

Laura laughed through her own tears.

"Oh, let me look at you." Clara dabbed her eyes, her gaze wandering over both Laura and Timmy. "I take it back. You have changed. Your hair's longer, and you finally put some meat on your bones. You got color in your face, too. And this one…" She poked Timmy's tummy. "You've grown!"

Timmy chortled, wrapped one small arm around Clara's neck and dropped his head on her shoulder.

"We've both arrived in a lot better shape this time." Laura smiled. "So, where is everyone?"

"Pete, Mitch and Dean went to fetch supplies in town. Brooks is still up at the house. Pete Stewart's old place, that is. Don't suppose he got a chance to tell you yet."

"Tell me what?"

But Clara shook her head. "Nope, ain't gonna ruin the surprise. Take my truck. Keys in the ignition. Oh, wait. Here. I fixed him a basket. Sun goes down so late, he gets on a roll and forgets to come home for supper." She bustled around the kitchen, Timmy on her hip. "Don't mind, do you?"

"No. No, of course not." She wiped her damp palms on her shorts, shy and eager all at once. She'd thought of little else on the drive—what she would say to Brooks, how she would say it, knowing the instant she laid her eyes on him again every well-rehearsed line would fly from her mind.

"Good. Head for the west pasture. Only one road there. Follow the compass."

"All right," she said. "I should be back—"

"No hurry. There's food enough for two." Clara rubbed her hand over Timmy's back, turning her gaze to the window with a faraway look, a ghost of a smile on her lips. "Best sunset you ever did see."

Brooks stepped back and surveyed his work. The Stewart place was shaping up nicely. A small two-bedroom, it had triple dormers and a wraparound porch, plus the option of adding two more bedrooms and a bath on the second floor.

They'd gutted it earlier that week and finished framing the rooms today. With any luck, they'd wrap up electrical, plumbing and drywall by next week. He'd gotten ambitious and power-washed the porch. Satisfied, he stripped off his shirt and turned the hose on himself to wash away the day's sweat and grime.

Excitement pumped though his veins when he thought of the finished product, picturing that catch phrase Laura had repeated in her plan: rustic charm with modern conveniences.

Laura.

He squeezed his eyes shut. God, how he missed her and Timmy. Just when it didn't hurt to breathe every minute of every day without them, when he could get through her weekly packets of photos and letters without wanting to bawl like a weaning calf, she had to call.

In the past months, he'd learned to embrace the pain, telling himself yeah, it hurt like hell, but it was a *good* kind of hurt, like the satisfaction of sore, aching muscles at the end of a hard day. The hole in his heart proved he didn't share his father's and brother's weaknesses. If he could survive this agony, he could survive anything.

He told himself all this. He thought he was getting better. Then she called. And his heart shattered again.

He couldn't even talk to her, too afraid he'd lose it right there on the phone, cut open a vein and start gushing all over the place. Tell her all the things he'd wanted to before, only he'd held his tongue.

No, it was going to take Brooks a lot longer before he could exchange polite chitchat with her. Like breaking and resetting a bone—that's how it felt in his heart. Now, he had to heal all over again.

He turned off the water hose and pushed wet hair from his face. Looking west, he calculated a few more hours of light. Might as well start on the railing.

He'd gotten back to work when he thought he heard the sound of gears grinding. He paused and listened. Nothing and then—there it was again.

He winced and looked up the road. Sure enough, Clara's pickup crested the hill, barreling straight for him, kicking up all kinds of dirt in her wake.

His pulse jumped. Clara didn't usually drive this fast. Or grind gears. Something was wrong.

Brooks dropped what he was doing and headed down the driveway. But when he squinted at the horizon, he realized it wasn't Clara in the driver's seat after all. It was…

No way. He was seeing things. He rubbed his eyes.

Laura!

His jaw hit the ground. He was sure he heard the thud. Then his mouth went dry with fear.

What happened?

He practically ran to the truck. She practically ran him down. He yanked open the door the second she stopped.

"What's wrong?" he demanded.

"Nothing's wrong. I—"

"Timmy?"

"He's fine. He's at the house with Clara."

"And you?" He stepped back to catalog her body parts, barely registering denim cutoffs and a red tank top. "Are you sick? Hurt? What?"

"No. Nothing's wrong. Everything's fine."

Without thinking, he hauled her into his arms, hugged her hard, then set her away. "Geez, woman." He raked his fingers through his damp hair and realized he was shaking something fierce. "Give me a heart attack, why don't you."

Her liquid brown eyes softened as she smiled. "It's good to see you, too."

He stared at her, unable to believe she was really there, in the flesh, not a product of wishful thinking.

She was more beautiful to him than ever. Her face had filled out, and it had a healthy, sun-kissed glow. The same could be said for the rest of her. She sat sideways on the bench seat of the truck, her long, shapely legs hanging out the door. Her hair went past her shoulders, the color of honey graham crackers, tied loosely with a red ribbon that matched her top—a tank that molded small, high breasts.

Perfect breasts. Perfect heart. *His* perfect woman.

God, he wasn't strong enough for this.

Then he realized those big, brown eyes were moving over *him,* and he *really* wasn't strong enough for that.

He stepped back and half turned toward the porch where his dirty shirt hung from the rail, wanting to put it back on but opting not to offend her with its odor. "Are you... Did you come for a visit?"

She nodded. "Timmy should celebrate his birthday with his family."

Brooks swallowed hard. "Great. That's...great." He turned his gaze to the Stewart place, more as an excuse to look someplace besides at her. "You, uh, want to see what we've been doing?"

"Sure." She slid down. "Clara sent a basket." When she reached back inside, the denim of her shorts riding up, he turned his back and sucked in a sharp breath.

"Leave it," he said between clenched teeth.

"Aren't you hungry?"

Famished. But what Brooks wanted, she wasn't serving. "No," he said, closing his eyes. Behind him, the truck door creaked shut. He needed to oil those hinges. He added the task to his mental to-do list. Now seemed like a good time to think about lists. Recite them. Backward and forward.

He started for the house. She fell into step beside him, close enough that he could reach her hand. He didn't.

"Wow." She peeked in between rail posts to see in the window. "This is great."

"Rustic charm with modern conveniences."

She spun around, the pleasure in her eyes unmistakable. "You're doing it?" Excitement tinged her voice. "The dude ranch?"

He shrugged but couldn't help the grin that tugged up one corner of his mouth. "Got this great business plan. Spelled everything out nice and easy. Thought we'd start simple."

"Phase one," she whispered, as if remembering.

"Two, actually. Sold a bit of land for an outrageous price. Paid off the loan and had money leftover to invest, so..."

"So I love it." She stepped past him onto the porch.

The air stirred beside him, and his gut pulled tight. He'd been dying to tell her, dying to hear this very reaction from her. So why did he feel so hollow inside?

Because nothing felt as good, as rewarding without her here to share it.

"We can do this later," he said gruffly. "You must be tired. Let's head back—"

"No." She gave a nervous laugh and leaned up against the post, rubbing her arms. "Sorry. It's just I've been rehearsing what I wanted to say because I wanted it to come out right. But I knew once I saw you, my mind would freeze, and I wouldn't remember any of my really great sentences. Except one. The one I was kind of hoping to lead up to…"

"Women." He smiled and blew out an exasperated breath. "Never can get straight to the point, can you? It's genetic or some—"

"I love you, Brooks." The words drifted on the breeze, soft and sweet with the slightest tremble, an iron mallet to his fool heart, smashing it into a million friggin' pieces. Again.

But. He knew she was leading up to a *but.* And God Almighty, he couldn't take it anymore. He shot from the porch.

"Damn it, Laura. What do you think, I'm made of steel?" He reeled around and rubbed a hand over his face. "We need new ground rules. *You* want me to stay away from you, you can't *say* these things to me. Come and go as you please, but give a guy some notice. And don't wear things like *that* around me. Because if *you* can't keep up *your* end of things, *I'm* gonna start spewing things like I love you, I want you, come back and *marry* me for God's sake." He turned his back and covered his eyes.

"Brooks—"

"I'm not there yet, okay?" he gritted out. "I don't know when I'm gonna be, if I'm *ever* gonna get over you, but I sure as hell can't do it this way. I can't *take* this…." he ground out, pressing the heels of his hands over his eyes.

"I see you in my dreams at night. I hear you when you're not even there. Sometimes, I *forget,* and I catch myself *talking* to you. I can still smell you. I can still taste you. I close my eyes, and it's like you never left. Then I remember." He drew a ragged breath. "Go back to the house. Just *go*…and let me…get a grip."

Around them, the sounds of spring grew louder. The whistle of the wind. The ripple of the leaves. The chirp of crickets. A meadowlark's mating call. And then, the sound of feet on the steps, coming down, coming toward him, stopping.

She stood so close he could hear her breathing, smell her scent on the warm breeze, stirring the hairs on his arm.

He didn't turn around.

He couldn't.

In another second, he was going to die.

"Do you remember when you told me your fear?" she asked softly, not waiting for his answer. "I never told you mine. I've gone through most of my life afraid of being alone. I thought anything—even a bad relationship—was better than nothing. As if *I* was nothing… I had to prove to myself I could survive on my own. Learn to like myself. Be happy in my own skin. Now I've done those things, and I'm not afraid anymore. I'm not here because I'm afraid of being alone but because what I feel is true, and I trust you—with my heart. With my life."

Brooks spun around, his eyes searching hers. "You…?"

"I love you. I *have* loved you from that day at the mall when I bought that lipstick. I've never stopped. So if there's any way you'd consider actually spewing some of those things—" her voice broke "—I'd really like to come home now. Did you mean…?" She gestured lamely with her hands. "What you just said…?"

He couldn't breathe. He didn't think. Blindly he reached for her, picking her up off her feet, burying his face in her hair, shuddering at the feel of her in his arms. "Yes. God, yes," he said, struggling to pull air into his oxygen-starved lungs. "I hoped… I prayed…" He kissed her head. "If this is a dream…"

"No dream." She wrapped her arms around him, her damp face against his bare chest. "I've missed you so much. And Brooks, what you said about your fear…? You have to know now you're nothing like Luke. You keep me in your life by making me happy." She pressed her lips to his chest. "I finally figured out you gave me a piece of your heart when you let me leave with Timmy—"

"Not a piece," he said, lowering her to the ground, framing her face in his hands, feasting his eyes on the woman he adored, the woman he'd waited for his entire life and believed he'd lost forever. "All of it, lollipop."

"I know," she whispered. "I know…"

"And *I* know I can live without you, if I have to." He wiped her tears with his thumbs. "But you give me a choice, honey, and I'll choose you every time. I love you *so much.*"

She smiled through her tears, reaching up to cover his hands with hers. "I know you do. You let me go. Now I've come back."

"I swear I'll cherish you forever," he solemnly vowed.

Her eyes softened. "I believe you."

Something loosened in his chest. All his life, Brooks thought himself unworthy of such trust. Because of Laura, he'd learned the truth about himself, and he knew beyond a shadow of a doubt, he would honor her until he died. "So we'll be hiring a manager for the dude ranch." He lowered his head, his lips hovering scant inches above hers. "Know anyone with hospitality expertise?"

She laughed, a puff of air tickling his face. "As it happens, I do. And you're in luck…. She's moving to the area.'' She tugged his head down and kissed first his top lip, then the lower. "Permanently."

Brooks groaned, capturing her mouth, tracing his hands along her waist, her rib cage and the sides of her breasts, reacquainting himself the shape of her, his woman. "I don't know if I can top her current salary..." His mouth moved to her neck, kissing and nibbling a path across her collar-bone.

She gave a broken sigh and tipped her head to the side. "You could offer benefits, in the *other* coin of the realm."

"I...could...do...that." He punctuated each word with a gentle nip, sliding her tank top off one of her shoulders.

She shivered and trailed her hands down his bare chest to his belt. "A signing bonus would be nice, too."

He laughed. "Whatever you want, lollipop. Whatever you want."

"I want you, Brooks. Forever and ever."

"Done." His mouth closed over hers, sealing his vow.

* * * * *

 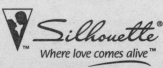

If you enjoyed what you just read,
then we've got an offer you can't resist!

Take 2 bestselling
love stories FREE!
Plus get a FREE surprise gift!

Clip this page and mail it to Silhouette Reader Service™

IN U.S.A.
3010 Walden Ave.
P.O. Box 1867
Buffalo, N.Y. 14240-1867

IN CANADA
P.O. Box 609
Fort Erie, Ontario
L2A 5X3

YES! Please send me 2 free Silhouette Intimate Moments® novels and my free surprise gift. After receiving them, if I don't wish to receive anymore, I can return the shipping statement marked cancel. If I don't cancel, I will receive 6 brand-new novels every month, before they're available in stores! In the U.S.A., bill me at the bargain price of $3.80 plus 25¢ shipping and handling per book and applicable sales tax, if any*. In Canada, bill me at the bargain price of $4.21 plus 25¢ shipping and handling per book and applicable taxes**. That's the complete price and a savings of at least 10% off the cover prices—what a great deal! I understand that accepting the 2 free books and gift places me under no obligation ever to buy any books. I can always return a shipment and cancel at any time. Even if I never buy another book from Silhouette, the 2 free books and gift are mine to keep forever.

245 SEN DFNU
345 SEN DFNV

Name	(PLEASE PRINT)	
Address	Apt.#	
City	State/Prov.	Zip/Postal Code

* Terms and prices subject to change without notice. Sales tax applicable in N.Y.
** Canadian residents will be charged applicable provincial taxes and GST.
  All orders subject to approval. Offer limited to one per household and not valid to
  current Silhouette Intimate Moments® subscribers.
  ® are registered trademarks of Harlequin Enterprises Limited.

INMOM01   ©1998 Harlequin Enterprises Limited

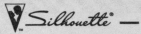

Silhouette —
where love comes alive—online...

eHARLEQUIN.com

your romantic
books

♥ **Shop online!** Visit Shop eHarlequin and discover a wide selection of new releases and classic favorites at great discounted prices.

♥ **Read** our daily and weekly Internet exclusive serials, and participate in our interactive novel in the reading room.

♥ **Ever dreamed of being a writer?** Enter your chapter for a chance to become a featured author in our Writing Round Robin novel.

your romantic
magazine

♥ **Check out** our feature articles on dating, flirting and other important romance topics and get your daily love dose with tips on how to keep the romance alive every day.

♥ **Learn** what the stars have in store for you with our daily Passionscopes and weekly Eroticscopes.

♥ **Get** the latest scoop on your favorite royals in Royal Romance.

your
community

♥ **Have a Heart-to-Heart** with other members about the latest books and meet your favorite authors.

♥ **Discuss** your romantic dilemma in the Tales from the Heart message board.

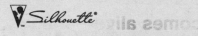

INTIMATE MOMENTS™

THE VALENTINE TWO-STEP, IM #1133

The first book in RaeAnne Thayne's new Western miniseries

♡UTLAW HARTES

This time they're on the right side of the law—and looking for love!

Available in February only from Silhouette Intimate Moments.

Be on the lookout for

TAMING JESSE JAMES, IM #1139 (March 2002)

CASSIDY HARTE AND THE COMEBACK KID, IM #1144 (April 2002)

Available at your favorite retail outlet.

Where love comes alive™

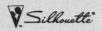

INTIMATE MOMENTS™

Where Texas society reigns supreme—and appearances are everything!

When a bomb rips through the historic Lone Star Country Club, a mystery begins in Mission Creek....

Available February 2002
ONCE A FATHER (IM #1132)
by Marie Ferrarella
A lonely firefighter and a warmhearted doctor fall in love while trying to help a five-year-old boy orphaned by the bombing.

Available March 2002
IN THE LINE OF FIRE (IM #1138)
by Beverly Bird
Can a lady cop on the bombing task force and a sexy ex-con stop fighting long enough to realize they're crazy about each other?

Available April 2002
MOMENT OF TRUTH (IM #1143)
by Maggie Price
A bomb tech returns home to Mission Creek and discovers that an old flame has been keeping a secret from him....

And be sure not to miss the Silhouette anthology

Lone Star Country Club: The Debutantes

Available in May 2002

Available at your favorite retail outlet.

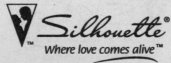

Where love comes alive™